Corpse on a Swing

Corpse on a Swing

A SEXY,
SCREWBALL
MYSTERY

Pepe Montecarlo

MochanVanilla Media

Contents

Contents

Dedication and copyright

Hic liber dedicatus est meae Reginae Nubianae.

This is a work of fiction. Names, characters, places and incidents are products of the author's imagination or are used fictitiously and are not to be construed as real. Any resemblance to actual events, locales, organizations or persons, living or dead, is entirely coincidental.

Cover design by CoveredbyMelinda.com
ISBN 979-8-9896488-0-1 (Paperback)
ISBN 979-8-9896488-1-8 (Epub)

Primary players

In order of appearance:

Miriam Margarita "Mimi" Vega: Her swinger profile described her as "nicely curved with more to love," but she had a dark side.

Peter Paul "Pepe" Montecarlo: His girlfriend, Laurel, sees him as "so god-damned sexy," but he's also a sexagenarian smart-ass whose absurd philosophy attracts unwanted attention.

Reynaldo "Rex" Vega: Laurel calls him a "gentle giant," and Pepe thinks him a fun conversationalist when he isn't shooting people.

Laurel Traeger: Pepe sees her as "like Halle Berry's younger, prettier sister," but she will definitely "cut a bitch."

Lt. Tiffany "Tuffy" Traeger: Laurel's sister, she's a competent detective with an appropriate nickname who brooks no foolishness, but she has her demons.

Raoul "Deuce-and-a-half" Jones Jr.: In Pepe's version of *Fear and Loathing in Las Vegas*, Deuce would be Hunter S. Thompson's lawyer.

The Right Reverend Theophilus Lenfant: He projects a "holier than thou" image. "Suffer the little children" is a phrase just a little too apt.

Delilah Samson: Her initial impression is one of embarrassment in a nudist resort, but she has dreams that would be nightmares for most people.

#

1

Mort de Mimi
(Death of Mimi)

Sunday, Oct. 9, 2022, 12:30 a.m.

Mimi's blood pooled on the parquet floor beneath the octagonal room's sole fixture, the "Great Sex Swing," a cross between a trapeze bar and a gynecological examination chair.

"Oh, lawd," I said to myself, unconsciously mimicking my beloved Laurel in the other bedroom. The ringing in my ears induced by the two powerful shots I'd just heard muffled the sound of my voice. "Another fine mess you've got me into, Laurel," I muttered, my head bowed.

Kneeling before the swing, I felt moisture on my left toes tucked underneath me. I looked up at the mirrors behind the swing and realized Rex's blood was spreading also. In one reflection, I saw through the door -- behind Rex's large, naked, crumpled, pale body — my beloved Laurel Traeger, tall, slim, ochre, naked, ever-present vodka-Sprite-cranberry cocktail

4

(we call it "Tito's Tart") in hand, striding with her long legs nearer from a bedroom across the bungalow's living room.

Laurel's pixie-ish pink hair stood even more erect on her round, caramel head. Her long black false eyelashes folded back like terrified caterpillars beneath her arched, bleached eyebrows.

Laurel's elegant feet skidded to a stop at the doorway before her ornately enameled toenails could be soiled by Rex's effluvia.

"Oh, lawd, Pepe," she whispered.

Her golden eyes, welling with tears, took in the scene:

Item No. 1: Mimi Vega, a salt-and-pepper-haired tawny woman of 50 with an eclectic and impressive appetite for sex. Her swinger profile described her as "nicely curved with more to love." Tonight, naked and spreadeagled on the swing, she had a hole in her face the size of a coffee mug, inflicted by a .45 Colt bullet traveling at 1,100 feet per second from a Taurus Judge revolver. Think of it as the cartoon gun used by Eddie Valiant in *Who Framed Roger Rabbit?*

Item No. 2: Rex Vega, 55, who Laurel had always described as "a gentle giant." Rex's tall frame was heavy — but not obesely so — with hairless tanned flesh. His left hand was missing, his arm ending in a scarred stump from a previous injury. Gravity caused at least one previously attached pound to creep down the mirrored interior of the death room as a through-and-through hole the size of a Bavarian beer stein opened his head from disintegrated ear to disintegrated ear.

Item No. 3: The offending weapon, two chambers empty, lying in the spreading pool of gore.

Laurel turned her horrified gaze upon my hooded blue

eyes, pursed lips and thin gray mustache, which was still sopping wet because I had been pleasuring Mimi orally only moments before.

"We gotta stop meeting like this, *chula*," I said, and started to gag. The after-effect of the shot continued to turn down the volume in my head. The odor of blood and gunsmoke began to overcome my Mimi-scented mustache.

"*Ay, caramba!*" Laurel whispered, her voice quavering with emotion.

I turned to the task of standing up while touching as little as possible, which is not easy for a sixty-something-year-old man, no matter how fit. My hands and legs started shaking from the fear, sadness and adrenaline of the violence catching up to my conscious mind.

I did my best to rise with my toes the way my high school judo teacher taught me. As I typically emit an automatic chuckle at my clumsiness, the reflection of my body -- tanned, except for feet and gym-short regions – highstepping like a flamingo out of the newly christened abattoir was almost, *almost* amusing.

"Tuffy ain't gonna like this," Laurel said, and as she said it, her sister, Pecan County Sheriff's Office Deputy Lt. Tiffany "Tuffy" Traeger, knocked insistently but not loudly on the cabin's thick, wooden exterior door, like Sheldon summoning Penny in *Big Bang Theory*.

"Just a minute," Laurel called out, as she turned to look for her thick white robe. She grabbed hers and tossed me mine, matching monogrammed items we had picked up at the Hedo II clothing-optional, swinger-friendly resort in Jamaica. I had just finished knotting the belt as Laurel opened the dark brown shellacked door and waved in Tuffy with her other hand, still holding the vodka-tonic.

Disheveled in her "mock" sexy police-stripper outfit with black knee-high motorcycle boots and a white furry handcuff linked to her right wrist, Tuffy turned her dark chocolate face up to my own usually plain vanilla face (closer to strawberry, probably, due to the circumstances, no doubt). She cocked an eye and waited for me to speak. I raised my light brown eyebrows, my eyes welling with tears, and let go a sigh. "Well …," I said, squeezing the bridge of my nose with a shaky hand and wondering where to begin.

As I hesitated, Tuffy sniffed the air and began to look around the white enameled main room, decorated with a couch, two armchairs and an ottoman, all Naugahyde, plus a coffee table and dinette set, all the same wood as the door. I smelled it, too – the ferrous smell of blood mixed with whatever Rex and Mimi's bowels were emptying on the polished parquet in the octagonal room.

It suddenly occurred to me I may be splattered with blood. As Tuffy walked across the dark wooden parquet floor to that room and stopped, I turned to a mirror next to the cabin door to look for blow-back. A solitary drop of blood anointed the border between my short grayish hair above my right ear and the tousled, inch-long blondish crown of hair atop my head.

I reached for an antibacterial wipe from a container on the coffee table and dabbed at the droplet. "Laurel, do you see any splatter at the back of my head?" I asked.

"Shut the fuck up and do not touch him," Tuffy said without turning. "Fuckedy-fuck-fuck-fuck." She took short steps toward the death scene, as if afraid of disturbing a sleeping infant.

We shut up and kept still for two full minutes as Tuffy took in the scene. Laurel and I screwed our eyes up, trying to blot out the memory of the scene, squeezing out tears. I started to gag again.

Tuffy told us to go sit in one of the two bedrooms, touching as little as possible. She pulled out her smartphone and made a call. Laurel and I grabbed tissues from a box on a hallway table as we entered the room, where we wiped away tears and sniffles.

"Wright? Tuffy. Get Monster and yourself down to NTOR ASAP. Call for the county medical examiner and a forensic team. We have a 10-31C in Cabin … hold on." Tuffy asked Laurel the cabin number. "Cabin 8. Just ask at the gate. Don't let anyone besides us in or out. Keep it quiet, no sirens. I'll fill you and Monster in when you get here."

NTOR is the acronym for Nut Tree Orchard Resort, usually pronounced "En-tor," but also jokingly referred to as "Not a Thing On Resort." NTOR is a "clothing optional" – i.e., nudist – adults-only campground with various "recreational facilities" popular among well-heeled swinging couples and their occasional "swingle" friends, known as "unicorns" (female) or "bulls" (male).

Most NTOR patrons arrive in recreational vehicles or keep them on-site on a permanent basis nestled among the majestic pines, the sensuously gnarled live oaks and the occasional stray pecan that migrated from the orchard at the back of the property. Laurel and I had not yet taken the plunge of buying an RV and preferred to rent facilities where we play. So much easier to let others clean up, right?

A few minutes later, we heard a sport-utility vehicle slide to a stop on the gravel drive outside the cabin and the quick footsteps of two men as Tuffy opened the door and let them in. We couldn't view them from the second bedroom. Tuffy told them to keep the cottage secure while she went to change out of her costume and into street clothes. They could look around, but could not touch anything and must say nothing to the couple sitting in the other room (i.e., Laurel and me).

That was when I realized Laurel and I would be suspects.

"Sheeuttt," I whispered, looking at Laurel, still sipping her drink between sniffles and wiping tears off her cheek.

"SHUT THE FUCK UP IN THERE, YA HEAR?"

Tuffy had very good hearing. We heard her close the door and trot away to her own cabin next door, which she had been sharing with our mutual friends Dean and Rose Franco. Dean's questioning voice came to us through the closed window, but not the words themselves or Tuffy's response. He was probably standing stark naked outside, his sunburnt, weathered 70-year-old skin goose-bumped and taut across his six-foot, wiry frame in the cool, dry Texas Hill Country night breeze of mid-October. Rose would be inside, gagged, tied and suspended in mid-air in a different kind of "playroom."

Fun people, the Francos.

#

2

Grin and bare it

Sunday, Oct. 9, 2022, 12:45 a.m.

Laurel and I stared at the open doorway to our temporary home's living room area.

The sound of two sets of footsteps came to us, one heavy and slow, and another lighter and quicker. The maker of the heavy footsteps filled the doorway with probably 250 pounds of muscle and bone. He was Caucasian, had a shaved head and face, thick eyebrows, thick arm hair under the light blue uniform shirt's short sleeves. The name tag over his left breast said "M.T. North," and the three stripes on both sleeves said he was a sergeant. In North's eyes, I saw the remains of the horror he must have felt on viewing Mimi and Rex, but also the beginnings of serious thought. The thick eyebrow on the left lifted as he looked over us both – me first, then Laurel. This guy wasn't all muscle and bone.

After giving us both the once-over, he walked into the room, observing the messed-up sheets, the clothes in the closet, Laurel's jewelry, my stinky running shoes, other things.

In his place at the door came a more average-size white, fit man, sleek and nowhere near as muscular as his colleague. He wore his dark brown hair brushed back from his face with no part and a thick dark brown mustache – what my friends have called a "porn-stache." He also wore a uniform. The name tag said, "B.O. Wright," and the stripes said he too was a sergeant.

Wright's porn-stache was forming a rather ugly smirk this evening as he eyed Laurel. It pissed me off.

"Got something to say?" I said, smiling broadly, raising my eyebrows as if I were greeting an old friend.

Wright's gaze slowly turned toward me, showing a mixture of contempt, hostility and dismissiveness. His head cocked like a curious Border Collie, and one eye squinted like Festus from "Gunsmoke."

"Like Tuffy said, shut the fuck up," he said, his voice stretching the "uh" sounds into a couple of lazy, extra syllables, the way people in the South sometimes do, but with a menacing monotone.

Wright strolled around the room also, taking in the sights but focusing more on Laurel and myself.

As Wright followed North into the main living room area, Tuffy re-entered the cottage, talking to the forensic technicians who followed her — a male and female, both Latino, both in their early 30s, wearing paper overshoes.

The next few hours alternated among periods of stupefying dullness, hair-raising spookiness, annoying exasperation and mortal fear. The techs took our fingerprints and administered a paraffin test to our hands. This showed I had indeed fired a weapon earlier and Laurel had indeed not.

It began to sink in: I was the only eyewitness to what I knew to be a murder-suicide; that made me a potential suspect, if Tuffy and her pals disbelieved the murder-suicide story.

Tuffy told Wright to take me outside for a preliminary statement and told North to do the same with Laurel in the bedroom where we had waited.

The cottage had a little stucco-pillared porch with a couple of light, brushed aluminum chairs and a small picnic table of the same wood as the door. Wright and I sat in the glow of the porch's red light (a subtle signal to fellow swingers not to disturb) and the local cops' cherry tops. I glanced out into the night toward the pine-straw-and-leaf-strewn gravel road and saw a gathering of naked or scantily clad people, most of them shivering, staring from behind the police tape as the red and blue lights played across their flesh like fairy sprites.

I smiled at Wright, who continued to give me the con-temptuous smirk. I told him what I saw and what happened.

"My first thought was, 'Well, I know what Philip Marlowe would have said in this situation,'" I said. "He would have said, 'Hi, Rex, is that a rod in your hand, or are you just glad to see me?'"

"So, you were just blissfully pleasuring this guy's wife on that crazy swing, and the guy walks in and blows her away and then he shoots himself?"

I smiled and nodded.

"Got any idea why he might have done it?"

I smiled and shook my head no.

"Why are you smiling?"

"That's my business," I said, continuing with the goofy grin.

However, dear reader, I'll share my little secret with you. I once saw a video TED Talk about body language, including how to convince others that one is a non-threatening, helpful member of a friendly tribe -- maybe the same tribe.

So, the goofy grin, raised eyebrows and open, palms-up hands ready to accept a friendly shake had become something of a habit for me, especially in stressful circumstances. So, there you are.

Wright either had seen the same video or was so evolutionarily stunted in his breeding that he could not pick up my signals. In any event, my goofy grin was confusing and angering him, just a little, which was amusing me, just a little.

But, to dispel any notion I was some kind of village idiot or giggling ghoul, I reshaped my face into a mask of sad concern for this next bit. A cute little old Machiavelli, that's me.

"I can tell you I'm deeply saddened by the death of two people I liked," I said. "They were the first swingers Laurel and I ever played with, a couple of years back."

"We found gunshot residue on your hands, meaning you fired a weapon recently."

"Sure. There's a firing range here at NTOR. Rex and I tried out his new Taurus – really a doozy of a weapon, by the way. A cheap a substitute for a penile implant, if you ask me. I had my own SIG Sauer there, as well. I haven't cleaned it yet. You'll find it inside."

"We found it. We'll hold onto it for a few days, if you don't mind."

"I kinda do mind," I said, resuming a delighted display my pearly whites. "However, I realize you need to eliminate it from what went down in there. I expect it to be returned by the end of the week, or you'll be hearing from my lawyer."

My lawyer, Raoul "Deuce-and-a-half" Jones Jr., later chided me for being so voluble with the police; I responded that the circumstances upset me.

"Shooting seems an odd pastime at a nudist camp," Wright said.

"This is Texas, sergeant," I said. "Shooting kinda comes with the territory. For your information, standing stark naked and taking potshots at a target can be a hoot. You should try it. Perhaps you already have?"

But shooting wasn't all Rex and I did at the range; there I learned of other recent deaths among our "usual sexpects," as Laurel and I called our regular playmates.

Recalling the conversation, I felt a shiver run up and down my spine like a German cockroach.

#

3

Gun smoke and mirrors

Saturday, Oct. 8, 2022, 1 p.m.

"Dave and Maeve died of gas poisoning in their trailer during the big freeze last January," Rex had said, staring through his wraparound sunglasses at the silhouette targets about 25 feet downrange, stapled to four-by-four wooden posts before a sand berm. After three decades of use, the berm was probably more lead than sand. He wore ear plugs attached to a string behind his neck, a watch on his gun wrist and some flip flops, but nothing else.

I wore black horn-rimmed sunglasses, ear plugs on a string, a Timex Ironman on my left wrist, a smart watch on my right wrist and a pair of flip flops. I felt overdressed.

Dave and Maeve Cena had been an attractive, tanned couple in their early 70s who had an immaculate 20-foot trailer permanently parked at NTOR, with attached wooden, covered patio and some sculptures of gnomes and cute woodland creatures arranged in sexually inappropriate positions next to their carport. Hard not to smile when visiting Dave and Maeve at home.

"Damn, that sucks," I said, extracting the magazine from my P365 pistol and loading it with ten more 9-mm Luger cartridges. I sighed. "I'll miss Maeve, and I'm sure Laurel will miss Dave."

Through the gap on my own horn-rimmed sunglasses, I glanced 50 yards to the right, over at the swimming pool full of naked bodies, most of them very drunk. Laughter, splashing, squealing and conversation yielded little sound-space for ZZ Top's "Legs" playing on the exterior stereo speakers. I looked down and felt a pang of sadness at the thought of explaining the Cenas' passing to my beloved.

Oblivious, Laurel danced on a pedestal next to the pool, rotating a Hula-hoop as she downed a shot of Don Patron with one hand and resumed sipping from her pineapple-shaped cup in the other hand. Talented lady, our Laurel.

"Yeah, we'll miss them, too," Rex said in a monotone, re-inserting an ear plug in his right ear and raising the revolver to point at the target. "Mimi wants to take over their trailer, if she can get their kids to give us a good deal. It shouldn't be too hard a proposition, but we haven't been able to make contact."

BLAM! The head area of the silhouette disappeared.

"I doubt their kids want any evidence of their swing lifestyle around," Rex continued, punctuating the sentence with another explosion from his right fist, removing the silhouette's lower abdomen.

"We're losing a lot of silhouettes," I said.

"We're losing a lot of playmates, too," Rex said.

My 9-mm semiautomatic sounded like a champagne cork after the explosion from the Taurus Judge .45 Colt revolver, which some people call a "hand cannon." My pea-shooter poked a neat hole on what would have been my silhouette's nose.

BLAM! BLAM! BLAM! The chest, left shoulder and right shoulder of Ron's silhouette disappeared.

"Oh?" I hit my target's right eye-space precisely. "What do you mean?"

Click. Rex's revolver was empty.

"Only problem with this thing," Rex said, setting the Judge on a chest-high table and rotating the cylinder out. "Only carries five rounds. Gotta reload too often."

I looked askance up at Rex. The Taurus Judge has a notorious reputation for being a painful weapon to fire. It carries a large charge and kicks like an ill-tempered mule with a frickin' Taser attached to its tail. But Rex's one complete arm was quite muscular, so it didn't tire like most people's. The other arm, amputated below the elbow, didn't carry much meat, but it provided a steady surface on which to support his strong arm.

I resumed shooting, clipping my silhouette's left ear.

"That's what I was aiming for," I said, which was true. "What do you mean, 'a lot of playmates'?"

"Where the hell have you been?" Rex said, looking askance down at me as I re-acquired the target on the silhouette's right ear, which my bullet excised precisely.

"Frank and Ruby Dahl?" Rex asked as he ejected the spent shells and inserted fresh cartridges.

Frank and Ruby were another swinging couple. Frank was a black retired university athletic director in his 60s. Laurel and Frank enjoyed each other a little too much. Ruby was a petite Latina of 50 with a smart mouth who squirted when you went down on her just right. Lovely woman and pretty funny in most situations.

"Where are they?" I asked. "We thought we'd see them here this weekend."

Singing along with the music, now playing Springsteen's "Hungry Heart," Rex said, "Went out for a ride, and they never came back."

The hair on the back of my neck rose. "When and where was this?" I aimed for the silhouette's Adam's apple.

"Memorial Day weekend, out of Port Aransas on a rented boat."

I had been running a half-marathon that weekend not far away in Corpus Christi. Yeah, way too hot for a half-marathon, but that's part of the challenge. The after party was fun.

The Adam's apple of my silhouette was neatly punctured, and my own Adam's apple rose and sank with the emotion I felt at Rex's new revelation.

"Gotta say, Pepe, your eye is as good as it ever was."

"Thanks. Any idea what happened to Frank and Ruby out in the Gulf?"

Rex sighed, loaded the last cartridge, rolled the cylinder back into place, acquired the target and pulled back the hammer for a single-action target shot.

"The boat was found in the Intracoastal Waterway about 30 miles south, empty. News reports said it drifted aground on the barrier island. No bodies found. They're listed as missing."

BLAM!

Angry about what I thought was the pointless deaths of four people I liked, I put three more rounds into the heart of the silhouette, and the slide stayed open. The magazine was empty. I closed the breach unloaded and slid the pistol into its padded carrying case.

Talking with Rex was beginning to depress me. I watched as he put four more rounds into the remains of his silhouette, then suggested it was hot enough for a drink. Rex agreed, and we gathered up our spent shells -- mine were on the ground -- then returned to our respective accommodations with plans to rendezvous at the pool in 15 minutes.

#

4

Blut und baumwolle (Blood and cotton)

Sunday, Oct. 9, 2022, 1:45 a.m.

As these memories crossed my mind, furrowed my brow and emerged from my mouth, Wright cocked his head and examined my face. Police, emergency medical people and the medical examiner trooped in and out of the bungalow's front door. Their passing shadows darkened the red silhouette glow around Wright's stiff, brushed hair.

Tuffy stepped outside with a pale, solid, brown-haired female deputy holding a camera and told Wright to get photos of me with and without the robe, front and back.

My grin was not something I wanted shown during any potential trial. A bit over the top, right? Straight-faced, I stood for front, side and rear photos with and without the robe.

The photographer blushed but took the time to get a

closeup of my back, pulled out a penlight and pointed out something to Wright.

"Did you scrape yourself on your back or anything?" Wright asked, to which I said no. I looked at the robe on the chair and saw some blood residue inside on the back, likely from when Rex shot himself.

"Hmm," Wright said, and it sounded skeptical. In his reddish shadowy reflection on one of the cabin's windows, I saw the smirk and head shake as I turned to start re-donning the robe.

But Wright had seen the bloodstains on the inside of the robe as well and said to leave it alone.

For some absurd reason, here in the heart of the Texas Hill Country, one of many destinations for the 19th-century German diaspora, something weird leapt into my mind, reeling from the horror of the night's surreal activity. In particular, I thought of Bismarck's "*Blut und Eisen*" (blood and iron) speech advocating war and industry as a path toward German unity. In this case, "*Blut und Baumwolle*" (blood and cotton) could present a path toward my being found somehow guilty in this night's series of unfortunate events, albeit wrongly.

Kinda sobers an old fart up.

After some negotiation, Wright and Tuffy allowed me to put on some gym shorts and a T-shirt from my luggage inside the cabin. They deemed the evidence value of these articles of clothing as nil, I assume.

"Why do you care about clothes?" Wright asked, as I stepped into the shorts. "This is a nudist place, right?"

"True." I grinned and gestured at the flustered, retreating

female photographer. "It's more for your colleague's benefit than mine."

I did not mention it, but I was beginning to think I would not be spending the night at NTOR, which was another reason to put on some clothes.

That foresight turned out to be correct. After a 20-minute discussion among Wright, North and Tuffy, I was escorted to a police car — though not in handcuffs — while Laurel started yelling absurd obscenities at her sister. A lot of it I did not catch. One of the advantages of sexagenarian ears is an inability to understand much of what one's lover is saying. I did catch the all-important "bet' not" admonition, however.

"Y'all bett' not bring him back here with the least, tiniest scratch on him, ya feel me?" Laurel said to the police in general, wagging an intricately decorated index fingernail at all present. She was still wearing her robe, which also appeared to lack evidentiary value.

After I cooled my buns on the hard plastic back seat of the cruiser for about 10 minutes, a young male deputy climbed into the driver's seat, started up the car, backed into NTOR's main circular driveway and turned toward the exit. Aside from talking into his radio, the young man with the blond crewcut said nothing during the 20-minute drive to the county courthouse, where I was placed in an interrogation room, offered refreshment and grilled nonstop until about 6 am, when I said I wanted my lawyer, laid my head on my wrists on the table and fell asleep.

About 10 a.m., Deuce escorted me out of the courthouse and I sipped a black coffee. He is my best friend, a former University of Texas fullback and the best man at my first wedding. Deuce-and-a-half is Army-speak for a 2.5-ton truck used to transport soldiers and their equipment. My lawyer is a big guy, all muscle, brains and heart.

I spied Laurel's smiling face. She wore skin-tight, expensively ripped and faded jeans, knee-high alligator cowboy boots, a sexy low-cut off-white thin cotton blouse and a wide straw cowboy hat. She shifted her sweet ass away from the door of my burnt-orange 1959 Corvette convertible, our vehicle for this "fun" trip to the Texas Hill Country.

She jumped on me, wrapped her legs around my waist, kissed my neck and whispered in my ear, "You're so god-damned sexy." She wore a cherry blossom scent. I leaned my hairy white ass against the car to support her weight.

Inasmuch as I reeked of a holding cell, had worse-than-usual morning breath, bore a whitish bristle of unshaved chin and wore the scruffiest t-shirt and shorts in my collection, I murmured, "You're so god-damned delusional."

Wearing a light gray suit appropriate for autumn in Texas, Deuce caught the exchange and cackled while he looked around to see what potential jurors might be watching from the quiet courthouse lawn area. A five-year-old girl walking with her thirty-something mother stopped and stared, but everyone else in the lily-white-and-Latino county seat of Pecan County scrupulously ignored the scene.

We rode in separate cars – learned counsel drove a Lincoln Navigator – to an IHOP next to Interstate 35. Inside I sat at a booth and filled some of the blanks in my story for Deuce that I had neglected when he met me in a legal consulting room down the hall from the main courtroom.

He knew about our open lifestyle, swinging, nudism, etc.,

and did not judge. He was happily married to a beautiful third wife with a couple of teenage daughters and just wasn't into what we liked, but he didn't condemn us.

However, he shook his short, curly, graying hair, and a chuckle emerged from his pale, crooked grin at this latest adventure.

"Dude," he said. "I mean, dude, really? You visit what is essentially a clothing-optional resort for retired Keebler elves, and find yourself hip-deep in what, to the ignorant bystander, looks like a jealousy-inspired bloodbath of a gun-fight. Here in the buckle of the Bible Belt, it also inspires the bat-shit craziest of conspiracy theories – like maybe it was a Satanic ritual in which you were sacrificing Mrs. Vega, and this Rex guy was just trying to save his wife. Dude."

"Oh, lawd," Laurel said, her voluptuous lips pursed in chagrin.

#

5

Wake up and smell blood in the water

Sunday, Oct. 9, 2022, 10:30 a.m.

I raised an eyebrow as I sniffed and sipped my delicious coffee, and a nervous little Latina, age about 17, set down a plate of eggs, bacon and toast for me, a plate of eggs and extra-crispy hash browns for Laurel and a bagel with a package of blueberry cream cheese for Deuce. No, we didn't need anything else, thanks.

The place was bustling, it being a Sunday after church in what was, as Deuce said, the buckle of the Bible Belt. It felt a little like scenes out of "Five Easy Pieces," "Reservoir Dogs" and "Pulp Fiction," with the underlying peep-show aroma of "From Dusk Till Dawn." I watch too many old movies.

After decades slogging through the newspaper journalism trenches, followed by a couple of successful business books and lucky investments, I've put a couple of million away in my career. I've been living off investments and the interest, but I didn't want to spend any more time or money than necessary on what I saw as none of my damn business, and I said as much.

"Ha!" Deuce barked, drawing the attention of the cashier and our waitress back in the staging area between the kitchen and the dining tables. Seeing the young lady carry a three-foot-wide tray of full-almost-to-overflowing plates, I realized Arnold Schwarzenegger has nothing on these diner waitresses for weightlifting. I gave her a friendly wave and she gave me a slight grin. She would get a generous tip.

"You are in this, bud," Deuce said, spreading cream cheese on his bagel. "Forget what I said about being hip-deep. You're up to your neck and the maelstrom of excrement is rising. You may be putting my youngest through Rice University before I'm done with you."

"Much as I like and admire you and your family, the prospect does not amuse," I said. "I don't understand. I was just a witness. I didn't shoot anybody. Don't they realize that?"

Deuce took a big bite of his bagel, washed it down with some orange juice and took a moment to chew and swallow before responding.

"They tell me the forensic evidence is inconclusive," he said, using a paper napkin to wipe a dab of cheese off his chin. He pointed the napkin at Laurel. "You're not out of this, either."

Laurel, whose hat was crown down on the fourth seat of the booth, looked quite shocked, with her spiked pink hair adding to the effect. "What the – why would anybody think I'm involved?" she asked.

"I gather they wonder whether you somehow conspired with Pepe, here, to conceal evidence – or maybe to compose some would-be exculpatory evidence," Deuce said. "It doesn't help – in fact, it hurts – that your sister was first on the scene, as a fellow NTOR guest."

Someone – Wright was implied – thought Laurel might have splattered blood on my back and have it transferred to the back of my robe to prove I must have had my back toward Rex when he killed himself. For some — ulterior? — reason, it beggared Sgt. Wrights's credulity to think I had my back to Rex when he killed himself – which of course is exactly what happened.

"You had your back to Rex when he shot himself?" Deuce asked. He was in his deposition mode, I could tell. The questions were dispassionate, laser-focused on the facts. He had questioned me and others like this before. It's one of the reasons I admired him as a lawyer.

"Yes," I said.

"Why?"

"Why should I turn around? I saw his reflection in the mirror as he put the barrel of the revolver in his ear and pulled the trigger. I looked away, because even I get a little squeamish, sometimes."

I was beginning to choke up — delayed reaction, I guess, to the loss of friends in such a violent circumstance.

"Oh lawd," Laurel said, her voice quavering. Tears welled in her eyes and ran down her cheeks. I pulled her to my side in a tight embrace and felt as much as listened to her sob.

I glanced aside at my friend, brow furrowed with sympathy. He pinched the bridge of his nose between his eyes. He was choking up in sympathy with Laurel and me. Lawyers have feelings, too, you know. He snorted, blew his nose and pushed away the remains of his bagel and cream cheese.

A few minutes later, Laurel had calmed down enough to blow her own nose and visit the lady's room. Having said, "No, *gracias*," to the fried baloney and powdered eggs offered at the Pecan County jail, I wolfed down my breakfast and gulped my coffee, while my suitably squeamish solicitor asked the waitress for a to-go box so he could resume breakfast at his suburban Austin office, about 20 miles away.

"We have a little time," he said. "Not much. Can you bear to stay at NTOR for a few more nights? The stronger security there might help you keep out of the news."

"Oh lawd," I said, doing a fair impression of Laurel. "I'm sure we can figure something out. That, of course, is the least of my worries. My big one is a classic: How do I prove I didn't do it? They have to prove I did it, in order to convict me, but in the court of public opinion, my life can easily be ruined by sheer speculation and an inconclusive cause-of-death result at the inquest."

"True enough."

"Maybe, just maybe, if I can find out why Rex did it and find proof of why he did it, I can convince people to leave me out of it."

Deuce's head bucked like horse's head will do when he smells something he doesn't like.

"Going to break out the old investigative journalist skills, eh?" The lawyer in him was skeptical about that part of my career, before I made my pile with a book describing exactly how the Great Recession happened, during which my own investments bloomed like algae in a South Louisiana lake.

"Tell me what you find," he said, jabbing his finger at me, "that's provable."

Truth is one thing; what is provable is something else. What is provable will keep you from losing a libel suit. I never lost a libel case in my journalism career, because I only used what could be defended in a court of law.

"Of course," I said. "You want updates on the directions I'm headed?"

"As your favorite fictional detective Nero Wolfe used to say, use your judgment guided by experience. As an officer of the court, I don't want to hear about you violating any laws, unless you're willing to pay me to defend you. Speaking of which –"

He produced from his inside jacket pocket the first invoice of my defense. I kept Deuce on retainer in part to help his cash flow. It had been a few years since I had needed to use any of the funds I had on deposit with his firm.

I removed the tri-folded high-quality paper from the letter-size Salazar & Jones law firm's envelope. I grinned broadly across at my old friend.

"You play offense," I chuckled. "I don't find this the least bit offensive."

"What's not offensive?" asked Laurel, who had composed herself and returned behind my back.

"This," I said, handing her the $1 invoice, and she beamed down at my friend. Laurel paid the bill and we walked out, promising to chat over the phone later, perhaps in a video call.

As I motored through the little town of Teresianstadt, the Pecan County seat, back toward NTOR, Laurel said, "See?"

"See what?"

"He loves you," she said. "I keep telling you, you're lovable."

I blushed a darker crimson than that police photographer had the night before.

#

6

Lenfant terrible

Sunday, Oct. 9, 2022, 11:30 a.m.

As we approached the turnoff from the highway to the gated NTOR entrance, I saw a couple of dozen people dressed in nice clothes standing beside the road, in front of two TV news crews. Some of those people without cameras held picket signs.

I assumed overnight cop reporters at the two stations overheard the homicide radio call and put out the word that morning, but I guessed it was possible somebody inside the resort was both "inside the tent," as LBJ would say, and "pissing in," which would be the inverse of his political dictum. To quote someone slightly more up-to-date (C+C Music Factory, to be precise,) it was one of those "things that make you go hmmmm."

"ABANDON ALL HOPE, YE WHO ENTER HERE!" one of the signs said. At least some of these folks knew how to read.

The rustic sign next to the resort's front gate paid homage to Dante Alighieri: "Abandon all inhibitions, y'all you enter here." So, yeah, not really a place for reverence and obeying silly rules about avoiding the fruit of the tree of knowledge of good and evil.

"THOU SHALT NOT COVET THY NEIGHBOR'S WIFE!" "Covet" is such a strong word, don't you think?

"DO NOT NTOR SODOM AND GOMORRAH!" Clever.

They saw our car coming and my turn signal, and one of them in a seersucker suit – a preacher? – stepped away from the microphone and spoke to the other people who were holding signs and makeshift drums and the kind of ultra-loud plastic clappers you find in big football stadiums.

As we slowed to turn in, they chanted: "You perverts! Won't convert! Then you will not find comfort!" The chant was pretty disunited, but the clappers and drummers had the rhythm right.

I asked Laurel to turn on her phone's video camera and point it at them.

I smiled at the protesters and at the TV cameras and slowed to a stop. A tall, pale blond TV reporter wore a burnt-orange tight, knee-length business dress and jacket on her slim, boyish figure. From within the heavy makeup, she looked with curiosity at me with the beginning of a grin but eyebrows raised as if in surprise, perhaps noticing how her suit matched my car. Hmmm. As if on cue, Laurel emitted a low growl.

"What's up?" I asked, not loud in comparison with the chanting, clapping and drumming. She stepped to the driver side of the car, motioning her disheveled camera woman to follow, and bent closer to my level, so I could smell the baby powder on her. She had a burnt-orange bow tie on her white pleated-front shirt inside the jacket.

The protesters were on the passenger side, and a scowling Laurel was busy swinging her phone's view from the protesters to the reporter and back.

As the woman began speaking, another on-camera reporter, a tanned woman with dark brown curly hair, more casually dressed in jeans, cowboy boots and a white dress shirt, motioned her cameraman to get closer as well.

"May I ask you who you are and whether you are a guest at Nut Tree Orchard Resort?" the blond asked, brushing lovely hair away from her face, which had assumed an appearance of serious concern, with a crease between her neatly arched dark-brown eyebrows.

"You may; I may not tell you," I chuckled. "I'm not dressed for prime time at the moment."

"His name is Peter Paul Montecarlo!" said the flush-faced man in the seersucker suit, who had approached Laurel's side while I discreetly ogled the TV reporters.

The chanting waned, but the clapping and drumming continued apace.

"You can find that out from his license plate," said the man. He was about 6-foot-2, skinny, with a long neck, salt-and-pepper hair neatly combed despite the rather breezy highway environment. Too much hair spray, I think.

Gesturing with a small black copy of the King James Version of the Holy Bible to the other reporter who was approaching, the man said, "Google him; you'll find some interesting background."

Pointing the bible at Laurel, he said, "You may want to know who she is, too." Laurel's hand reached toward her purse, where she kept pepper spray, among other things.

Out of concern for the professional vulnerability of Laurel's sister, I shielded Laurel's face from the camera with my hand and presented an icy grin to the TV cameras.

"Leave her out of it," I said. "If you don't, this interview is over."

As the cameras turned back toward me and Laurel hid her face with her hat, I raised my eyebrows and turned back toward the man who used a bible like a pointy stick. My work on the Great Recession had made me a minor celebrity for about six weeks. Somebody had been doing his homework, and sharing with a fraternity brother who shouldn't have all the answers to the test just yet.

I wondered who.

"Did you kill Rex and Mimi Vega?" the man asked. His little congregation had fallen silent.

Laurel snorted, her hand in her purse.

"Uh, three things," I said with a slow cadence and a warm smile. This guy's willingness to make unthinking leaps of faith diminished my estimate of his intellect, which reassured me as to his relative impotence in the current situation.

"First: No," I said. "Second: Who the hell are you? Third: Who gave you the authority to ask me that question?"

A busty, overweight blond woman with a florid complexion – overexcited much? – stepped up beside the questioner and said, "He is the Right Reverend Theophilus Lenfant, and don't you forget it!"

I didn't know her name then, but she became Karen to me

thenceforward. I admired how she gave the name Lenfant a nice French accent.

Lenfant put a calming hand on the pastel pink sleeve of her sensible, light pantsuit. She wore sensible shoes, too, brown and comfortable, like nurses' shoes.

"We're concerned about what happens in this establishment, not just to their bodies, but their souls as well," Lenfant said. "Therefore, you could say we all were ordained by God to ask that question."

I nodded, still smiling. "Very thoughtful of you. We're all grownups here, and to the extent some event here involves the broader public interest, the Pecan County Sheriff's Office has done an adequate job of defending that interest."

Lenfant stepped closer and leaned over Laurel to give me an infuriated glare. "We're not so sure," he said, and I caught the scent of cheap hairspray. His face had become flushed, as well, but the nostrils whitened as he took in air. He gave an almost imperceptibly quick nod toward Laurel.

"You might want to step back," I said. My icy grin was becoming uncomfortable. "I wouldn't want these tires to dirty your nice, shiny, Sunday-go-to-meeting shoes."

"Mr. ... Montecarlo is it?" the dark-haired reporter asked. I turned my now more genuine smile toward her. "Can you give us your account of what happened last night?"

"Forgive me, ma'am," I said. "I'm not from around here, or I might recognize your name. Would you mind telling me?"

"Joanna Metzger," she said, holding her hand out to be shaken. The wind pulled a stray curl toward her green eyes in a frankly attractive way – at least to me -- and I caught a scent of Chanel No. 5. The gear was in neutral, so I shook her hand politely and slowly. In my peripheral vision, I caught sight of Laurel's raised, suspicious left eyebrow and pursed lips.

She nodded toward her cameraman, a stocky, swarthy older gent with a Houston Astros cap turned backwards over his collar-length gray hair. "This is Bob Black." I smiled at him and waved.

"Ms. Metzger, if you'll give me your card, I'll contact you this afternoon, and we can chat for a while, since you asked," I said.

"I'm Stevie Sabin," the blond said, grabbing in her pocket for a card and handing it to me. "We'd like a chance to talk to you, as well."

Noticing that Ms. Sabin declined to identify her male, Latino, middle-aged photographer, I took her card and I gave Joanna a chance to hand me her card.

"No offense, intended, but if and when I consent to be interviewed, it will likely be via video chat, and you'll both be on the call," I said. "I understand about deadlines, and I realize you'd like to get what you can as soon as you can, but accuracy must be top priority, right?"

Both nodded. "Of course," Joanna said.

"And while I know what I saw and heard, I am puzzled by the meaning of it," I said. "Also, my lawyer, Raoul Jones Jr., may tell me not to participate or, at the very least, insist on auditing the session."

Lenfant had walked around the back of the car and was standing between Ms. Sabin and her videographer. As a veteran of too many impromptu press conferences, I can tell you: One interposes oneself between on-air talent and their lenses at one's peril.

"You ladies are missing an important point," Lenfant said. "This is a rich man, a powerful man, a man who pretty much does what he likes, no matter whose lives are ruined."

"Careful, padre," I said, still smiling, but hearing Laurel unsnap something inside her purse. I sure hoped it was the pepper spray holster, not the little Beretta .32-caliber "purse gun" she kept in the same location. "You wouldn't want to fall victim to a slander suit."

"The truth is an absolute defense to slander," Lenfant said.

"As my lawyer was telling me this morning, what matters is what's provable," I said, starting to put the car in gear and looking out the windshield to find a line of Lenfant's supporters blocking the way.

"Excuse me, ladies and gentlemen," I called out, still smiling. The two drummers appeared to be in a high school marching band, and two of the females holding clappers looked like they might be in the high school baton team, while the other people -- white, stocky women -- might well have been parents of the youngsters. Out of the corner of my eye, I saw the busty lady on Laurel's side nod vigorously at her fellow protesters, who resumed their chant.

"You perverts! Won't convert! Then you will not find comfort!"

Laurel pulled a can of pepper spray out of her purse and began to point it at the busty lady.

"*Mierda*," I said under my breath as I shifted into reverse and skidded the car backward just as Laurel's spray started shooting out, hitting the woman's bosom instead of her face.

The lady screamed and started scrambling for something in her purse. By the time she had it out, I had sped around to her rear on the grass next to the highway shoulder and entered NTOR's driveway, waving and smiling at the little crowd, still making a racket.

Ever cognizant of the state of my car, I realized the aptness of my grille-ornament longhorn plowing through high grass.

As I came to a skidding stop in front the gate, I glanced in the mirror and saw Lenfant struggling with the woman over something in her hand. I learned from a TV report later it was a .38-caliber revolver. A security guard leaning against a cruiser blocking the gate stepped forward to verify our identity. He backed up the vehicle and let us get close enough to punch the entrance code for the camp. We entered, and the chanting, clapping and drumming slowly disintegrated

"Not the best and wisest use of your hot sauce, darlin'," I said.

"She had it comin'."

"And she might not have been prosecuted for shooting both of us," I said. "Texans – especially rural Texans – tend to be well armed."

"Huh," Laurel scoffed, her lips pursed. "She oughta know I'll –"

"Cut a bitch," I finished the line for her. "Yup."

#

7

Naked? Pray!

Sunday, Oct. 9, 2022, 12:15 p.m.

Laurel had arranged for us to stay in a rented travel trailer, since our old bungalow was a crime scene, and it was to that RV we drove. I wanted to get naked, clear my head, jump in the pool and plan my approach to proving our innocence.

Clearing my head entails running nude along the pine-straw-paved roads and paths of "Not a Thing On" Resort. Nude. Not shoeless. I needed those shoes, as well as a hydration backpack and my sunglasses to navigate the warm, dry, shaded Hill Country lanes. Also, by the way, I keep a Kel-Tec .380 semiautomatic pistol (all of 11 ounces, loaded) in the hydration pack, JIC IJS (just in case, I'm just sayin').

Laurel and I agreed to meet in an hour or so at the pool, after I had logged my five miles.

When I run alone, I mutter mantras or prayers. In Latin, I pray for faith, hope, love (*fides, spes, caritas*) from the Father,

Son and Holy Ghost (*ex Patre et Filio et Spiritus Sanctus*). I make affirmations in Spanish: I'm a good, worthy person (*Soy bueno y digno*). In Spanish, I also sometimes affirm I'm good enough (*Soy bastante bien*). I say the Hail Mary in English. Weird, I realize. It's something my therapist recommended.

I rarely have an opportunity to run naked, but I dig it. My first exposure (pun unintended) to the idea was an old Cornell Wilde adventure movie, "Naked Prey," in which his character had to run a long distance across the African savannah to evade certain native warriors trying to kill him.

One inspiration for me to try nude running myself is an old Italian language instructor of mine when I was a college-level exchange student in Australia. Professor Agnelli liked to run along Tasmanian devil and wallaby trails nude in the Tasmanian bush, far from any human civilization. He also taught me Judo, causing one of my eyeballs to pop out of its socket during one boisterous choke-hold. But I digress.

As I ran past my temporary neighbors, the Cornell Wilde movie's plot came to mind, amid my mindless muttering of mantras. Trotting past the camp of a guy named Chuck Woodward, who simply stared at me, I wondered which camper would chuck a spear at me, if one was handy.

How many wooden spears would a nude Chuck Woodward chuck, if Mrs. Woodward wouldn't suck Chuck Woodward's woodie?

I crack myself up.

The musing did dispel any nerves I felt during the run as I encountered the following:

--Four pointed fingers from people who turned to chat with their *compadres* about me

--Four faces appearing to be shocked to see me doing the same damn thing I did the day before as if nothing had happened

--Three friendly waves

--Two attempts to stop me for a chat

--Two shaking heads accompanied by chuckling

--Two couples who appeared angry enough to circulate a petition to have me stoned to death

I'm pretty sure I had the attention of most of the 400-some-odd (OK, some odder than others) guests and residents of NTOR.

At the end of my second circuit -- third mile -- of my usual route, Jesse Raslon, a retired Navy pilot, also in his 60s, jogged up beside me.

"Hi, Pepe. How's it hangin'?"

What can I say? Dad jokes rule in nudist camps.

I glanced at my 5'10", not-an-ounce-of-fat-on-him, white crewcut, 100% tanned friend and gave him what my kids call the "Montecarlo Cackle," a copyrighted combination of Bela Lugosi's Dracula and Bart Simpson. It sounds sort of like this: "Bwah! Ha-haw-haw!"

"Want to race, old man?" I asked.

"Give me a half mile to get warmed up," he said. "Seriously, I guess you're OK, right? How's Laurel?"

I snorted.

"Laurel's way tougher than me," I said. "But it hurt her. She liked Rex."

"Yeah," he said, not the least bit winded. Sweat was pouring down my hairy back as usual. "Hard to fathom."

"Deep talk from an old Navy veteran."

"I of course believe your story, that he shot her and then himself."

I wondered where he had learned that. Cops tend to be closed-lipped about such things. I looked at him and raised an eyebrow.

"Franco overheard you when you were telling your story to the cop out on the front porch."

"Ah."

"And of course, I know you and Laurel well enough to realize just exactly how straight you are."

"Wow, you're a barrel of laughs today, Jesse."

The running program on my phone, which was in my hydration backpack, notified me I had just completed 3.5 miles.

"I normally try to speed it up for the second half of each mile," I said. "You up for that?"

"*Por supuesto*," he said, and he lit out for the end of the lane and turned into the woods around the often rowdy younger residents' neighborhood.

A cloud of marijuana smoke drifted over us as we passed a group of twenty-somethings passing around a bong between sips of Pabst Blue Ribbon. They hooted and laughed at the floppy old farts jogging by.

I glanced back at them, grinned, yelled, "Pussies!"

More whoops and cackles hounded us into the next turn back toward the cabins, including the one rented as a mere playpen for Mimi, Rex, Laurel and myself.

I struggled to catch up with Jesse. I sped up a bit and

had caught him when Siri, the voice of my running program, announced I had completed four miles. Bless her.

"This is where I gotta stop for something to drink," I said, not realizing we were approaching the cabin where it all went down, if I'm not being too subtle.

Two deputies in sheriff's office light gray felt cowboy hats leaning against a cruiser looked up from their coffee as we slowed in front of the white Spanish Colonial style stucco structure. They moved off their vehicle and approached us, standing on the side of the one-lane road. I fumbled for the drinking tube of my hydration backpack.

"You gentlemen looking for something?" asked one deputy, white, in his 40s, about 5'10" and about 230 lbs., wearing a similar uniform to deputies we met the night before, but without stripes. I think that meant they were reserve deputies – i.e., qualified peace officers but only paid when hired for traffic control or some other duty the full-time officers did not want to do. I don't think they recognized me.

"Naw," I said. I had passed them twice before without stopping. "Just getting something to drink." I offered the tube to Jesse, you looked disgusted and shook his head no.

Curious what these guys might know, I asked, "Can you tell us what happened here last night?"

The other man, Latino, in his 30s with a salt-and-pepper mustache, 5'8" and about 210 lbs., chuckled. "You probably know more than we do," he said.

The first man – his name tag said B.O. Baxter (Think he went by Bob? Or was he called "B.O." behind his back?) – scowled at the younger man, V. Guadalupe.

"Any information you can offer would be a great help," Baxter said to me.

I shook my head, and Jesse looked down the trail where we would be running next.

"Thought maybe something unofficial might be circulating among the deputies," I said, wiping sweat from my eyes.

"Couple of people shot," Guadalupe said, scowling back at Baxter. "I think they took somebody in custody, but a smart lawyer got him out already. They're pretty sure he did it, though."

"No shit?" I said and started trotting up to Jesse who looked eager to finish the run. I get it. Running with slow old farts can be tedious.

We passed by the pool, where Laurel's wet back sparkled like a polished copper vase on the side of the pool as she lifted a pineapple drink cup to her lips. No one was at the shooting range as we passed by.

We sped up the last half a mile before we got to Jesse's RV and he beat me there, of course. My excuse was this was his first two miles, while this was my fifth and final one for the day. And I got almost no sleep the night before. Slow runners are always quick with excuses.

Raslon's stereo exuded some sexy rhythm and blues music. Grace Raslon, Jesse's wife, a lovely blond in her 50s, looked up from her book as she sat in a lawn chair in the shade. "Hey there sexy man! What your name is?" she sang along with the tune.

I mimed as if she was looking at me, looked around as if she must be talking to someone else. "Uh, Ted," I said. "Ted Cruz."

Grace and Jesse laughed. Politicians get no respect in Texas, especially douches.

Grace set the book she was reading, E.L. James' "Fifty Shades of Grey," on a folding table next to her chair. "C'mere, Ted."

My eyebrows raised, I moved toward her tanned, still-firm body, and she reached for my cock, which dripped sweat.

"Your poll is sagging, senator," she said, as she leaned forward and began stroking my penis.

"Gotta warn you, I sweat like a—"

"Shut up, senator." She put the cock in her mouth and began sucking hard. Trying hard not to recall the last time Mimi did something similar for me, I looked at Jesse, who chuckled and went inside for a towel.

Little Pepe stood at attention even as I heard a battery-powered golf carts approach behind us. It was one of the ladies who cleaned the cottages, a twenty-something blushing brunette with a baseball cap, jeans and an NTOR nut-brown golf shirt.

"Mr. Montecarlo?" she asked, looking only at my sunglasses. Grace was not distracted from her oral machinations. Controlling where one looks is something one learns in a clothing-optional, swinger-friendly facility. I nodded. "Ms. Clarke, the manager, would like you to stop by the office at your earliest convenience."

"Now is not a good time." I pulled Grace's head closer to my crotch, and I closed my eyes and leaned my head back, thrusting into her mouth.

"I understand," the woman said. "When you do come

…" She hesitated, suddenly aware of the double entendre. "I mean, when you stop in, bring Ms. Traeger with you, and –"

"Mmm-mmm-mmm," Grace said, obviously enjoying herself. I glanced down and saw her left hand caressing her vagina.

"You should wear some clothes to the meeting," the woman said, starting to roll the cart forward.

"We'll be there," I said. "It won't be long."

To the extent that a low-powered golf cart can burn rubber on a one-lane, pine-straw-paved path, the NTOR worker burned rubber. My eyes were closed, but a couple of seconds later, to my ears came sound of a commotion as if some slow-walking pedestrians had to move out of the way.

#

8

The gracious dead

Sunday, Oct. 9, 2022, 1:30 p.m.

Stepping into *Casa Montecarlo temporal*, I found Laurel splayed out on the bed, her eyes closed, moaning, as her "wand" vibrator brought her to what would likely be the first of many orgasms that day. I have pretended an intense jealousy of the wand, which we called "Juan."

To set the scene, Laurel's flattish belly featured a 12-inch scar, an unfortunate souvenir of a previous, criminally stupid lover. That gentlemen now resided in a medical ward at a high-security prison unit in Huntsville, Texas, under the appellation "Prisoner No. 02264085." One angered my Nubian Queen at one's peril.

I had texted her earlier we needed to meet Ms. Clarke, and Laurel responded she knew already, as the swimming pool was the closest recreational amenity to the office.

I pushed the vibrator away with my nose and put my

47

eager tongue to the task of bringing her to another level of ecstasy. And then we did the hokey-pokey, and I turned her butt around…

And we did some more hokey-pokey.

The room had a sweet, sweet funk of lovemaking. That's what it's all about.

So, it was more like 2:30 pm by the time Laurel and I entered the Pine Sol-scented, air-conditioned, white paneled office of Ms. Clarke. The nameplate on her desk said "Jonquil Clarke" – the first Jonquil I'd ever met. I wondered what people called her for short. Jonnie?

Refreshed and cleaned in the poolside shower I had shared with Laurel after our lovemaking, I wore khaki cargo shorts with a Gerber multi-tool (a combination knife, pliers, scissors, etc., similar to what Hank Hill carries in the TV show *King of the Hill*) in one pocket and the Kel-Tec pistol in the other, an off-white *guayabera* shirt untucked and sandals. If it matters, you have to be pretty intimate with me to sense the gun's presence.

Laurel wore a low-cut light blue sun dress, sandals and a smile. She carried her ubiquitous pineapple cup and the small purse containing a switchblade in addition to pepper spray and the .32-caliber Beretta Tomcat. *Semper parata* (always prepared), our Laurel.

"Mr. Montecarlo, Ms. Traeger, thanks for coming," Ms. Clarke said, and stood with a somber expression to offer her hand. A slim, tanned woman in her 40s with thick, shoulder-length salt-and-pepper hair, she wore the NTOR shirt and jeans that must be the camp's uniform -- when they do wear clothes. Sometimes the deejay or bartender at night or out by the pool were as nude as anyone.

"Pepe," I said, holding onto her hand a little longer and catching her light scent of suntan oil.

Ms. Clarke's eyebrows rose behind her large, plastic-rimmed glasses.

"Call me Pepe, please," I said, releasing her hand and sitting in one of two arm chairs facing the glass-topped desk, which carried a computer, some files, and an organizer tray. It had no drawers. I guess "You can see everything!" is a running joke at nudist camps. She wore royal blue Sketcher walking shoes.

"OK, Pepe," she said with a shy smile. "You can call me Quil."

"Huh," I said, grinning back. "I wondered what would be short for Jonquil."

"My older brothers tried to call me Jonnie, but I wouldn't have it," she said, reaching for Laurel's hand.

Using her "Eartha Kitt" voice, Laurel purred, "Call me Laurel," rolling her "r." Laurel likes to let other women know I'm her man, but she smiled behind her sunglasses and took a sip from her bronze straw.

Quil held onto Laurel's hand an extra second, decided to be amused, let go and sat down at the same time as Laurel.

"We've been meaning to have this chat with you since you arrived, but things have been … well … busy, with the Columbus Day three-day holiday festivities and the usual fall rush," Quil said with a dejected sigh. She handed a manila folder to Laurel.

"This chat?" I asked, a bit surprised.

"What's this?" Laurel said, bristling. She set her drink on the desk and dug reading glasses out of her purse. How she gets all that stuff in there is a miracle. Her eyebrows scrunched together in concentration as she read.

"NTOR's lawyer — also the Cenas executor -- sent this to the last address we had for you, but we got no response," Quil said.

"We've been traveling a lot," I said.

As Laurel read and turned to the next page of what appeared to be a letter from a law firm, Quil said, "You may have learned of the recent death of Dave and Maeve Cena."

"Yes," I said, having explained to a weepy Laurel before the previous night's excitement. "Oddly enough, it was Rex Vega who told me yesterday. Gas poisoning?"

"It appears so," Quil said. "That's what the coroner concluded. It was brutally cold, and they had both their gas heater and their stove on, and some critter appeared to have built up a nest in their main ventilation system."

Laurel frowned and handed the folder to me.

"They left me their trailer?" Laurel asked. "And what's this description of the land in the letter?"

I read the letter as Quil explained.

"That land is occupied by Nut Tree Orchard Resort," Quil said. "A lot of people don't realize it, but the Cenas owned NTOR, and let us manage it. We – I say 'we,' but I mean our firm, C.O. Resorts – operated the camp and paid them a comfortable income from the net proceeds. They hired me about 20 years ago and at one point let me set up this arrangement for them, so they didn't have to worry about the day-to-day operations."

"Huh," Laurel said, scoffing. "How much debt on the land? I don't have anything to pay off any mortgage with, and Pepe shouldn't have to, either."

"That would explain it," I interrupted, finishing up my reading of the letter.

"Explain what?" Laurel asked.

"Why Rex and Mimi were unable to make contact with the Cenas' kids about acquiring their trailer," I said, and explained what Rex told me at the shooting range the day before.

"Yes, the Vegas did reach out to us for contact information for the Cena family, but we kept putting them off until we could talk to you," Quil said. "As to debt, the property is free and clear, and we take care of property taxes from gross revenues. Since we allow hunting and indeed have some nut trees at the rear of the land, next to the El Camino Real, it is classified as agricultural, so the taxes are not a big burden. The Cenas received about $120,000 a year in rent, which you'll now receive."

Quil opened another folder on her desk, extracted a commercial-size check and handed it to Laurel, whose glasses had slipped down her nose and whose mouth was agape. Tears were welling up in her eyes.

"We owe you for six months," Quil said. "You understand, this is taxable unearned income, and you'll have to pay the tax at the appropriate time. If you want us to make those payments for you on a quarterly basis, we can talk about it at another time."

"Wow," I whispered. "I'm going to be a kept man."

Laurel punched me lightly in the shoulder, and I heard

her sob. I knelt beside her and held her as she cried into my shoulder.

"I can show you the will, but you would probably get a kick out of the video," Quil said, standing up and moving toward a TV on a low file cabinet next to a window over-looking the pool. Through the wall, thumping music – Barry White? – came to us, but most of the sound was deadened.

Quil picked up the remote, turned on the TV and the nearby DVD player and returned to her seat. I moved my chair closer to Laurel and sat with one arm caressing her balsam-scented bare shoulder.

On screen were Dave and Maeve, nude and tanned, as usual, smiling at the camera. Maeve's teeth ("store-bought," she called them), gleamed as white as her hair. Behind her wire-rimmed glasses, her eyes crinkled with genuine affec-tion. Dave grinned through his short gray beard, humor in his brown eyes. His narrow chest shook with a gentle chuckle.

"Laurel, if you're seeing this, we're not here to enjoy you in person," Maeve said. "Hell, we're not even on the planet in any real sense. Just know we love you, and think of you often – so often, in fact, that we wanted to do what we could to give you as much pleasure on a continuing basis as you did us on those occasions when you and what's-his-name visited."

Dave waved his hand at the camera and said, "We hope Pepe's with you, but that's your business."

"To be clear," Maeve said, getting serious, "we're leaving NTOR to you, not to anyone else. Our kids and grandkids are well taken care of. They don't want to have anything to do with this, and that's OK. We're not including Pepe in the will for two reasons: One, he doesn't need it. Two, you might kick him to the curb someday, and then where would you be?"

Dave looked seriously at the camera, pointed and said: "The fact is, you, Laurel, are a huge asset wherever you are. You have been a huge asset to NTOR. Every time you have shown up, people talk about how much fun they had, and they invite more people, and the business just blossoms."

Laurel's tears ran down her cheeks as she smiled. I was getting choked up, too.

"So, it's not just for your benefit we're leaving the property to you," Maeve said, still smiling. "It's for the benefit of Jonquil Clarke and all the other people who work and depend on Nut Tree Orchard Resort. We want it to continue to thrive and bring joy to couples for decades to come, and at least while you're alive and when you're here – which we hope will be a lot – we believe that's going to happen."

Dave nodded and waved at the camera, and the video stopped. Quil sniffed, grabbed a tissue off her desk, blew her nose and handed the tissue box to Laurel, who blew her nose, handed the box to me, stood and said, "I need to go to the ladies' room," as she exited the office.

The inheritance included the Cenas' trailer, Quil reminded me, but I said we didn't want to have to relocate again from the rental trailer we were occupying currently. The rental would come out of what we had been paying for the cottage.

This happened to be the Sunday of a three-day Columbus Day weekend, so we could not meet with the Cenas' lawyer and sign papers before Tuesday. I said late morning or early afternoon on Tuesday would probably be OK, if Quil could make those arrangements, and we prefer to meet in the camp's office, if possible. Quil agreed it may be best, to avoid having to exit the front gate under the watchful eye of media and potential protesters. She would try to get the attorney on the phone so we would know the meeting time by lunchtime Monday.

As we finalized these arrangements. The time was about 3:30 pm as Laurel returned, her tear-tracks wiped, lipstick straight and sunglasses over red eyes. She held a tissue in her hand as she grabbed the pineapple cup off Quil's desk. I stood to say we needed to go.

\#

$$9$$

Camus pour deux (Camus for two)

Sunday, Oct. 9, 2022, 3:35 p.m.

Phoning Deuce as we walked to our rental trailer, I told him I'd like to set up a video call meeting with the two reporters by 4:15 pm, and I asked him for his advice.

"As your lawyer, I advise against it."

Says He Who Introduced Me to the Collected Works of Hunter S. Thompson.

"Thanks, Dr. Gonzo," I said. "But I kinda wanna get ahead of this thing in the court of public opinion."

The line went silent. The charcoal-scented wind rustled through the trees. Our footsteps crushed leaves and pine straw underfoot. Laurel sipped the last of her drink, making the slurping noise that happens with straws and ice in metal cups. Deuce's sigh came through the smartphone to my ear.

"Therefore, as your lawyer, I advise you to have me on the call, with only you seeing me, and with my microphone muted," he said. I could almost hear the judgmental frown in his voice, as if he were talking to an errant preteen. "Keep a close eye on my screen, because I'll be signaling you if I see you're straying into dangerous legal waters."

"Okily-dokily-doo!"

"As your lawyer, Mr. Flanders, I would fear less for your continued freedom if you would stop being so annoyingly amused by your circumstances."

"Okily-dokily-doo!"

He hung up.

With the continued pastoral near-silence of NTOR's Hill Country setting, Laurel had heard both sides of the conversation. She eyed me askance from behind her sunglasses.

"He's got a point," she said, as we rounded the corner and saw the rental trailer ahead.

"Ah, but he's too deep in the esoterica to see the Battlestar Galactica," I said.

She snorted, pursed her lips, shook her head as if my bullshit had attracted too many flies to the area. "What am I going to do with you?"

"The situation is absolutely absurd," I said. "I find the best way to approach absurd challenges is to notice and draw attention to its absurdity, via humor."

"Way to go, Monsieur Camus," she said. "You do realize dear old Albert is dead, right?"

"Absurdly irrelevant," I said, as I opened the door to the trailer and followed her inside.

You may want to know how I concluded life is absurd. Here's the story:

The love of my life, before Laurel, was Francesca "Frankie" Montecarlo, *nee* Perez, who died in March 2020 — yes, the March the world shut down due to the novel coronavirus pandemic — of a cerebral aneurysm.

Consider: Frankie had been an absolute positive force in the world throughout her life. She had been a fantastic daughter, sister, wife, mother and friend. In her work, she had saved dozens of marriages and even more lives by preventing suicide or helping people overcome addiction. She wasn't perfect, but if anyone I knew had a claim on a direct entrance to heaven — do not pass Go, do not collect $200 — it had to be Frankie.

In contrast, I had been an adequate son, brother and father, but a quite imperfect husband and friend. In my work, my big contribution was, in effect, advising the 1% richest people in the world about how to make more money and avoid losing it. I had also acquired a big pile of money myself, but I realize that occurred at the cost of thousands who bet wrong in financial markets and likely suffered significantly after the Great Recession. Therefore, I considered my fortune infinitesimal on the scales of human value.

So, between Frankie and myself, if you were an omnipotent God who wanted to maximize the value of humanity on earth, which one of our lives would you end?

I agree.

But as I came to accept the idea that one's contribution to others' lives would not necessarily add to the bottom line of human value, at least in the grand scheme of things from the viewpoint of an omnipotent deity, I thought, what the hell? Why should one abide unquestioningly by the various conventional mores, as long as violating such standards did no harm to others?

To sum it up: Life is short. Eat dessert first.

I don't mean simply live for pleasure. I mean, if one wants to get something done, quit fooling around! Do it! As dear old Albert might say, that boulder isn't going to roll up the hill by itself. I'm not going to become the best Pepe Montecarlo there ever was or will be without intense passion, effort, thought and, dammit, a sense of humor.

But in light of the pandemic year of 2020's absurdity and my own spiritual, emotional and libidinous malnutrition, I perceived a "foolish consistency … the hobgoblin of little minds," to quote Emerson, for me to eschew meeting new women in person, mourning and pandemic be damned.

The result of pursuing this new freedom from social limits? The joy of meeting and loving Laurel Traeger — and dozens of her swinging friends and lovers. Fuck the consequences.

I could be wrong. I often am.

#

10

Meat for the press

Sunday, Oct. 9, 2022, 4:15 p.m.

It took a bit of doing with help from a paralegal to coordinate the two TV stations in a video call from inside our rented trailer. Those news directors were unhappy about sharing an interview on such a sensational crime. As we convened the web conference, Deuce was only visible to me. I agreed the call was on the record. My attorney showed me his businesslike, witness-deposition face. I gave him a discreet "OK" hand gesture to signify I understood the situation.

We flipped a coin, and Stevie Sabin won the toss and chose to ask the first question: "What happened last night, regarding the death of Mimi and Rex Vega?"

"Mimi and I were in a room, enjoying each other's company. Rex walked in with a gun, shot her in the face and shot himself in the head."

"Can you give us –" Stevie started to ask.

I held up a cautioning hand and pointed to the other reporter's screen. "It's Joanna Metzger's turn."

"Sh—" Stevie started saying before muting her microphone. On her lips, I read the end of the word, "—it!"

"Mr. Montecarlo, can you give us any more details about the scene, such as the expression on each person's face?" Joanna asked, snapping off her microphone.

I frowned. As a former journalist, I understood where she was coming from. She wanted "color" for the story. I disliked it, but I understood it, and it couldn't hurt Mimi to satisfy Joanna and whatever ghoulish viewers she had.

"Before Rex entered, Mimi's eyes were closed, and she was giggling. When she realized Rex was there, she opened her eyes, look surprised and, I guess, angry. Rex's face looked, well, resigned, sad, disappointed and in the end, a bit frustrated."

Deuce, who had been writing something out of my view, looked up at me to make sure I was paying attention. I gave him a quick questioning raised eyebrow, and he wagged his head ambivalently, as if to say, "not great, not bad."

Stevie started talking without unmuting herself. I pointed down at the microphone, she pushed a button and said, "Sorry."

"What was everybody wearing?" she asked, and muted her microphone again.

"It's a nudist resort. They had not a thing on." I nodded at Joanna to ask her next question.

"How long had you known Rex and Mimi Vega, and what do you know about their – I think you call it – 'vanilla' life history?" Joanna asked.

"For those of your viewers who have not heard the word 'vanilla' aside from a culinary context, a person's 'vanilla life' is the mode of living outside the open sexual lifestyle enjoyed by Rex, Mimi, myself and tens of millions of other Americans, almost all well hidden from the public eye.

"To answer your question about Rex and Mimi, all I can say is they were the first couple we played with, which must have been, what, about two years ago?" I looked up with raised eyebrows at Laurel on the other side of the laptop computer in the trailer's dining table. She nodded that it was about right.

Deuce stared at the screen, not writing.

"I think that's right, two years ago, in the summer. As for their vanilla life, Rex worked in information technology, and Mimi worked in some form of life-coaching field. I don't really know anything more about their background, I'm afraid."

I looked at Stevie Sabin, who unmuted her microphone.

"How did you meet the Vegas?"

"We met at what we call a 'meet and greet' event for couples in this open lifestyle at a Houston-area restaurant. Several other couples were there. We found Rex and Mimi both charming, down-to-earth people."

In Stevie's florid face, a crease formed between her expertly threaded eyebrows, her lips pursed and her nostrils flared. I concluded my allegro/staccato answers were not charming one particular news beast. I was answering her simple questions but with insufficient salaciousness.

Joanna, in contrast, switched from looking at her notes and to looking at me. Both Deuce and Laurel regarded me sideways, as if they thought I was about to pull a fast one. Joanna unmuted her microphone.

"Mr. Montecarlo, we have learned Mimi had several lawsuits filed against her for fraud and embezzlement in various courts outside Texas, including Florida – where she is from, by the way – and Louisiana. Allegations include misrepresenting her credentials, misappropriation of funds, identity theft and others. How do you respond?"

At a certain suburban Austin law office, a large attorney was going ape-shit, pulling his hair straight in both hands, then waving his hands at the screen, giving the thumbs-down sign.

"Complete dismay. Was Rex implicated in any of this?"

Stevie unmuted her microphone. "Hey! That's not part of the deal!"

Joanna mimed "No" at the screen.

"Sorry, Ms. Sabin," I said, smiling. "I don't believe my asking questions was part of our agreement. Do you have a question?"

Stevie's left eyelid drooped as she exhaled in frustration. "Mr. Montecarlo, sources close to the investigation say you are a 'person of interest' in the death of Rex and Mimi Vega. How do you respond?" She muted herself.

I cocked my head. Deuce shook his head violently at me. Laurel's eyes grew wide and she set her pineapple cup down with a slight bang on the dining table.

"Who says I'm a person of interest?"

Stevie unmuted herself.

"I'm asking the questions, and I'd like an answer. You said you would give us the naked truth."

Her lips curled in appreciation for her own *bon mot*.

"Will you give us the truth, warts and all?" she continued down the bad-pun lane. "Will you answer the question?"

Deuce had scribbled in three-inch-high capital letters "STFU!!!" sideways on a legal pad and held it up to his computer's camera. I couldn't help grinning a little.

"In effect, I've answered the question. That's at least part of my response. The rest of it is this: 'Person of interest' is a phrase we hear on TV detective shows, but in my experience, its meaning could not be more clear, which is to say that a person of interest is someone who officials think may have some useful information about a noteworthy event. Indeed, as I am the only eyewitness to the events we've been discussing, I'd be very much surprised if I was not considered a person of interest. If I were you, I would not –"

"EXCUSE ME!" Deuce had unmuted his microphone and interrupted.

"—read anything more into that piece of information than what I just described."

"Excuse me, ladies, but Mr. Montecarlo has an appointment to discuss St. Thomas the Fulsome of Ulster on another call right now," Deuce said. Joanna and Stevie could not see him, but I found it hard to hide my amusement.

"Pardon me, Joanna, Stevie, but it appears church matters require my immediate attention. I hope we can discuss this situation further as more information comes to light."

Learned counsel had muted his microphone again and was punching the "STFU!!!" on his legal pad violently with his index and middle finger while glaring at me from the side of the screen.

"Thank you, Mr. Montecarlo," Joanna said, and muted herself.

"Yes, thank you, Mr. Montecarlo," Stevie said, muting herself. I read her lips shouting, "FOR NOTHING!" to me in the screen. I let loose with the Montecarlo Cackle.

All screens went dark for a minute, and Laurel whistled in surprise.

#

11

Rex's losing hand

Sunday, Oct. 9, 2022, 4:35 p.m.

A signal sounded for a new video call from a certain suburban Austin law office.

"SHUT THE FUCK UP, YOU IDIOT!" Deuce shouted.

"That was hilarious," I said, chuckling. "St. Thomas the Fulsome? Was he exaggeratedly doubtful? Offensively Aristotelian? HA!"

Deuce shook his head. "I hope you'll be half as amused when they stick a needle in your arm in Huntsville."

"That would be an outcome even more absurd than I consider our situation to be," I said. "However, I am often wrong. If so, would you come to watch me die?"

I looked at Laurel. "Would you, baby?"

Laurel rolled her eyes, pursed her lips and shook her head in frustration.

He assumed what I call his "Sunday come to Jesus" face:

65

a frown, eyebrows pointed toward his straight Roman nose, lips turned down.

"I know you need to learn as much as you can about the victims – " Deuce started.

"Rex and Mimi," I interrupted.

"The Vegas."

"No, Rex and Mimi," I said. "Laurel and I only just this week found out their last names. People in the lifestyle rarely learn each other's whole names. I realize it appears odd, not knowing the full names of the people with whom you're exploring the depths of carnal knowledge, but that's part of the culture. I'm not saying it's right or good. It just … is. That doesn't change how we felt about them."

My friend, now in his cynical attorney mode, cocked his head.

"Okaaaay. I know you need to know as much as you can about Rex and Mimi, but you need to do so as discreetly as possible. The fact is, the cops are very serious about you two conspiring to kill them. The district attorney over lunch advised me to make sure you stick around. They don't want to have a manhunt for people they had in their hands this morning, despite the flimsiness of their case now."

Laurel, who was sitting on my side of the RV's table, looking at the screen with me, snorted. "Gee, I'd hate to put them to any trouble."

"You don't want to unnecessarily piss these guys off," Deuce said. "They know you normally carry a concealed weapon."

"I think of it as a concealed weapon of love," I said, glancing down at my lap, which Laurel was fondling.

"You two are hilarious," said the man desperately seeking serious clients, who shook his head. "No, really. You'll be the hit of the cell block. They'll probably give you an extended engagement."

Laurel chuckled.

"The point is, if they issue a manhunt, they could identify you both as armed and dangerous, which could go south real damn quick," he said.

"Fair enough," I said. "We have no intention of leaving the area. I think we can make good headway right here at NTOR."

"Or get good head, anyway," Laurel said and winked at me as she sipped from her Tito's Tart. Did I mention she had been drinking since about noon?

"True dat," I said. After all, Grace Raslon is a pretty skilled fellatio practitioner.

"Jesus, you guys," Deuce said, looking out the window of his office, trying to dispel the fog of innuendo Laurel and I spouted as part of our daily banter and re-enter the mundane world of law, the courts, writs, office overhead, etc.

"I'm curious what you thought about the revelation Ms. Metzger gave us about Mimi's checkered past," I said.

"At last, a reasonable topic of discussion," he said. "Yes, we knew about that. Her name comes up in PACER, the federal court records look-up system. The nut doesn't fall far from the tree."

Before retiring, I used the federal Public Access to Court Electronic Records in my reporting. Every federal court feeds filings into PACER. God help the poor archaeologist a hundred years from now, having to dig through mountains of what can be the driest, most deadly dull legalese imaginable, to find one significant nugget of truth.

As a nerdy reporter, I thrilled at having access to all those files without having to visit local courthouse, the practice before PACER was launched. On previous occasions, I could hit a dead end because a file got lost or a fire destroyed documents for the years I was researching. Today, looking at that mountain of data, most of it meaningless and unimportant, I think, I bet somebody set those fires on purpose, just to save the rest of us the trouble of deciding whether something was important enough to save.

"She was in PACER?" I asked.

"Not as a defendant, criminal or civil, except as a matter of interstate extradition. However, she was identified as a witness in relation to her father, who was a real piece of work."

Laurel stood to refill her pineapple cup with Tito's Tart, removed her clothes and started to sit beside me again. I asked her to make me some coffee before she sat down.

"Remember the Dullestown Bank scandal?" Deuce said.

Wow, there was a leap in history, to be sure. The Dullestown Bank went bankrupt under the leadership of its main owner, Truett "Truly" Dulles, whose nickname was hilariously ironic. As my daddy said at the time, he was "as crooked as a dog's hind leg." The scandal ended the careers of several top Democratic politicians around 1970 and could be blamed – or appreciated, if you swing that way – for helping transform Texas from a Democratic stronghold into a two-party state, at the time.

"Vaguely," I said. "You and I must have been at Paulson

Junior High at the time. I was working at my dad's gas station, in between dislocating my kneecaps on the football field."

"Remember Jim Bob Kefauver?"

"All I remember was people always said Jim Bob Kefauver must be sitting on a beach somewhere in the Caribbean with all the cash embezzled from some ritzy Catholic high school in Houston."

"Cassidy Basilian Academy," he said.

"Whatever."

"Guess Mimi's maiden name."

"I thought it was Comemos. It isn't?"

"That's the name he gave the family when they came in from Cuba with the Mariel boat lift." Deuce leaned back and looked at the screen on his desk next to the one where he saw me, just as Laurel set a steaming mug of coffee in front of me and sat down beside me. "In fact, her Cuban birth certificate says …" He slid his reading glasses on and looked more closely at the other computer screen. "Miriam Margarita Kefauver. Jim Bob married a beautiful young mulatta down there, Iris."

He gave it the Spanish pronunciation "eerees."

"She's still living in Florida, although the COVID-19 put her in the hospital for a while," he said. He looked back at my screen and caught sight of Laurel, which made him gasp in shock, the poor little innocent.

"Ma'am. Really?" he said. "You gotta go topless now?"

"Hey, I'm bottomless, too, if you want to see," she said, giggling.

"My wife wouldn't appreciate it."

Laurel brought her breasts up in her hands and shook

them at the screen. "Tough these-ies." As I say, she had been drinking for almost five hours by now.

"Really, Laurel?" I said, rolling my eyes. "We're trying to have a serious business meeting here."

"Really, Pepe? You yourself said this whole situation is absurd. Why should I put something on?"

I looked at the 61-year-old attorney. "She's got a point," I said. "You're a grownup. Stifle your libido in the presence of such bodacious tatas, for once in your life."

Deuce's eyes rolled like pictures of blue diamonds on a slot machine, and his head shook like Lurch shivering in The Addams Family, but he rejoined the topic. "I'm sending you our file on Mimi and her family."

"Thanks. Anything on Rex?"

"Did you know how Rex lost his left hand?"

"I try not to pry under two circumstances: when a man's shtupping my woman and when he's brandishing a gun."

"I was just confirming what I thought would be the case," he said. "I'm sure Mimi didn't want the story repeated. My God, the man was pussy-whipped. It was basically Mimi's fault he lost his hand."

"Whuuut?" Laurel asked, letting the straw drop out of her mouth for once.

"It would be funny if it were not so sad," Deuce said. "I'm going to tell you because you need to understand how twisted the pair of them had become. Some documents in the file touch on it, but I talked to a lawyer friend down there in Florida who represented the aggrieved party – the plaintiff in an identity theft case against Mimi – who gave me the

Howard Cosell-type deep-background commentary on how Rex lost his hand."

"Howard who?" Laurel asked.

"Deuce and I used to watch a lot of Monday night football together," I explained. "Howard Cosell could spend half the game giving the deep background on some minor benchwarmer just to hear himself talk."

Deuce rolled his eyes as if everybody should know who Howard Cosell was.

"The short version is this," he said. "She had taken over this million-dollar mansion on Miami Beach from a sweet old widow named Boucher who thought Mimi could coach her into finding just the right new husband. The old widow's kids had gotten mama away from the house, and came back with a couple of deputies to evict Mimi. Rex wasn't living with Mimi then, just spending lots of time with her. They were frolicking nude in the hot tub when the widow Boucher's son arrived with the deputies and, oddly enough, a couple of the son's Doberman Pinschers."

He bowed his head and stared at me to emphasize the latter two words.

"The son was pissed, so as soon as he heard the couple cavorting in the hot tub, he set the dogs loose on them," he continued. "The deputies were negligent, and the Miami-Dade County Sheriff's Department paid a price for it, but that's a minor sidebar, as we say in the legal trade.

"Well, Mimi and Rex jumped out of the tub and made a beeline for a gate leading to the driveway where their car was parked. Mimi got through first and pushed the wrought-iron gate shut on Rex's wrist, leaving his hand exposed to the dogs, which proceeded to not-so-neatly chew it off his left arm."

"Oh. My. God," said Laurel.

"The story goes that he begged Mimi to let go of the gate, so he could pull back his arm, but she said if she did that, the dogs would get both of them." The attorney's face was dispassionate, his voice monotonous.

"The hand came off, and Rex and Mimi stumbled – naked, mind you – to the car, hopped in and sped away. By now, the deputies realized they had let the situation get out of hand, as it were."

"Jeez, dude, a new low," I said.

A little sheepish grin then appeared. "Sorry. Couldn't help myself. Anyway, they tried to get the hand from the dogs, thinking there might be some way to reattach it. However, the two dogs were fighting over it, and eventually the male ran off with it and hid under some bushes so thick no one could reach it."

I sighed. "And … of course … the male dog's name is …"

"Don't say it!" Laurel shouted.

"You got it in one," he said. "The dog's name was Rex, so thenceforward, it was still Rex's hand, just a different Rex."

"That's some mo' shiggedy," Laurel said.

"*Algo de mierda oscura, seguro,*" I said, feeling just a bit squeamish. Looking at Laurel, I could tell she didn't understand. "Some dark shit, for sure."

"So, it's safe to say Rex had motive for killing Mimi in spades," he said. "But he stayed with her. I have no doubt she could be hella persuasive and manipulative, but … damn!"

"No doubt at all," I said. "Having probed every cubic

centimeter of her body with gusto, I can understand how a guy like Rex – who probably thought she was out of his league – would do whatever he could to keep that woman in his life."

"Sad," he nodded.

"She was definitely out of his league," Laurel said, steam faintly rising from her angry pink spiky hair. "She was a low-down cunt, and he deserved much better."

"As I say, the nut doesn't fall far from the tree," Deuce said. "Wait until I tell you what her life was like growing up."

My turn. "Even mo' shiggedy," I said.

#

12

Nuts falling from trees

Sunday, Oct. 9, 2022, 5 p.m.

Arriving with the Mariel boatlift in Miami in 1980, the renamed Comemos family ("let's eat" in Spanish) moved into a dingy motel a half mile from the beach, Deuce said. They set up house by buying the place, which took a considerable fraction of whatever money Jim Bob still had.

"The place was a dump — a hot-sheet hotel, really — but Jim Bob saw its potential, it appears," he said, his voice only slightly distorted by the video call. "One of the more frequent visitors to the ladies regularly staying at the motel was a TV cable technician who helped Jim Bob install hidden cameras in every room.

"Things went swimmingly, at least on the surface. For four years, until 13 years of age, little Mimi attended St. Mary Magdalene Catholic School from fifth through eighth grade.

The motel had no debt, so Comemos renovated it. Senora Comemos learned how to cheat at the dice game bunco with some church matrons."

Laurel, who liked to gamble, snorted with contempt.

"Jim Bob, as one might expect from such a paragon of ethics, blackmailed the occasional well-heeled patron of the motel's frequent female guests," Deuce continued. "He also helped arrange meetings for narcotics deals — secretly video-taped — for a cut of the proceeds, my lawyer friend says."

"Your lawyer friend has a very sensitive ear for Miami's underworld," I said.

"He owes me a favor for keeping a client's kid out of prison," learned counsel said.

To watch his back, Jim Bob hired a fellow Marielito who could keep old cars running but earned most of his money as a small-time hood and leg-breaker for a gambler who kept to the old, pre-Castro ways, Deuce said.

"Carlos Marron, known on the street as either '*El Mecanico*' or 'Charlie Brown,' became enchanted by Mimi, whom he called '*mi Mimi*,'" Deuce said, making it sound like an opera singer preparing to sing with the note "meemeemee."

"Cute," Deuce said with a modicum of sarcasm. "Charlie Brown would buy her candy, help her avoid punishments, etc., and drive her to school in the hotel's Lincoln Continental every day. Around then, Mimi hit puberty with one might say a spectacular bang. She basically used her budding hormones and sexuality as a license to exploit quite a few people in her circle — kids, teachers, nuns, priests. By the time she moved into Our Lady of Fatima High School three years later, St. Mary Magdalene's headmaster had resigned his vocation, two nuns had left their order to become Lesbian activists, three teachers had become drug addicts, and several classmates had been traumatized for life."

"What the hell?" Laurel asked, her eyebrows raised in surprise. "Pooberty ain't a license to sin."

Laurel always pronounced puberty "pooberty," the way Harry Morgan's Olly Perkins character did in the old western comedy, "Support Your Local Sheriff." I found that quite endearing, but I also was disturbed by what I was hearing and cocked my head at my friend inquisitively.

"Wait, I'll explain in a minute," he responded. "It's a helluva a story, I shit you not. Mimi's tenure at St. Mary Magdalene School served as a tipping point toward the eventual closing of the high school and its conversion to a parking lot. In the last of those eventful three years, the Diocese got wind of it and tried to minimize liability by offering medical and psychological services to help Mimi deal with the sexual abuse she had suffered at the hands of adults at the school. Through those files, now available because of Mimi's death with a little help from my lawyer friend, my investigators learned the hellish shit that had happened – at least according to Mimi. She lost her virginity soon after arrival from Cuba when a female guest at the motel enticed her from the swimming pool and played with her with some unusual toys, and Mimi said she liked it."

"Da-amn," I said, glancing aside to Laurel. "That's fucked up."

"Exactly," Laurel whispered, her eyes horrified.

Mimi enticed two other young classmates, a boy and a girl, to meet with this same woman for similar "play" at a different location, Deuce said, and Mimi had participated in what she thought of as "playful torture" of those preteens.

"The boy hung himself that summer," said the attorney in a monotone as he continued reviewing his notes..

"Oh lawd," Laurel said, her eyes brimming with tears. I could feel the anger and sadness welling up in my gut.

"The parents were too traumatized to pursue the case at the time, so Mimi's story was the first explanation of the boy's death," Deuce said. "The girl, Rubia Trevino, became Mimi's chief lieutenant as darling Mimi proceeded to sow chaos at Our Lady of Fatima High School. Through a battery of what were then fairly sophisticated psychological tests, the Diocese determined Mimi was a budding sociopath, without using that word. She had no moral compunction, no sense of guilt, no inhibitions, no empathy, no fear."

"Ahaaaa," I said. In *The Far Side* version of my life, a light-bulb clicked on above my head.

In my role as a business journalist, I had regular contact with several CEOs who wound up on the wrong side of the law. In trial testimony, several attorneys described their defendant clients as being full-blown narcissistic psychopaths with Machiavellian proclivities — labeled by their expert psychological witnesses as having the Dark Triad. Alas for those defendants, juries thought the accused considered the Dark Triad a feature, not a bug. As a reporter, I tried to remain open-minded about it.

Deuce hesitated at my utterance, but dismissed it with a shake of his head and continued in monotone.

"They called in Jim Bob and Iris and told them Mimi was a danger to herself and others who needed immediate and vigorous treatment, to avoid winding up dead or in prison," he said, flipping the page on his legal pad. "Wait a second — what the fuck?"

He held up a news paper clipping next to his screen, looked at me, looked at the clipping, and turned it around for us to see.

I was staring at a face that could have been my own — dark hair, thin mustache, smart-ass toothy grin, cocked eye-brow — above a caption stating, "Jim Bob Kefauver leaves the Harris County Courthouse on bail."

"OK, now I know you are a vampire," Laurel said, turning from the photo to me, and sipping from her cup.

"I-I-I — Ay-yi-yi!" I said. "That's just so, so random. Some-body up there finds me a barrel of laughs."

Deuce returned the clipping to his manila older and resumed reviewing his notes.

"Iris, as you might expect, was in denial — enraged, in fact. She said this was just a ploy to try to keep the church from taking responsibility for the atrocities at the school. Jim Bob knew better – more about that in a minute – but he sniffed a potential financial jackpot, so he backed up Iris' rage with a threat of a lawsuit."

"*Mierda*," I muttered, beginning to feel nauseated. I saw it coming: Kefauver's exploitation of his own child for his own benefit. A dark triad, indeed.

The church authority in the case wanted no lawsuit, and said as long as Mimi went to a different school, they would take no action. Jim Bob said it was unacceptable. Not only would Mimi continue to go to Catholic schools, she would do so for free, and the Diocese would pay for all therapy Mimi needed throughout her schooling.

"The last part was key, from Jim Bob's standpoint, sick puppy that he was," Deuce said. "He had a girlfriend who was a down-at-heel psychologist who could bill the Diocese almost any amount. You'll never guess who the girlfriend was."

"The Whore of Babylon?" I said.

"Kenya Moore from *Real Housewives of Atlanta?*" Laurel said.

"Oooh, burn," I said, grimacing.

"I have no idea who that is, and I don't want to know," my friend said. "It was the woman who seduced Mimi at the age of 10."

"That's some mo' shiggedy, right there," Laurel said.

"*El juego continua,*" Deuce said.

Laurel gave me a questioning glance as my attorney flipped through the file.

"You're a gambler," I muttered. "You should know 'the game continues.'"

"So, Jim Bob — as I say, one sick puppy — is shagging this Ms. Dr. Evil, as it were," said the lawyer, ignoring our little explanatory exchange. "Her name was Alexandra Freeman, and she was quite a freak. At one point, she has Jim Bob bound, gagged and probed with God knows what at her apartment when who shows up?"

"Don't say it," Laurel muttered, looking out one of the RV's windows toward the pool, where our friends played with each other's naked bodies in innocent joy.

"Darling Mimi," Deuce said in a sort of breathless monotone. "You'll find out in a bit how this all came to light. She's about 17 now, high as a kite on some killer sinsemilla – remember that? Good stuff. Anyway, Mimi finds all this quite amusing and participates in the daddy torture. A whole litter of puppies at play, for sure.

"But a few days later, Mimi is at the motel, high again, giggling and hinting around about it in front of Charlie Brown – remember him? And daddy slaps the shit out of her, as daddies are wont do."

"Some do, and one can't say he wasn't provoked," I said, looking down at my hands folded before the computer keyboard. "But my God, what the girl had been through already! And from what you've already told me about Jim Bob, he deserved whatever pain he suffered. To let your daughter be used that way? *Que monstro!*"

Laurel looked aside at me quizzically. "What a monster," I mumbled.

"Charlie Brown was not amused," he continued. "He had no idea what Mimi was hinting about, and from Charlie's perspective, Jim Bob had stepped way over the line. *El Mecanico* got medieval on his ass but good. Beat and kicked him to death then and there, next to the motel ice machine.

"The cops came. *El Mecanico* was *silencioso*. Mimi was just high enough to tell the whole story. They found some dope on her, so she said she'd tell them all about it if they'd forget about the dope. She was on the one hand proud of Charlie for defending her but complaining now she had no father. It was classic sociopathic conflicting manipulation."

"Still a kid, but damn, she was a piece of work wasn't she?"

I said, shaking my head, squeezing the bridge of my nose to stop tears from flowing.

"There was some good come out of it," Deuce said, sighing. "Ms. Dr. Evil went to prison. She had videotapes of her encounters with Mimi and her classmates, Jim Bob and others. She died in prison when Hurricane Andrew swept through Florida in 1992 -- murdered by a cell-mate, I gather."

"Jeez, this is depressing," I said with a sigh. "Infuriating and depressing."

"True dat," whispered Laurel, completely sober and teary-eyed.

Mr. "Bill-'em-by-the hour" looked at his watch. My laptop computer screen said 6:15 pm.

"It is getting late, and Yvonne will be wondering whose tits I've been staring at by now." The lawyer lowered a comically stern eyebrow at Laurel through the video screen. Yvonne was Mrs. "Bill-'em-by-the-hour." "I do have some actual legal work to do here, rather than relating some disgusting Marquis de Sade-level ancient history – which you're being billed for, by the way. As it is, I won't get home before 8, so try not to bother me unless something urgent comes up, please."

"Of course," I said, shaking my head. "I'd say 'Good work,' but I kinda wish you hadn't told us all that godawful shit. As Nero Wolfe might have reluctantly said, 'Satisfactory.' I'll text you tomorrow, my friend, and I hope we'll discuss something more pleasant. Shouldn't be too difficult."

#

13

A pool reception

Sunday, Oct. 9, 2022, 6:15 p.m.

Looking at Laurel, I said, "You know, we need to start paying more attention to our usual or potential sexpects. It wouldn't hurt to do a little cyberstalking to make sure we're not about to play hokey-pokey with someone who is infinitely more pokey than hokey."

"I have no idea what that means," Laurel said.

I cocked my head and looked at my beloved, whose face was much more somber than usual.

"You OK?" we asked simultaneously. "Jinx!"

She snorted and pursed her lips. "I ain't studying' that bitch no more."

"Yeah, I get the impression we're not quite as torn up about her death as we might have been last night," I said, shaking my head and looking at my hands, closing up the laptop computer on the RV's dining table. "Still sad about Rex, though."

"Don't start," she said, tears welling up in her eyes. We held each other for a long minute, sighed and stood up from the table. Laurel approached the blender and began composing another magic elixir, while I opened a fridge smelling of onion and sadness.

Our appetites diminished by the nauseating story our solicitor had just inflicted on us, Laurel and I walked my tablet computer and a cooler of beer and margaritas over to the pool, where the crowd was smaller and much less boisterous than the previous night, typical for a holiday weekend's Sunday evening. This was different. DJ Ted, the aging hippie brother of Jonquil Clarke with the Magnum P.I. haircut and George Hamilton tan, waved and smiled. But when I jumped in the pool, swam a couple of laps, stopped and stood, I peripherally saw people slowly turning away from me – not all, but enough to notice.

Laurel, bless her, had been welcomed effusively, and a well-tanned shapely blond of about 30 pushed a shot of peanut-butter whiskey into her hand with a half-dozen other aging hipsters. Can't stand the stuff myself, but to each his own.

Of course, this is when DJ Ted started playing Mel Waiters' blues song, "I got my whiskey," which prompted Laurel to cheer him, rise slow and majestic out of the pool, and give him a sopping wet kiss. See what I gotta put up with? I suspected my beloved Nubian Queen was trying to keep the horror story we had just heard from ruining everybody else's vibe, and I admired her for it.

With an artificial bonhomie, I shrugged and grinned at

the blond who had pressed the shot on Laurel, and she smiled back shyly.

What the hell? We're all naked as God made us, and she's gonna be shy? I took it for a sign she needed encouragement, so I moved toward her, but as I did so, a man who was a little taller, darker, beefier and much younger than me moved between us and gave me a "get back" stare.

"Want something?" he asked.

"Don't we all?" I grinned.

"Haven't you done enough damage this weekend?" The girl put a hand on his mahogany-brown shoulder, and he started to turn away.

"I'm not nearly done yet," I said, grinning. "I plan to leave as many women exhausted with orgasms as will have me this weekend. Perhaps your friend there is looking for something more stimulating than --" I looked him up and down "-- beef and peanut butter whiskey."

The woman waded clumsily around the guy and said, "OK, OK, OK! Let's not do the penis measurement today, shall we?"

Her fellow shot-drinkers – two other women in their 30s and a white-haired, sunburned, tattooed rugby scrum-half in his late 40s – laughed.

"Roight!" said the scrum-half, who had introduced himself to Laurel and myself as "Shawn from Manchester" the night before. "Anybody here heard of shrinkage?"

I smiled up at the big, brown, male intervenor, and he started a little grin, as well.

"Juanda!" shouted my darling Laurel behind me. "Juanda! You made it!"

"Of course I made it, my love," said Juanda Falcon (pronounced "Fal-CONE"), who happens to be the usual third wheel when we're playing three-handed penis-bridge, if I'm not being too subtle.

A statuesque woman of 46 with the milky, freckled skin of someone who grew up on Michigan's Upper Peninsula let go of her rolling suitcase and returned Laurel's enthusiastic hug, heedless of how soggy it was making her summer cotton crepe blouse and jeans.

"Goodness, girl, you've been partying pretty hard, haven't you?" Juanda said, smiling at her and shaking her brown-and-white curls, which only occupied the top and left side of her head. She had shaved the other side, and she had a small tattoo of a butterfly under the yummy little lobe of her right ear.

"Hello darlin'," I sang, beginning the Conway Twitty tune. "Nice to see you. It's been a long tiii-ime!"

Juanda jumped in the water, clothes and all, and gave me a wet, passionate kiss that tasted like Cherry Coke.

"You're just as lovely, as you used to be."

I quit the song at that point, as DJ Ted started playing Twitty's version. Mine was pretty bad, I'll admit.

Instead, I began unbuttoning her clothes and nuzzling her butterfly tattoo and inhaling her strawberry-scented shampoo mixed with the pool's chlorine as Laurel explained to DJ Ted, "That's Juanda, the girl I was telling you about last night."

Little Pepe was starting to get pretty peppy as I glimpsed Juanda's pale, perky breasts.

"Mammaries ... light the corners of my mind," I started

singing again, and nibbled her swelling nipple, which elicited a little squeal of delight and giggles from Juanda, laughter from the peanut-butter whiskey gang and a Midlands-English "Too roight, mate!" from Shawn.

"C'mon, girl, the rules say you gotta be naked in the pool," I said. In fact, the rules did not so specify, but I nevertheless dove under water and helped her unbutton her jeans and pull them and her little thong away from a yummy pussy. I stayed down to pull the jeans off completely, put my head back in her crotch with her legs over my shoulders and stood up, to the delighted laughter and squeals of my fellow pool party players.

"Pepe, you can't!" she said, but she held my face in her crotch all the same, and hooked her feet around my waist from the back.

Seeing that no one was behind her, I tumbled us into the water on her back, dunking her, and standing afterward with mock sheepishness.

"You're right, I can't," I said. "At least not right now."

Juanda shook the water out of her hair at me and slapped my shoulder. "You're so naughty!" she said.

"You have no idea," I said, giving her my Groucho Marx grin and eyebrow wiggle.

"Oh, I most certainly do, don't I, Laurel?" Juanda said, as Laurel had waded back into our wet little circle.

"If he's so bloody naughty, his punishment should be to take a shot!" Shawn-from-Manchester shouted.

"Shot! Shot! Shot!" chanted the women in the group, and the big guy who glared at me earlier carried a four-ounce plastic cup over to me plus one for himself.

"No hard feelin's?" he said, grinning down at me.

"I got nothin' hard for you man," I said, chuckling. "It's all for those ladies. Give me the damn shot."

I knocked it back and made a face. Too sweet. To the extent I like whiskey, which is sort of barely, I like whiskey to taste like whiskey.

"There you go, bud!" the big guy said. He gestured to his girlfriend and stuck out his hand. "That's Janis, and I'm Ben, and we all know Laurel. You must be her boo-thang."

"Boo-thang, am I," I said, imitating Yoda in a demented pastiche of a bad Star Wars prequel. "Pepe, am I called."

Ben laughed. Juanda, Laurel and I gathered around the pool-side chilled shot dispenser. They also happened to have Patron tequila, which I do shoot, so I downed one, stepping out afterward to carry Juanda's drenched clothing over to the reclining pool chair where we had deposited our cooler, towels and my tablet computer. Laurel had rolled Juanda's suitcase to the same area.

The alcohol took some of the edge off my anger and sadness over the earlier pitiful tales. Nevertheless, I remained sober enough to scowl at the prospect of reading more about Mimi, about whom I wondered how I could be so deluded. I blamed the influence of Little Pepe.

But I'm one of those conscientious, neurotic fools who does his duty, which I reckoned entailed finding out enough about both Mimi and Rex to determine the rationale for their deaths. I grabbed a Hopadillo India Pale Ale out of our cooler next to a reclining pool chair and our towels. Little Pepe had lost some of his pep, to be honest. Mind-flashing a memory of the previous night's *pesadilla de sangre* (bloody nightmare),

I sat down to read some more about Our Mimi of Miami. I had made it through her 10th-grade report cards -- all A's of course, but how much of them were due to her actual brains and how much of them entailed manipulation and blackmail of teachers? – before I dozed off.

#

14

Unicorn a la mode

Sunday, Oct. 9, 2022, 7:15 p.m.

I dreamed of a faceless Mimi slapping my face with her cold, blood-slick breasts and awakened to find Juanda straddling me with her wet naked body and slapping my face with her chlorine-scented boobs, as Laurel laughed. The shadows were long, but I soon recovered my composure.

"Thank you, Jesus!" I said, nuzzling the giggling Juanda's left breast. "I didn't think I'd make it to heaven, at least not without a few eons in purgatory, but here I am!"

"We hungry," said Laurel, having doffed her sobriety in the pool over the previous hour. "Jesse and Grace invited us over for some barbecue they had delivered."

"They didn't cook?" asked Juanda, a caterer who was ever thinking about food and its preparation.

I pushed her up so I could turn sideways on the chair.

"Grilling is a ticklish matter at a nudist camp," I said. "'Put another shrimp on the barbie' can have multiple meanings in a nudist camp, innuendo-wise."

Shawn-from-Manchester laughed to his friends behind me. "I like that bloke," he said. "He's funny!" He might have consumed a little too much peanut-butter whiskey.

"I'll probably be here all week, folks," I said, standing and bowing to the crowd exiting the pool in the gathering dusk. "Remember to give good, hard tips to your waitresses."

Laurel, Juanda and I walked down the gravel and pine straw road to our rental RV to drop off the baggage and my tablet. With remarkable foresight, considering how tired and groggy I was, I collected a couple of flashlights with lanyards we could hang around our necks or whatever. I carried the cooler and Laurel threaded her pineapple-cup-carrying hand through the lanyards while she continued informing Juanda about the previous night's excitement.

"If I'd a known what a cunt – what a stone-cold cunt – that bitch Mimi was, I never would have let my boo-thang near her," Laurel said, finishing up the Tito's Tart in her pineapple cup with a loud sucking noise.

"I got my own reasons for despising the bitch," Juanda said grimly, but she grabbed onto my free arm – the other carried the cooler – and hugging onto me as if I was about to run away. "Plus, we shouldn't share our man with such a sicko. But Rex was so sweet!"

"That's another thing," Laurel said, twirling the straw in her mouth and looking into the distance. "I'm convinced Rex was a good man. I think she had it comin'."

I started humming the tune "Cell Block Tango" (refrain: "He had it coming") from the musical "Chicago," but I don't think the ladies got the joke. Laurel, as I've said, had been drinking since noon (it was approaching 8 pm), and Juanda, a Type 1 diabetic, was tipsy.

In the shadows, we passed several naked middle-aged people gathered around a lit wrought-iron *chimenea* fire pit emitting a spicy scent of mesquite. I smiled at them. They stared at us for ten seconds and resumed low talking, smoking and sipping cool drinks.

"Huh," Laurel said. She is sensitive to people paying unfriendly attention to us.

"Baby, am I going to have to kick somebody's ass tonight?" I asked.

"You just might," she said.

As we approached the Raslons' RV, I stopped, which brought the women up short. "I know it's hard – not as hard as you'd like it to be--"

Juanda giggled. Laurel snorted.

"— Hard enough, I guess, to maintain an even keel in this situation, but it's important that we avoid making more waves this weekend," I said.

"Hey!" Jesse called out from the picnic table laden with the evening meal. "Nautical metaphors are my shtick!"

"Forgive me, O Captain, my Captain," I said, bowing deeply as he approached. Laurel swatted my behind with her free hand. "Oh! Not yet, my Nubian Queen! First, we feast!"

Jesse wore a chrome cock ring around his penis and testicles, which was having the desired effect of bringing it to at least half-mast.

"Oh, yum," Laurel said as she bent over to kiss it.

I swatted her behind clumsily with the hand of the arm

Juanda still clung to. "Not yet, my Nubian Queen! First we feast!"

"Mmm-mmm," Laurel said, as she knelt in the grass and started sucking on it harder, and Jesse leaned back a little and closed his eyes. "I got my feast here," she mumbled after a couple of seconds, and handed her pineapple cup to me.

Little Pepe was enjoying the view and getting a little peppier when Grace exited the RV and approached with a platter of dinner rolls.

"Y'all!" she scolded half-heartedly, as Juanda giggled and fondled my cock. "These boys need to keep their strength up."

"True dat," I said, as I found a place for the cooler and flashlights and introduced Juanda.

"So, are you bi?" asked Grace, who has no shy bone in her body, and enjoys women almost as much as men.

"I'm bi-curious," Juanda said, blushing prettily. "I prefer men, but I occasionally enjoy the attention and taste of a lovely woman such as yourself."

"Lovely," Grace said, and turned to the moaning Jesse and Laurel. "Jesse, stop that this minute! Sit your white ass and swollen red cock in this chair and start eating. You were the one who said you were hungry."

Laurel sat back and gave the circumcised head of his cock a little peck, and Jesse helped her to her feet.

"I'll see you later, Red," she said to the penis.

"I think of it as my mast," Jesse chuckled. "I look forward to hoisting it to full sail in your little boat later."

I started humming Karrin Allyson's samba tune, "Little Boat," but again, my musical witticism fell on deaf ears. Or maybe not. Laurel, who knows the tune because I've made her listen to it on long drives when I was controlling the Pandora, looked at me, shook her head and rolled her eyes.

As we ate, of course the conversation turned to Rex and Mimi.

"I can't get over how many of us in the lifestyle have died over what – the past nine months?" I said. "The Cenas' deaths look pretty innocent, but then there's Frank and Ruby and then Rex and Mimi. Do you think there's a pattern? Could somebody be out to get us? It's too absurd to contemplate."

Juanda knew about Frank and Ruby but not about Dave and Maeve, so we had to fill her in.

"Were you at NTOR when Dave and Maeve died?" I asked Jesse and Grace.

Jesse nodded as he swallowed some brisket and washed it down with a Michelob Ultra. "Yes, we were here. It wasn't a great time to be at a nudist camp, as cold as it was, but we spent some time in the hot tub, partied in DJ Ted's Clubhouse and then in the Playhouse."

I explained to Juanda that the Playhouse was a place where swingers had orgies. In one room five beds were lined up along one wall and porn played on a big-screen TV facing the beds. Another room was part dungeon with an X-frame St. Andrew's cross for restraining "victims" and a variety of chains, manacles and whips. Yet another room had various unusual apparatuses, including another swing like the one where Mimi died.

"Don't think I'll ever want to play with a swing again, but oh, the fun Ruby and I used to have on it!" I said, shaking my head in wonder and sadness, choking up. "Phenomenal."

"Exactly," Laurel said.

"Maeve did a great naked pole dance in the clubhouse that night," Grace said.

I found the image of 70-year-old Maeve Cena, lovely though she was, doing a pole dance as amusing as you probably do, and I grinned, but I could tell Grace was getting emotional.

"Anything strike you as odd that night or the next day?" I asked.

"Such as?" Jesse asked.

"Anyone at NTOR you didn't expect to be there?" I said. "Any unusual noises or altercations? Any dogs that didn't bark or horses that didn't whinny?"

Jesse cocked his head and bobbed it as if nodding at a slant.

"Rex and Mimi were here then, which surprised me. That's the first time we've seen them during bad weather," he said, standing and gathering up plates. The "mast" was much lower than it had been when he sat down (one notices). In this, I suspect the death talk played a role. "I always thought Mimi was a fair weather nudist."

"Interesting. Anything else?"

"About two in the morning, I stepped out to take a leak, not wanting to fill up my dark water tank any more than necessary, and I saw them bundled up, walking back to their trailer," he said. "We didn't speak. I don't think they saw or heard me, because the wind was blowing pretty hard, the trees were making noises, and it was starting to snow."

"I remember," Grace said. "You stepped in and said it was snowing, and I looked out and saw them walking away, crunching on the gravel."

"Do you remember where you and they had your RVs

parked?" I asked. "Were they walking toward the Cenas' trailer? Or away from it?"

"Away from it for sure," Jesse said as he dropped the paper plates and utensils in the trash and started into his own trailer. "A navy man always knows his position."

"*Por supuesto!*" I said, grinning. Jesse was pretty cool, even if he was better looking, smarter and in better shape than I. He bobbed his head toward the interior and gestured to me to follow him.

"These men," Laurel said, as I stood up. "Get a room, you two!"

I pranced in the most politically incorrect way over to the trailer and called out in an effeminate voice, "Oh, Jesse! I'm right behiiind you!"

The ladies laughed.

In fact, he had some "magic powder" (not cocaine) which helps men of a certain age keep it up. It's not illegal, and it is all natural, but the shit works. We mixed it with a cup of water for each of us, and the ladies murmuring outside could hear our spoons rattling in the cups.

"Jesse, are you doing what I think you're doing?" Grace called out to us.

Again with the effeminate voice, I called out in a theater-filling whisper, "Hurry up or she'll catch us!"

"I thought so," Grace said, chuckling. "Just clean up afterwards, please."

Grace made explanatory noises to Laurel and Juanda.

"Oh lawd!" Laurel said loud enough for the people in the next campsite to hear. "We'll never stop them now."

#

15

Just a-wobblin'

After some more undignified nudge-nudge, wink-wink, the five of us departed toward DJ Ted's Clubhouse, still feeling remarkably energetic, given the rigorous workout we gave the Raslon RV's suspension system. The festive atmosphere of the campsites we passed with strings of *faux* Chinese lanterns along their awnings brightened our smiles.

Grace was arm-in-arm with Juanda, and Jesse was swinging Laurel's free hand back and forth like fourth-grade puppy lovers. Laurel's other hand still carried the ever-present pineapple cup.

Your humble servant carried the flashlights and the overfilled little cooler, augmented by the Raslons' chosen spirits, Cabernet Sauvignon and sparkling Moscato. DJ Ted's Clubhouse had a bar for setups and a bartender, but it was BYOB for alcohol. In Texas, any fool can testify against granting a liquor license by the relevant local government authority, so seeking one for a controversial place such as a nudist resort would be an exercise in futility.

"I thought I saw somebody I know in that protest crowd outside the gate when I drove up," Juanda said.

"Oh, really?" I asked, pointing a flashlight at her face.

"Thanks, asshole," she said, and I turned the light away. "Yeah, you got a preacher up here named Theophilus Lenfant?"

She also gave the family name a French pronunciation. I guess on Michigan's Upper Peninsula, one is close enough to Canada to hear plenty of French.

"As a matter of fact, we met him on the way back from the courthouse," I said. "Charming fellow."

"So charming, I almost busted a cap in his ass," Laurel said.

I started to tell what happened at the front gate, but Juanda stopped me.

"While you were napping –"

"I was not napping," I protested. "I was studying an electronic file on my tablet computer containing the school records of one Miriam Margarita Vega, *nee* Comemos, alias Mimi Kefauver."

"Really, Pepe?" Juanda said, giving me a gentle shove with her yummy booty. "Well, that file must have been on the inside of your eyelids, because when I started slapping your face with these babies –" she lifted and wagged her breasts at me "—your eyes were closed, and you were snoring like a well fed baby."

Grace chuckled but held onto Juanda's arm.

"So, while you were studying the file magically imprinted

on the inside of your eyelids, Laurel was telling me about it, but she didn't mention Lenfant's name," Juanda continued.

"Once that bitch told us to never forget his name, I magically forgot it," Laurel said. "Huh!"

Juanda giggled. "I wish I could forget it," she said.

"Why?" I asked.

"I can't go into details," she said. "I got a nice settlement to sign a non-disclosure agreement, but suffice to say, he's a real son of a bitch. I can say the NDA is with Sol Rosensteen's East Mount Houston Church."

"Wha?" Laurel said. "I got people who worship there."

"Pretty much anybody who lives in Houston knows someone who attends that church," I said.

East Mount Houston Church was one of those super-churches preaching "prosperity gospel." During and after the Enron scandal in the early 2000s, membership of EMH (christened "Everybody's Money is Here" by cynics) and coffers exploded. EMH bought a failing indoor amusement park to accommodate tens of thousands of worshipers for at least two sermons each Sunday. Something about the stench of failure drives some Christians to church, hoping for a reprieve from economic reality.

Rosensteen drove a Bugatti Veyron, when he wasn't taking a helicopter over Houston's notorious traffic jams. Those poor souls stuck in traffic in 100-plus-degree heat with 90% humidity never knew when they looked up and prayed for relief, they were praying to Rosensteen, flying by. The brutal Texas sun and humidity oppresses the just and the unjust. Blessed be the name of Texas.

"Interesting," I said. "Can you give me a hint?"

"To not give you a hint, I got $250,000 – oops, I wasn't supposed to say that," she responded.

"Da-amn!" Laurel said, stretching it to two sing-song syllables. "Well, you can't say that prosperity gospel stuff didn't pay off for you, at least."

"True dat, honeychile," said Juanda, who had spent enough time as Laurel and my unicorn to enjoy using Laurel's Deep South, down-home *patois*.

"What was he doing when you drove up?" I asked. "Was he still trying to wrestle a gun out of the grip of a rather busty middle-aged lady?"

"What?"

I explained what I saw in the mirror when we were going through the gate.

"No, it looked like he was talking to someone from NTOR who had driven up on a golf cart," Juanda said. "No big-boobed middle-aged lady was there."

"Cops may have hauled her off or said they wouldn't do anything, if she would leave and disturb the peace no further," I said. "Probably Jonquil Clarke, NTOR's manager, trying to negotiate an end to the protest. Tall lady in her 40s, salt-and-pepper hair with glasses?"

"Nope, youngish brunette with a baseball cap!" Juanda called out as she opened the clubhouse door for me, which let the beat of Cardi B's WAP out into the fresh, dry, cool and quiet Hill Country air.

We were, of course, still nude – got to stay consistent, right? – but we were the first people to arrive in such a state. Everybody else – a dozen or so couples -- wore something they thought was sexy that they could easily slip off.

A cheer rose up, led by Shawn-from-Manchester.

"LAU-REL! LAU-REL! LAU-REL!"

I turned to Laurel, shook my head, and said, "Can't take you nowhere."

She gently pulled the cooler out of my hand, set it on the ground, jumped up and wrapped her legs around my waist, and howled like a wolf, which elicited the expected renewed cheering. I staggered and danced us over to the dance-floor, where I let her reach her legs down, stand up, turn around and start to twerk in front of me to the beat of Cardi B's suggestive (OK, pornographic) lyrics.

That's when I started howling and softly spanking her lovely ass.

See what I gotta put up with?

By the end of the song, Jesse had found us a table and laid towels down for us. Somehow, Juanda had grabbed the pine-apple cup, and now was the time for Laurel to take a last sip of her Tito's Tart.

Jesse and Juanda had struck up a conversation, and Grace had wandered off to chat with a group including Ben and Shawn-from-Manchester. In a few minutes, DJ Ted was playing V.I.C.'s "Wobble," and Laurel had to show all those women, including Ben's girlfriend, Janis, how to line dance.

By the way, Ben was topless, wearing what appeared to be firefighter's pants held up by suspenders and firefighter boots. Shawn-from-Manchester wore shorts, flip-flops and a t-shirt with a Union Jack printed across the front and the sleeves torn off.

I don't line dance. The last time I did, it was "Cotton-Eyed

Joe," which may not be politically correct these days. I neither know nor care.

Still somber over the previous night's violence, I watched the fun and pondered how Laurel could party anyway, even as she struggled to compartmentalize the searing memories of the previous night. I knew she was not shallow. I was puzzled, but put it down to the fifth of Tito's she had finished that day.

I carried the soft-sided cooler over to the bar, where a short mustachioed Latino named Sven Horsen (that's what he said it was, anyway), wearing a black leather vest and, I suspected, nothing else, took charge of our provisions after I extracted my phone from the cooler's side pocket and an ice-cold Hopadillo IPA from the ice chips at the bottom.

Returning to my seat, I saw Laurel had whipped most of them into the beat, except Ben and Shawn-from-Manchester, who were way off, but enjoying themselves, nonetheless. I loved – and was mystified by -- how Laurel could introduce little variations on the steps without missing a beat. Talented lady, our Laurel.

Sitting down, I saw a text message from the uber-serious solicitor.

"Hey, shit-head, seen the news yet?" He used the "shit" emoji for one word. Clever.

"?"

"Your little encounter with Monsieur Lenfant and his fascist wife led both local stations at six, and your interview was touted for the 10 pm slot."

"Oy."

"Watch your back, man. That Stevie Sabin hates your guts now."

"Lovely. I thought she was kinda cute."

"Don't start."

"And how did Ms. Metzger treat us?"

"It was fair, balanced, focused more on Mimi's chaotic life, while still somehow sympathetic to a murder victim."

"Damn. That's a very fine line to draw. Impressive."

"It's the smart ones you gotta watch out for."

"True dat."

A commotion arose behind our table, which was one of those closest to the dance floor. I glanced around and saw an overweight white man in his late 60s, wearing typically Texan jeans and cowboy boots. I guess he was the one guy not expecting to get laid that night. He was attempting to rise from his table as a pale, mousy woman with glasses pulled on his sleeve to keep him seated.

"No, I won't, dammit!" he shouted over the music, and he gestured toward me. "That dirt-bag millionaire probably killed those two people, and we're going to sit here and let him party with us? I don't think so!"

Oh, shit, I thought. Here it comes. Out of the corner of my eye, I saw Sven looking at the guy and reaching for something under the bar. Shawn-from-Manchester was oblivious, but Ben was watching what was happening and starting to fall even further off the beat.

"Stand by," I texted to Deuce.

"?"

The guy – receding hairline, clean-shaven -- pulled loose

from the woman and started toward me. I looked up and smiled.

"Hey, asshole!"

"You bellowed?"

The word he used in the next sentence is what you think it is, so I'll just use the first letter

"Why don't you take your house-n_______ and get the fuck out of here?"

I felt the blood rushing to my head and stood up, but kept smiling. "We're having such a lovely time."

#

16

A Soulwood Train of thought

Sunday, Oct. 9, 2022, 10 p.m.

"Don't you realize nobody wants you here?" the unpleasant fellow said with a frown, a little less loud, as he leaned down toward me close enough to convey the odor of Jim Beam. "Everybody here thinks you killed those two people."

"I don't think everybody does," I said.

"And your house-n____ helped you do it!" he said, hitting my eye with a little whiskey-scented spittle.

I blinked but saw in my peripheral vision Laurel stop dancing and stare at us. I also I saw Ben approaching from the dance floor, and in the peripheral vision to my right, I saw Sven – who was wearing cowboy chaps, boots but no pants -- approaching with a small baseball bat.

The next activity took about two seconds.

"I said, get the fuck—" the guy started, pushing my chest

104

with his left hand and reaching toward the small of his back with his right.

I was a little concerned he might bring a gun from that location, this being Texas. I took hold of his hand on my chest with my right hand and pressed the center of his hand hard against my chest with my thumb, which I know from experience is painful. I bent over forward and said, "Let me show you something down here." I was still smiling.

I had nothing on the ground I wanted to show him, except the folly of trying to strong-arm a more sober Montecarlo. From experience, I knew this move caused a painful twist of his arm and elbow. I was still mindful of a weapon, if it existed. So, having shifted him to balance forward, I circled around him and tossed him on his back.

If he had not had his arm behind him – yes, he was reaching for a gun – he would have been in some pain and embarrassment but OK. His unfortunate wrist landed between two unyielding surfaces – the floor and his pistol – with his 240-odd pounds slamming on top, so despite the music, I heard and felt through his bulk something crack and realized something had broken.

I stopped smiling. Doing damage not fixable outside a hospital was not my goal.

I still held his wrist and was twisting it, but tears had popped into his eyes, and I hoped he would be no further trouble to us. The arm behind his back did not move.

"You done?" I asked. "You going to be nice?"

"ASS-HOLE!" said the little mousy woman who had come up behind me.

"Who are you talking to, me or him?" I asked, with *faux* surprise.

The dancing had stopped, and Laurel was striding toward us.

The little woman swung her purse at me.

"Oh shit," I muttered. "It's gonna get messy now."

I twisted the poor schmuck's hand and wrist a little more. "Make her stop," I said. "She's going to get hurt if you don't."

"SHUT UP, WOMAN!" he bellowed, almost tearfully, and his lady knelt down beside him and held a napkin from her purse to his forehead, sweating Jim Beam and furrowed in excruciating pain. Her scent of Johnson Baby Powder almost overpowered the whiskey sweat.

"You just bett' not touch my man one more time!" Laurel said, her head and fist shaking. "Or I'll –"

"Your Royal Highness, your humble servant is well aware of your penchant for violence," I said to her, still holding the guy's wrist. "Have you forgotten your hostess responsibilities?"

I turned down to him in genuine sympathy. "If I help you up, you gonna behave? You need a doctor. I think you broke your wrist."

I swung his left hand up to his face and said, "Not this one. The one behind you."

He squirmed, groaned in pain, looked angry at me, but then at his woman. "I'll be good," he muttered.

"I don't think that 'house-n____' you were talking about heard you."

"I'll be GOOD!" he shouted, his voice quavering. "I'm sorry!"

"OK, I'll let go and we'll see what we can do to make you more comfortable," I said. "We may have to call for an ambulance. Don't move your body for a minute, OK? I think you broke something, and we don't want to make it worse."

Ben, as it turned out, was a firefighter who knew scads about first-aid, so he took over from then on.

Jonquil Clarke appeared like magic beside us and watched as Sven and Ben administered first aid, getting this fellow as comfortable as possible. She went out to a golf cart and returned with a first-aid box.

"Asshole!" yelled the red-faced little woman, quivering with anger and tears in her blue eyes, magnified by thick glasses. She rose to stand and look worried at her man as Ben, Sven and Quil straightened out the injured arm and wrapped it to a temporary splint. Looking at Jonquil and me, she said, "We're never coming back here again!"

"That's unfortunate," I said, giving her a pearly white grin from my seat, where I had resumed sipping my Hopadillo. "Under different circumstances, we might have all had a delightful orgy."

She started toward me, but Laurel stepped in her way and put her heavily-ringed hands on her hips, ready for a fight.

"Don't, just don't, Donna!" the injured man said. "Don't make it worse. It's gonna be OK."

In about 15 minutes, the injured man — Abe -- and Donna rode away to the emergency room in Jonquil's car, and DJ Ted was playing a song I had suggested, Keith Frank's "Soulwood Train," a Zydeco tune to cheer up Laurel and therefore everybody else. It worked, although the crowd had thinned a bit. I do dance Zydeco with her, albeit badly, and my mood was better, too. Juanda, Jesse, Grace, Ben, his girlfriend Janis and Shawn-from-Manchester were out there doing their best to keep up.

Good times.

#

17

13D5M.com

Sunday, Oct. 9, 2022, 10:30 p.m.

Dean Franco sat at the chair next to mine, when I returned. Rose had earlier joined the Wobble dance, disrobed and returned to the table formerly occupied by Donna and her douchebag. Dean still wore a spiked leather vest, spiked leather wristbands, a spiked leather thong, black knee-high motorcycle boots with a mirror finish and English Leather aftershave. What a guy. Vegan, I believe.

"Sorry that happened, Pepe," he said. "I tried to convince Abe what was said on TV was a crock of shit, you couldn't have killed Rex and Mimi, but he wasn't having any of it. I think learning you made your fortune during the Great Recession pissed him off too much. He lost his shirt."

I frowned. I guess I have what they call "survivor's guilt" with so much lost in the crisis. How many divorces? How many suicides?

"If he had literally lost his shirt – I mean, if he had been naked when he walked in here, like me – he probably would have been in a slightly better mood," I said, gesturing toward Dean's own wrinkled chest. "Who knows? He might have got laid. Weirder things have happened."

"Ah, well, he might have been a little more comfortable in his leather gear," Dean said. "Abe and Donna get a little freaky now and then -- our kind of freaky, I mean."

Laurel and Juanda sat next to us at the table.

"Really, Dean?" asked Laurel, who enjoyed some BDSM (bondage, discipline, sadism and masochism for you vanilla folks) when the mood strikes. Pun intended.

"Really, Laurel?" I said, turning to my Nubian Queen. I wondered what fresh mischief twinkled in those lovely, clear but clearly inebriated brown eyes.

"Hush, Pepe," she said, putting an decorated right index fingernail to her lips. "Grown-up people talkin'."

"*Mierda*," I muttered.

Juanda giggled, grabbed her cigarettes out of the cooler side pocket and jumped up to greet an approaching Shawn-from-Manchester. She kissed him, and they went outside for a smoke.

Dean and Laurel told stories for about 15 minutes. They talked about the kinky stuff they had enjoyed (not my bag, man), mutual friends in the BDSM lifestyle and how she could get more involved.

I tried to resume my text conversation with my scatological solicitor, but I think Mr. Potty-mouth had gone gently into that dark slumberland.

"Your sister's into this stuff pretty deep," Dean said to Laurel, as I returned my attention to the conversation.

"I know, I know, and that's why I gotta be careful," Laurel said. "We don't want to wind up in the same dungeon sometime. That would be fucked up."

"Awkward!" I sang in an effeminate falsetto voice. I'd finished my Hopadillo and was halfway through my second, and I'm a lightweight in the drinking scene.

"Yep, yep, yep," he said, chuckling. "She's had enough awkward shit in what I call her 'Fifty Shades of Blue' period."

"Whuh?" Laurel and I said simultaneously.

"Jinx!" we said, also simultaneously.

What can I say? Sexagenarian preteens, that's us.

Dean held up his hands, backing away from the table in his chair. "I'm not saying anything more," he said. "It's not my place. You can ask her, but I'd just as soon you not mention my name in the conversation. No tellin' what new welts she'd raise on my ass, if she knew."

I shook my head and grabbed his leather-bound wrist, almost cutting my palm on the spikes.

"Oh, no, you can't stop there," I said.

"Yes, he can," Laurel said, suddenly a bit more sober.

"Nah, nah, nah, we're not going to hurt Tuffy," I said, turning to Laurel. "For one thing, learning more would help us avoid any awkward encounter with her in the BDSM lifestyle. For another thing, we will be able to look out for her, protect her, if necessary. And --"

I nuzzled her delicious left ear with my lips, and whispered, "You want to get more into it, and this way you can do so without encountering her."

"It doesn't really matter," Dean said, as he wrote something on a napkin and pushed it toward me. "I'm not sayin' anything more. All I can say is, if you're not already on this website, join it, and you'll learn more than you want to know."

He stood and walked toward the stripper pole on the raised stage, where Rose — firm, tanned, sexy auburn-haired Rose -- squirmed upside down, her muscular thighs (how old was she again?) holding her ass against the pole as she fondled her breasts. Standing on the dance floor before her, a half-dozen 30-something guys, grinning like idiots, tossed dollar bills beneath her.

As I say, fun people, the Francos.

I looked down at the napkin.

"LtChocolock on 13D5M.com."

#

18

A well of tears

Monday, Oct. 10, 2022, 8 a.m.

The next morning, having sated little Pepe with Laurel, Grace, Juanda and Janis in and around the hot-tub, I was a bit slow moving around in the RV's queen-size bed. When I reached out to both sides, I was surprised to find myself alone with Laurel. In the past, Juanda and Laurel made a Pepe sandwich on such special occasions as this weekend.

Oh, well. Juanda liked Shawn-from-Manchester a bit more than the usual play partner. Good for her, but she was probably just turned on by his accent. Jealous? Me? Nah!

As I delight in jogging in the nude and despite a slight headache, I dragged my lazy white ass out of bed to prepare for a run. Laurel's breathing yielded a low-volume snore. Bless her heart.

With my running shoes, pistol-packin' hydration harness and sunglasses, I went outside to take a leak and stretch. I was on the road by 8:30 am in the cool morning air, still a bit humid. My energy revived as I pondered my next move in the quest to prove my innocence by proving why Rex did what he did, which meant figuring out that relationship.

Rex was a smart guy. He was amazing with computers, which can be a solitary pursuit. Sometimes so much solitude can screw up one's psyche. I'd seen it in introverted copy editors in more than one newsroom. No matter if you were in a room with dozens of other people, if you stared at a screen with no particular reason to engage with other people, you get lonely. Your sense of self corrupts, like a bad computer file, which in my experience seems to happen spontaneously, like a bad person bursting into flames. With the computer file, one knows one had something to do with the damage, but one can't figure out what.

I happened to know Rex spent most of his work time in the refrigerated computer room of his print shop in Houston, alone. Who knows what weirdness lurks in the hearts of men? The computer knows, methinks.

I, for one, look forward to our new artificial intelligence overlords.

What I needed was someone who knew Rex from the beginning. He had told me about growing up in the West Texas Oil Patch, although not as an upstream oil-and-gas industry kid. The law firm of Salazar & Jones probably had a paralegal or private investigator working on that.

I finished my first loop and made a mental to-do list: call Deuce about Rex, finish reading Mimi's file, check on the douchebag whose arm I'd broken the night before. Starting my second loop, I encountered Ben at a tent campsite, also in running shoes. He had seen me running the morning before and thought it looked like fun.

"How do you think that idiot is this morning?" I asked, referring to the injured man.

"His name is Abe," Ben said, going less than half his normal running pace. He was muscular, in his 30s, an even caramel-brown all over. If he ran even three-quarters of full speed, we would have had to talk like a livestock show auctioneer — extremely fast — as he lapped me three times to my one circuit. "I suspect he has a hangover and his arm hurts, but he'll be all right."

"*Hoc posset esse peius*," I said.

"Excuse me?"

"*Hoc posset esse peius*," I repeated. "Latin for, 'It could be worse.' Montecarlo family motto I made up."

"Ha," Ben said. "I doubt Abe's thinking that way, but that's his problem."

"It is, for a fact, right?" I said. "We should be thankful for what we have, rather than bitter about what we lost. I dare say he has a pretty good little helpmate in the woman who called me an ass-hole."

"If he'd brought out the artillery, shit would have gone south real fast."

"True dat," I said. "Somebody could have gotten killed, and it might have been him."

"It was an impressive move you made on him. What was it?"

"*Aiki-jiu-jitsu*. I'm not expert, but it's one useful thing I remember from some classes I took while my kids were studying karate."

"I'd like to learn that one. Could you teach me?"

"I'd like to, but I'm too old, and I'm afraid I might teach it to you wrong."

I was also afraid of somehow mixing it up with some more recent self-defense training I had taken when shit hit the fan during the Great Recession. I received some scary death threats. I resolved that my family should not suffer because of anger directed at me. So I took some personal defense classes combining hand-to-hand, firearms and non-firearm weapons training over a dozen weekends in 2009.

I had also learned about practical shooting competitions combining a level of fitness with shooting which made it more of a loud, live-action role-playing game shooting at targets, not people. A lot of fun, but I don't like chatting with people I don't know about it. You're the exception. You're welcome.

Ben and I talked about where he might find an *aiki-jiu-jitsu* instructor and about martial arts in general for a few minutes. We kept running until I'd finished my five miles and said I wanted to jump in the pool to cool off. He said it sounded like a good idea. We were at the shooting range by this point, so we walked over to the pool area, thinking to shower the dust off before jumping in the pool.

The delicious odors of sausage and coffee spread across the campground from an exhaust fan in the roof of the dining hall some distance away. Being not completely dense, I concluded the staff had prepared some breakfast, which likely meant biscuits, gravy and grits, as well. It was lovely Texas Columbus Day Monday morning.

There was just one shower head, so I told Ben to go ahead

while I took off my hydration backpack and shoes. I glanced over at the hot tub, which was in an open patio area next to the gymnasium. I did a double-take.

I walked over to the hot tub, looked down, and my eyes filled with tears. I fell to my knees and sobbed.

Ben trotted over to me. "What's wrong?" I gestured toward the hot tub, but could not talk, because of the crying.

Inside, lying mostly underwater was Juanda, her dead eyes open.

Ben pulled her pale nude body out and laid it on the concrete next to the hot tub, where the water had turned cold, and poor Juanda had emptied her bowels. I couldn't bear to look at her face, but her feet, ruddy and swollen as a symptom of her diabetes, had scratches on the soles. I looked further up and saw scrapes on her knees.

I stopped crying so hard, as my curiosity took hold. How did those happen?

"She said she had Type 1 diabetes last night," Ben said. "Do you suppose she had a seizure in the tub and drowned?"

I shook my head and shrugged, still too choked up to talk. Ben trotted toward the main office. I knelt by Juanda's head, caressed her cold cheek and prayed for the Good Lord to embrace her in heaven and let her know how much she was loved on earth.

Our RV was within sight of the pool and hot tub area. Laurel stepped out, looking for Juanda or me or both. Despite the distance, she saw me kneeling next to Juanda, and she started running toward me. About 20 feet away, I looked up at her with tears in my eyes, and she started to stumble and said, "No-no-no-no NO NO NO! It can't be!"

I shook my head and pursed my lips. "She's gone," I gasped, and started sobbing again.

The next couple of hours are kind of a jumble, to me. An ambulance showed up, and they treated Laurel and me for shock. Deputies showed up, but had no immediate questions for us, as their initial conclusion was it was a natural death, with no defensive wounds. Ben filled them in about how he and I found Juanda and about her diabetes. Ben and Janis escorted Laurel and me back to our RV and sat outside while we went inside, laid down, cried in each other's arms, talked about how much we had loved her, reminisced about some of those good times.

Fuck death.

#

19

Requiem for a unicorn

Monday, Oct. 10, 2022, 11 a.m.

Laurel and I had just wept ourselves to sleep when a loud thumping commenced at our RV door. "Mr. Montecarlo! Ms. Traeger! It's Sgt. Wright and Sgt. North. We'd like to ask you a few questions." It was North's earnest voice.

"That's some mo' shiggedy," Laurel said. "What on earth would those boys want now?"

"I'm sure they want us to fill them in on what happened last night, when we saw Juanda last and so on," I said in a low tone. Louder, I said, "Be right with you. Just a minute."

I washed the tear tracks from my face, still dusty from the run, and stepped outside as Laurel moved into the RV's kitchen area.

Ben and Janis sat in folding chairs outside. They had put on some shorts and t-shirts. I began to feel underdressed, as if I was somehow being disrespectful of the dead. Maybe not. Juanda would have done the same.

"How can I help you?" I said, stepping over to the camp-stove where someone had brewed some coffee. I didn't feel like smiling, but the coffee was good.

"Could you give us an account of when you last saw Ms. Falcon?" Wright said.

"Fal-CONE," I corrected his pronunciation. "The last I saw of her, she was relaxing in the hot tub as I was carrying my lady back to the RV."

"Carrying?" North asked.

"She was wiped out. It had been a long day. I'm kind of a lightweight, compared with her, in drinking, so I lifted her up and carried her back to the RV." I mimed picking up a body and carrying it face up, like Boris Karloff's Frankenstein monster carrying a drowned little girl in the first movie. But I held onto my mug of coffee.

Laurel, also naked, stepped out of the RV with a frown on her face.

"What you boys want to axe us?"

Flushed, North looked up at the trees and said, "Ma'am, we're just trying to reconstruct the events of last night around the last time you saw her."

"Last time I saw her, she was in the hot tub, riding the cock of that dude from England," Laurel said.

"We've spoken to him," Wright said, staring at my lovely woman's breasts. I didn't blame him, and I smiled for the first time since we found Juanda.

"He and Mr. Ben Bryant and Ms. Janis Marlowe left the tub while the victim, Mr. Montecarlo and you were still in the hot tub," Wright said. "There are some suspicious circumstances about Ms. Fal-CONE's death –"

"Oh shit," Laurel said.

"—And this is the second time in as many nights in which you two were among the last to see the body while it was still breathing," Wright finished.

Laurel started toward him, her red-rimmed eyes furious. "You bett' not –"

"Oh shit," I muttered and stepped between her and Wright, facing her and dropping a hot mug of coffee on my bare foot. "Ow!"

This was enough of a distraction, because Laurel backed up, reached for a towel and tried to dry my foot while handing the cup back up to me. I peered over at North and grinned, as if to say, "Notice how I defused that bomb?" His lip curled in the beginning of a grin, but he went back to looking back up at the trees. Kind of a prude, our Sgt. North.

"Thank you, babe," I said, and turned back toward Wright, gave him a weak smile and shrug. "Pepe unlucky, I guess."

"We're not fond of coincidences, Mr. Montecarlo," Wright said. "Would you both come back to the police station and answer a few more questions?"

"In truth, we have some things to do here, so why don't you just ask us what you want to ask, and we'll go on about our business," I said, smiling more broadly. "Or, I can have our lawyer meet us there and he can continue to build his case for a harassment and defamation-of-character lawsuit against the Pecan County Sheriff's Office. Since I had nothing to do with Juanda's death, I expect I'd double my nontrivial fortune if I let Mr. Jones pursue the matter."

Wright looked at North. They moved toward their police cruiser to chat for a minute. The tic-tic-ticking of their engine contracting as it cooled in the drying air drowned out their whispers. They returned, and Wright said, "That's acceptable, but if you don't mind, would you two put on some clothes? We'd be more comfortable. It's a small favor to ask."

I looked at my Nubian Queen and cocked an eyebrow. She shook her head side to side. "OK," I said. "We'll be back out in two shakes of my Nubian Queen's tail."

Ben looked at me sideways. "What did you call her?"

"Nubian Queen," I said, and leaned in to explain quietly. "That's because she's usually royally high."

Ben and Janis chuckled.

I thanked them and said they need not stay.

"We don't mind," Ben said.

"I doubt you intended to spend another day or night here, since this is Columbus Day," I said. "Give me your numbers and I'll call if we need you, but I don't see how."

Impersonating a politically incorrect Hawkeye Pierce with an attractive nurse, I said, "We may want you, but not while these guys are here."

Ben chuckled and Janis shook her head and rolled her eyes. I entered Ben's number into my phone's contact list, and they left.

My attorney had texted me to call him. Although I was not an attorney representing myself, I foolishly ignored his request. I was too emotionally spent to deal with an overprotective mouthpiece. I was also probably less than lucid after the previous night's excesses, alcoholic and carnal.

A few minutes later, Laurel and I munched on cantaloupe

and drank Tito's Tart and coffee, respectively, as North described the state of Juanda's body, as far as they knew.

"She drowned," North said, "but she had fresh scratches on her feet and knees – even a splinter in both places. Her left big toe was broken perimortem. It's like she had been walking in the woods and tripped. You know how she got those?"

"Not at all," I said, and looked at Laurel, who shook her head as tears started welling in her eyes.

"NTOR has lots of woods and woodies, but no wooden floors, so she didn't get those splinters from the built-up areas," I said. "If I remember my forensic-show jargon, perimortem means it happened near death, so close that the toe had no time to start swelling or healing."

"Well put," Wright said. "Why might she have gone into the woods in the dark?"

"I left her a flashlight," I said. "Who knows? She went out there to check out a raccoon or something, got frightened and tripped?"

Wright looked skeptical.

"No, I'm not buying it either," I said. "Sorry, can't help you."

"Tell us about your relationship," Wright said.

"Juanda was our unicorn," I said.

"Excuse me?" said North, who was taking notes.

"In the swing lifestyle, a unicorn is a single woman who plays with couples or single men," I said. "I say she was 'our unicorn,' because we had a pretty close friendship –"

I looked at Laurel, who was wiping tears off her cheek with a paper napkin.

"It was love, to be honest," I said, starting to choke up, myself. "I had hopes that we three would grow old – older, in our case – together, settle down in one spot and have our grandkids visit. It might have been awkward, but it might have been pretty nice."

Laurel's tears ran down her face, and I squeezed the bridge of my nose, and wiped an errant tear away from each eye.

"Beautiful," North whispered. Wright frowned at him.

"Yes, she was," I said. "Not in a conventional way – she was too much the Bohemian artist – but she was strikingly attractive, funny, a good woman with a strong moral sense, and a good Christian."

"No shit?" North said. Wright frowned at him again and added a cocked eyebrow.

"Yep," I said. "She knew the Bible backwards and forwards, sang loud and off-key in any choir that would let her and volunteered at a food bank in Houston."

"Ms. Traeger," Wright said, looking at Laurel. "What was your relationship with Juanda? Were you lovers, too?"

Laurel dabbed the tears from her eyes with the napkin on her lap while I took a sip of coffee. Coffee is good for defusing conflict, you know? She glared at him a moment but decided to forgive Wright's ignorance and insensitivity.

"I loved her, but we were not lovers," Laurel said. "We were very good friends, and we shared the joy we take with this man here." She pointed her plastic fork in my general direction. "To be honest, although it's none of your business, I do like women. I like having sex with women. Juanda wasn't that into it, and I think if she was, I would not have played with her. It might have ruined what we had."

I reached out for her hand, brought it to my lips and wept.

Laurel caressed my neck with her other hand and kissed the top of my head.

#

20

A fierce love

Monday, Oct. 10, 2022, 11:45 a.m.

After North and Wright left, Laurel informed me that she had recorded the interview on her smartphone.

"You are so much smarter than me. Why do you put up with me?" I said, pulling her toward me in a bear hug.

"Little Pepe has me hooked," she said, smiling up at me and thrusting her pelvis at mine.

We laid out our plans for the day:

No. 1: Check on Abe-with-the-broken-arm.

No. 2: Check if Jonquil or her staff had any idea what happened with Juanda, and when we will meet the Cenas' lawyer.

No. 3: Check in with Deuce, inform him about Juanda and ask if he has any more background on Rex.

No. 4: Check on the other recent deaths of Frank and Ruby, whether any connection exists.

No. 5: Finish reading the Mimi Comemos file.

Laurel and I saw no need to wear clothes, so we stripped, finished breakfast, cleaned up and headed toward the main office to see about No. 1.

"Mr. Cole is back at his campsite," said Quil, fresh and professional as always, emitting a light scent of cherry blossom. Nice. "He had a 'green-stick' fracture of both bones in his right forearm. He's in pain, but he'll be alright -- just embarrassed. He's planning to move his RV back home today, but I told him there's no rush. Even so, I sent Sven and Ted over there to help him. He won't cause you any trouble – any more trouble, I mean."

"He bett' not!" Laurel said, sipping from her pineapple cup. It may even have had pineapple juice in it. "Nor that bitch with him!"

We were standing at the registration counter in the main office. A couple of clothed weekenders stood nearby, trying to check out of the resort with the receptionist, who happened to be the twenty-something brunette who had interrupted Grace's fellatio of me the day before. She was blushing, but still trying to help the couple.

I put a calming hand on Laurel's waist.

"Babe," I muttered, "you need to be nice for your customers."

Laurel glanced at the other couple, in their 40s, overweight, sunburnt, in matching guayaberas, Panama hats, khaki shorts and tan Skechers.

"Oh, I forgot," Laurel muttered. She looked at the couple staring at us, smiled and said, "Hi, how was your weekend?"

Surprised, the sunglass-wearing man with salt-and-pepper

hair said, "It was great, but wow! We're not used to so much death."

"No shit," I said, smiling sheepishly. "This is one Columbus Day weekend I won't soon forget. You two be careful going home, OK?"

"You're staying?" said the red-haired woman, also wearing sunglasses. She looked at her man as if she wanted to stay, too.

"Afraid so," I said, as Laurel smiled and sipped her drink, probably reloaded with Tito's Tart. "Got a few things we need to attend to. Nothing fun."

I wanted to check on Abe Cole and his wife personally in hopes of salvaging something positive out of our unfortunate confrontation. When I asked about Cole, Quil cocked her head like I was crazy, but pointed out the Coles' campsite location on the resort map on the wall of the reception area. Laurel and I went looking for the Coles.

When we arrived, Ted and Sven had attached the fifth-wheel trailer to Abe's idling big Dodge Ram Cummins Diesel pickup, in which sat the woman I assumed was Mrs. Cole. From behind the trailer, Abe, Ted and Sven approached the truck on the passenger side, with Abe's arm in a sling. The lady jumped out of the cab of the pickup and started toward us like an angry Chihuahua.

"Why don't you people leave us alone?" she said, the pink and shiny silver visor bobbing as she spoke behind her large sunglasses. "Haven't you done enough?" She wore blue jeans and a thin pink hoodie over a blue t-shirt.

"Donna, be quiet," Abe said, as he continued to advance

on us. He wore a green-and-white checked shirt, bib overalls, sunglasses and a Houston Texans baseball cap.

Donna hesitantly walked back to get into the truck with the window open, and Laurel went up to the side to keep an eye on her. They began talking after a minute, but I couldn't catch any words over the engine.

"I want to apologize for what I said last night," Abe said. "Sometimes, I just shouldn't be drinking."

"No problem," I said, smiling. "I've been there, done that. I'm sorry I hurt you."

"I'm kinda glad you did," he said. "It could have been a lot worse."

"I have been thinking the same thing. How can I help you? This rig is daunting even when you have all your limbs intact. I can't imagine what it must be like without the use of one of your arms."

"It's not bad, as far as driving and parking are concerned."

"Ah, but you need to empty your black and gray water, right?"

Black water is wastewater from an RV's toilet system, while "gray water" is from the shower and kitchen.

"That's true."

"Let me help you do that, and we can let Ted and Sven go on about their business."

"I was going to do that for him, but if you want to do it, I'll sure find something else to do," Ted said.

Laurel and I walked alongside the truck as Abe drove it to one of the slots that had a septic tank. With gloves offered to me by Abe, I took the long three-inch-diameter expandable hose out of the hollow bumper, attached it to the trailer's black water drain and stuck the other end into the septic tank opening. The hose's exterior was untainted by what flowed within, so I wasn't too concerned about doing this task in the nude. Laurel and Donna resumed their soft conversation, and Laurel chuckled as Abe and I stood by the emptying trailer waste tank.

"I understand you had a pistol in your holster at the back," I said, leaning my hand against the trailer's spare tire. "I'm kind of a gun aficionado, myself. Mind telling me what it was?"

Abe blushed. "Yes, I did," he said. "It's a Colt 1911 .45-caliber."

"That would have done the trick," I said, my eyes widening. "My martial arts friends would have said, 'Pepe, why didn't you just go?' But see, I had nothing to do with those deaths, other than just being there and witnessing them. So, I saw no reason for us to leave, and then again, I was a bit impaired myself, between pussy and beer." I grinned sheepishly. "Then, you said what you did about my Nubian Queen."

Abe looked away, his face flushed. "Again, I apologize. That was shitty. I'd heard you made money during the Great Recession, and that about wiped me out, so I was spoiling for a fight."

"I understand," I said. "I'm sorry that happened. I was lucky that I made the investments I did when I did, because I had been living pretty close to the edge before that happened. I have many friends and relatives who were in your shoes, and some of them didn't make it. Suicide. Marriages destroyed. Drug overdose."

"Same with me, with relatives and friends. I'm lucky I had

a good woman who could support us while we got back on our feet."

"She's pretty fierce in her love for you. Good for you."

A gurgle indicated the tank was empty. Abe checked the gauge to make sure. We shut off the valve to the black water and hooked up the now-malodorous hose to the gray water drain and opened that valve.

Afterward, I typed my phone number and contact information into his smartphone, and he said he would be in touch if they were in the vicinity. As Abe drove away, Laurel started toward me from the passenger side of the truck and said, "She's not so bad."

#

21

A millionaire girlfriend

Monday, Oct. 10, 2022, 1 p.m.

"I've no idea what happened to Ms. Falcon," Quil said, when we asked in her office. "All our people had made it to various beds by about 1 a.m. I gather you folks were still enjoying our facilities at that time."

"*Tempus fugit cum ludis,*" I said. "Time flies when you're having fun."

"*Laissez les bontemps roulez,*" she responded with a sad smile. Having lived and worked in Louisiana, I was familiar with the "Let the good times roll" mantra, so I smiled back.

Looking at Laurel, she said, "Since you own the property now, I'll tell you we recently placed some unobtrusive cameras around the property, so that under certain circumstances, we can review what's happening. That's how I got to the club so fast when you had your confrontation with Mr. Cole."

Laurel's eyes widened and bleached eyebrows rose toward her pink spikey hair. "What the –"

"I only use it for emergencies," Quil said. "I destroy the recording every day unless something happens that might result in a lawsuit, like last night. It's in the liability waiver you signed when you checked in."

Turning toward me, she said, "By the way, I heard what you did for Mr. Cole. I doubt that situation was ever going to be a problem for us, but I think you just guaranteed it won't."

"Thank you," I said. "No biggie. Would have done it for anybody."

"The point is, those recordings are still available to me, and you can view them, if you want," Quil said. "Maybe you'll catch sight of something."

I said I needed to finish reviewing the Mimi Comemos file and talk to Deuce, so Laurel agreed to fast-forward through the videos in Quil's office. It was past lunchtime, so I ordered some Thai food for delivery, and returned to the RV to retrieve my tablet computer and a couple of towels. I thought we might take a sober swim in an empty pool, for once.

As I walked back to the resort's main office, I punched a quick text to my pal on my phone to arrange time to talk. By the way, when I'm naked at nudist facilities, I wear a sturdy nylon black fanny pack most of the time. I keep my phone in its front pocket and the Kel-Tec P3AT pistol and a couple of spare magazines in the main rear compartment. Altogether, it weighs at most two pounds; the pistol and full magazines weigh about half that.

Rather than answer the text, my counselor called me.

"What the fuck, Pepe?"

"Huh?"

"You had another death last night out there, or maybe it was early in the morning, and you don't call, you don't text. It's like you don't want to stay out of jail anymore."

I brought Deuce up to speed, including the interview with Wright and North, at which point my zealous advocate said, "You might want a different lawyer."

"*Por que, amigo?*" I said. "*Tengo un abogado muy excelente.*"

"You knew better than to have those guys interview you without me."

I scratched the back of my neck with the hand holding the phone. He was right.

"You're right. I apologize. We had just dozed off, when they started banging on our door, so I guess I was a bit groggy to be making important decisions. They wanted to haul us down to the police station, and we just didn't want to do that, so I agreed to a chat here. If it makes you feel any better, Laurel recorded the conversation with her phone."

"That wasn't dumb, at least," he said. "Maybe I'll keep her on as a client, asshole."

"That would be lovely," I said. "She can afford you now." I filled him in on the Cenas' legacy for Laurel.

"Interesting, verrrry interrresting," Deuce said, rolling his Rs and doing a fair imitation of the recurring Nazi character on the old *Laugh-In* TV show. "But not funny."

That made me cock my head and look at the phone. What was he thinking? I politely chuckled, but said, "By the way, until I see it in writing, I'll assume you still want to be my lawyer."

"Yeah, but my rates for keeping assholes out of jail are higher."

"Fair enough. I'll try to work my way back to the discount."

"It's harder to work for someone you can't expect to behave with common sense," he said. "It's also harder on my blood pressure, which ain't as good as it was when I played on the second string for the Longhorns. If defending you gets me in the hospital, or worse, Yvonne will be pissed at both of us. So, have you done your reading assignment?"

"Ummm, kinda distracted last night, so I'm still in the middle of her time at Our Lady of Fatima High School."

"I'll just bet you were busy," said the solicitor with more than a scintilla of sarcasm. "I know nights at a nudist swing resort can be 'hard on' you." In my mind's eye, I saw the air quotes.

"Ha."

"The high school file, in case you haven't noticed, is much thinner on details than what we discussed yesterday. I gather she figured out how to keep her 'permanent record,' as it were, spotless. However, my investigator turned up some news items that may or may not be relevant – a girl's suicide here, a young teen couple's fatal car accident there, one of her teachers' arrest for child pornography –"

"Oy."

"Yeah, that teacher died in jail awaiting bail. Other inmates got to him."

"But nothing official linking Mimi to any of those, I assume?"

"Got it in one. Carlos Marron was not convicted in her father's killing, and I think he was still protecting her. Iris promoted him, which is surprising, since he killed her husband. She may not have been all that fond of good ol' Jim Bob. Cops say Marron gained some power in the Miami underworld as a political fixer and procurer after kicking Kefauver's keester."

"Still watching Perry Mason, I gather," I said. "Love that alliteration. Listen, unless there's some point you need to make now, I want to save myself some high-dollar legal bills by finishing the file before we talk about Mimi anymore. You good with that?"

"Of course."

"What I need is as much background on Rex as you can find. It would be great if I could interview someone who was close to him."

"Well, you could turn over in bed and talk to Laurel."

#

22

My queen's other consort

Monday, Oct. 10, 2022, 1:30 p.m.

"Whuh?" I stopped outside the poolside entrance to the resort office and plopped down on a reclining lounge chair.

"Since he listed your Nubian Queen as a contingent beneficiary in his will and life insurance, after Mimi, I think they might have had a pretty close relationship," Deuce said. "Since Mimi died first – as you know – that means your Nubian Queen gets a cool million plus whatever his printing business is worth."

"Whuut?"

"She won't need to hang around your cheap ass now. She can find a real boy toy."

"I hardly think the around-the-world trip we took last year counts as cheap, but I see your point," I said. "I foresee

Santa being especially generous to her kids, grandkids and great grandbabies this Christmas."

"Assuming we can keep you two out of jail that long," he said. "That's one piece of information that establishes a more solid motive for murder than the cops had before. They couldn't quite figure out why you would kill two people with whom you had just enjoyed sexual pleasures. Now, they have a 'why.' You can expect them to come back out or call to ask you to visit again."

"At which point, we will call the eminent law firm of Salazar & Jones, without fail," I said.

"Good man," Mr. 'Bill-them-by-the-hour' said. "Listen, I do have other clients, so if you don't mind –"

"Of course, of course," I said. "I think we three – you, Laurel and I – need to have another chat today about Rex's legacy."

"OK, but my schedule is pretty busy," he said. "Could you and Laurel stop by my office about 4 pm today?"

"What else are we going to do?"

"I'm sure you could think of something."

"True dat. We'll be there. I'll go one better: I'll make sure Her Royal Highness is not quite so high. If I can stop her drinking now, she should be good to go. I'll promise some evening dancing in town afterward; works every time."

We rang off, and I entered the office, where my Nubian Queen was enthroned on a towel (still nude, remember?) on Quil's chair behind the desk, looking at a computer moni-tor and manipulating a mouse to fast-forward through the recording. The other hand periodically raised her pineapple cup's bronze straw to her lips.

"I got good news and bad news," I said. "Which do you want first?"

She looked askance at me, pausing the video, which provided a shadowy view of the entrance gate from above and to the driver's side of where access codes are entered into the gate keypad.

"Bad news."

"I need you to stop drinking the rest of the afternoon, until about 4 pm."

"And the good news?"

"After we go chat with our lawyer for an hour or so, I'll take you out for dinner and dancing at the Teresienstadt Hofbrau."

She cocked her head. "Good deal, but we go shopping first."

"Okily-dokily."

She started scrolling through the recording again, but I still stood, looking at my beautiful millionaire girlfriend. Never thought I'd use that phrase in a sentence, for sure. She looked askance at me again as she sipped.

"Still drinking?" I asked, trying to sound non-judgmental.

"This is water. Want a sip? I didn't want to have to go back to the RV."

"There's more."

"Good news and bad news?" I nodded. "Give me the good news first."

"You're going to be a millionaire."

The bronze straw dropped out of her lips and made a little "clink" in the bottom of her empty cup. "Whuuut?"

"Yes, Rex named you as a second beneficiary in his life insurance and will, right after Mimi, and since Mimi died first, you're elected. Deuce said you get a million from the life insurance plus his printing businesses in Houston and Miami, which have not yet been appraised."

She squinted her eyes. "What's the bad news?"

"The cops now have a motive for us killing Mimi and Rex."

"Sheeeutt."

I spread one of my towels on the chair facing Laurel and sat down.

"Now, baby, you know I'm not the least bit jealous, but were you close with Rex?" I chuckled. "Should we have been picking out China for a new throuple lifestyle? Why would he pick you?"

Laurel set down her drink and looked down.

"I have no idea," she said. "I had played with them at swinger parties before I met you, and we always had great butt-naked sex, but I wouldn't say I knew him well enough – or he knew me well enough – to leave that much money to me. Maybe he just didn't have anybody else he wanted to leave it to."

"Maybe. I remember thinking you were being pretty cool to play with him, given his arm injury."

"Everybody needs love, and he was good when you got him going."

"So, you weren't 'taking one for the team' with Rex? Because you knew how hot I thought Mimi was?"

"Of course not," Laurel frowned. "Don't ever ask me to take one for the team with a couple because you want to get in the woman's pants. Not gonna happen."

"We haven't talked in detail about the night of the killings. What was he doing with you before he left that bedroom?"

Laurel paused, pursed her lips, closed her eyes, pinched the bridge of her nose, then looked at me with her hand over her mouth, as if thinking.

"We had played for a while, and he started to go limp, so we just cuddled for a few minutes. He appeared to be distracted. We heard Mimi giggling, and he jumped up, dug what must have been that gun out of his 'ho bag' and left. Then, two big bangs, one right after the other."

A "ho bag" is some kind of bag – tote, gym, backpack – in which people in the swing lifestyle keep condoms, lubricants, sex toys, erectile dysfunction drugs and towels to have handy when one is *in flagrante delizioso*.

We were silent for a full minute, reliving the horror of those few seconds that changed so much in our lives. I stared at the wall, recalling the noise, the sort of explosive shock of the two big bangs, the deafening ringing in my ears, the thud of poor Rex's lifeless body on the floor, the slow awareness of the moisture of blood, the odor of body fluids.

I shook my head and looked over at Laurel, whose eyes had filled with tears. I went over to her side of the desk, knelt and took her in my arms.

"Baby ... baby ... I know, I know," I said. "It's going to be all right. I got you. You got me. We're going to get through this."

#

23

Murder porn

Monday, Oct. 10, 2022, 2 p.m.

Behind Laurel's spikey pink head, I saw something on one of the four squares in Quil's screen, timestamped 5:15 pm. One square showed DJ Ted's Clubhouse, and another showed the dining area.

A third square showed what appeared to be a panoramic view of the main open area of the camp, encompassing bird's eye views of the pool, covered outdoor pavilion for dances and barbecues, tennis court, gym, segments of the road, and the entrance to the 1,500-square-foot "playhouse" where orgies often erupted.

The fourth square is what drew my attention. I saw a thin man with the baseball cap of a barbecue restaurant pulled low over his face, so the brim obscured most of it. What surprised me was he was in the act of punching the code into the keypad.

I moved back from Laurel and touched the mouse to let

the video advance. He completed the code and drove on in as if he were a guest. On previous visits to NTOR, I had found myself caught behind other restaurant delivery people at the gate who had to punch the keypad's communications button and wait for somebody to open the gate.

"Hmm, that's odd," I said. Laurel stood up and went to the lady's room, encountering the brunette who had informed us of the previous day's meeting with Quil. The worker had a file and went around the side of the desk to set it on an in-box as I took Laurel's place in Quil's chair. I sniffed her light scent from an expensive Chanel Chance perfume.

"You've seen me naked," I said to her. "I think maybe we ought to learn each other's first names, at least."

She blushed, pointed a red-lacquered fingernail at the name tag on her uniform shirt. "Delilah," she said. "What'cha doin'?"

"Probably wasting time," I said, as I advanced the recording.

Delilah seemed surprised by what she saw. Maybe Quil had not informed all employees of the cameras' existence?

The panoramic view didn't show the delivery guy's vehicle, a dirty, late-model silver Kia Soul, moving around the park. I guess that meant he drove straight to the office, which was not in the panoramic view.

I advanced the recording, saw the little brunette worker heading across the compound with the golf cart and what I reckoned to be the barbecue Jesse and Grace had ordered earlier.

"That's you," I said, pointing to the cart.

Delilah blushed more, excused herself and left.

Why did the Kia Soul not exit at that time? Delilah returned with the golf cart. A few minutes later, the Kia Soul exited, the driver not visible through the tinted windows.

I fast-forwarded through the evening and saw our little five-person party's arrival at DJ Ted's Clubhouse. Six people headed to the playhouse for a small orgy. Funny to watch people walking like Keystone Cops naked. It was dark, and the pixilated faces were unidentifiable, at least to me.

Just after the happy couples entered, I saw a clothed man exit in a way I can only describe as furtively toward the shadows at the tree line. It could have been the delivery guy, but with the pixilated images, I could not recognize him, even if I had seen his face before. I suspected Quil could identify every guest or employee in the park without having to point out birthmarks.

I fast-forwarded into the night, spotted Jesse and Grace leaving hand in hand from under the awning over the hot tub. A few minutes later, Ben, Janis and Shawn-from-Manchester stumbled away, crossing the grassy area. A couple of minutes later, I watched myself staggering under the weight of Laurel's exhausted body back toward our own RV, around 1:30 am.

About 2 am by the time stamp, I spotted Juanda backing away from the hot tub. At this close range, the fear on her face was obvious. She stumbled but kept her footing as the baseball cap of the barbecue delivery guy came into view. He appeared to be carrying a semiautomatic pistol with a sound suppressor at the tip. A puff of dirt jumped between Juanda's feet. She turned and ran toward the back of the property, where peaches and pecans grew.

The man trotted behind her. The lack of sound was maddening.

My face flushed and tears obscured my vision as Laurel re-entered the room.

"What's going on, baby?" she asked. "What you seeing?"

"Juanda getting killed."

"What?"

I slowed the recording down to normal and explained what I had seen before. By the time I had finished – about 15 minutes later – we saw the man carrying Juanda back from the orchard. It appeared that she had a diabetic seizure, because her feet and hands moved spasmodically. He held her in a fireman's carry, with her head and shoulders over his back, and his face was well-hidden. He carried her back under the awning over the hot tub.

We fast-forwarded the recording through the discovery of Juanda's body by Ben and myself, but never saw that son of a bitch again.

#

24

Curriculo vitiorum (Career of vices)

Monday, Oct. 10, 2022, 4 p.m.

"So that's it, you just left the video there?" Deuce asked. We were sitting at a conference table in his practice's law library. I love the smell of old books and lemon-scented wood polish.

"I trust Quil to keep it safe," I said. "She said it's in the cloud, protected by a complicated password that no one but she could know. We wanted to tell you about it in person before we did anything else with it."

The solicitor sat back in his chair, tapping a legal pad with his mechanical pencil, thinking. His eyes had darkened rings, his hair was more disheveled than usual, his University of Texas tie loosened, his Phi Beta Kappa tie pin askew, his collar open, his sleeves rolled up over his meaty forearms.

"Jeez, I may need another lawyer to help me keep up with

you guys," he said, glancing at Laurel's demure face, then taking in the rest of the view like Miles Archer admiring Brigid O'Shaughnessy.

I didn't blame him. She wore a pink and white sundress that matched her hair and so much jewelry on her wrists and fingers that the clink of metal on metal almost drowned out the clomp of her pointy-toed pink cowboy boots when she walked on Teresienstadt's cobblestone sidewalks. Dior's Addict perfume was the only other thing touching her satin skin. Pepe a lucky man.

"I'll consult with my partner about it," Deuce said. "It could be exculpatory, but the inability to identify who is the person chasing Juanda out to the orchard and bringing her back could be a problem. Who is to say it's not you? On the other hand, the medical examiner is not quite sure whether the death has any foul play associated with it at all. And if the medical examiner concludes it's natural causes, it would be courting disaster to bring up something that could be used against you, no matter how innocent you are. As your pal Nero Wolfe used to say, it's a pickle."

"OK, we can come back to that tomorrow," I said, my blue jean legs crossed, tapping my left cowboy boot with my right hand. "As I said, I'm confident the video is going to be available to us, but we came here to chat about Rex and why he left Laurel so much money."

Deuce nodded, raised his eyebrows and looked at Laurel, who shrugged.

"Tell me about how you met Rex, what kind of relationship you had with him, etc., without getting into the sordid details," the lawyer said.

She looked at me, and I shrugged my denim-clad shoulders. She set her Pure Leaf tea bottle on the glass desktop, looked out the window, folded her arms and said she met Rex back in 2017 when she went to a swinger house party in a little Gulf Coast town between Houston and Galveston. Laurel met Rex and Mimi now and then for a meal and dancing at one of those funky tiki bars in the area. On more than one occasion, Laurel took her own swinger date to meet Rex and Mimi to play at a hotel afterward.

After Laurel and I became a couple in the summer of 2020, we went to a lifestyle dinner at somebody's house – "Meat and Greet" would be the technical term – that Rex and Mimi were attending. Texans were pretty loose on pandemic restrictions back then. Afterward, Mimi reached out for us to play that night, which we did.

"I never got the feeling he was 'in love,' with me," Laurel said. "In the lifestyle, we sometimes say stuff like 'Love you guys' or whatever, but it's more of a friendship kind of love. We may have said that to each other when parting for the night or whatever, but I never got the sense there was anything special about it."

I felt a need to enlighten my friend about my Nubian Queen's special charms outside the bedroom.

"You've never seen Laurel in her element, which would be dancing or partying to music," I said. "She's a phenomenon. I can't take her anywhere without her becoming the center of attention. People love her almost like it's a pheromone in the air."

He cocked an eyebrow. "Really."

"I kid you not," I said. "If you don't believe me, you and Yvonne meet us at the Hofbrau. We'll show you."

"It's a thought," he said. "I'll ask."

"I finished that file on Mimi you sent me," I said. "Wow."

That file — Mimi's CV (*curriculo vitiorum,* or "career of vices"), if you will — contained some 400 pages of documents, and I had only finished about 100 of them on Sunday, so I had to read fast after viewing Juanda's murder. Skimming through the rest, here were some highlights:

—Graduated with honors from Our Lady of Fatima High in 1987.

--In 1992, graduated *cum laude* with a degree in business from the University of St. Mary of Bethlehem -- known by alums as "Bedlam," a real party school – in Baton Rouge, Louisiana, where she hobnobbed with politicians later convicted of corruption and/or sex crimes.

--One of those officials who showed up in the "celebrity citing" pages of the Baton Rouge Advocate newspaper was an insurance commissioner involved in covering up embezzlements. Jail officials said he committed suicide after his indictment. The cops thought he was covering up for a girlfriend, but they wouldn't say who. Did it involve *El Mecanico?*

--On the day Mimi graduated from college, three sorority sisters swore out a complaint to the East Baton Rouge district attorney saying Mimi stole their identities, using them to charge tens of thousands of dollars at Lord & Taylor, Neiman Marcus, a riverboat casino and three jewelry stores. After the district attorney presented the case to a grand jury, the case was "no-billed" -- not enough evidence to prosecute.

--Within the next month, each of those sorority sisters

died: one from rabies, one from drowning (partially eaten by alligator) and the third by car accident. *El Mecanico* again?

--After graduation, Mimi returned to Miami. She did this ostensibly to help her mother but also to extract her smokin' hot ass from the Louisiana Tabasco she had been brewing, as it were. She also returned to enjoy her nightlife. Cocaine flowed. By the end of the summer, someone had shot Carlos Marron to death, and Mimi had fled to the Houston area, where she found work in a hotel in Clear Lake City, near the National Aeronautics and Space Administration's Johnson Spaceflight Center.

--In 1993, she met Rex, moved into an apartment next to him, and started working part-time as a teller at Rice Growers' Savings & Loan.

--In 1994, she left the hotel and worked full-time at the S&L, and Rex took out a loan to start a printing business. Later lawsuits claimed his business printed checks in the name of S&L patrons cashed at Miami banks when Mimi and Rex were visiting Iris.

--In 1996, Rice Growers' Savings & Loan started to fail, so Mimi and Rex moved to Miami, where Rex opened a second print shop and Mimi worked with both Rex and her mother, now with a more upscale hotel on Miami Beach.

--In 1997, after learning about life coaching at a seminar at Iris' hotel, Mimi got a mail-order life coach certificate, hung her shingle and acquired a few older female clients. A half-dozen lawsuits ensued (sorry for the pun) over the next two years. They claimed identity theft, fraud and theft of property greater than $5,000 in value.

--In 1998, the incident that cost Rex his hand happened,

and they decided to move back to Houston. This was ostensibly to get expert care for his arm but offered the extra handy benefit (ahem) of extracting Mimi from Florida courts' jurisdiction.

--With her old S&L dissolved but her cash-handling and accounting skills undiminished, Mimi found another bank teller job in Houston. The file cited no charges of fraud or identity theft, but she resumed her life coaching, which appeared to take off after the Enron scandal. If she was scamming these people, she was careful.

--After 9/11, Mimi and Rex involved themselves in the Veterans Outreach Patriotism Project at Sol Rosensteen's East Mount Houston Church. Two years later, someone blew a whistle on that program's disappearing funds. Rex and Mimi left the church, but faced no other consequences, and the funds never reappeared.

The file's last document date: Feb. 4, 2004.

Responding to my "wow," Deuce said, "Yes," and resumed tapping his pencil on the legal pad. "She was a piece of work. I can't see how you didn't sense her twisted nature, but I'm sure that milieu you guys thrive in has its own distractions."

"True dat," Laurel said.

I shook my head, grinning, and turned to Deuce.

"So you have a pretty good picture of Mimi now, but we need to know about Rex, and because he flew much lower under the radar, that's going to be tough," he said, sliding a manila folder over to our side of the table, and started reading off his notepad.

"We got a birth certificate, high school diploma, some newspaper clippings from his high school football career and the beginning of his San Angelo State college football career, including his career-ending knee injury, some tax returns, his college transcript, his addresses, but no criminal record and nothing aside from the lawsuits he faced with Mimi, which you have already seen."

I took a couple of minutes to flip through the thin file and closed it.

"What we need is someone close to him or – even better – his own diary or something like it," I said. "Has anyone or anything like that come up?"

"His mother is still alive, but they had been estranged since he took up with Mimi," he said. "One option: at the same time the two of them attended Rosensteen's church, Rex attended a nearby Catholic Church, Our Lady of Guadalupe. He wrote them some checks for donations and addressed a $1,000 check to Father Dan O'Keefe with a happy birthday notation in the corner."

"Dang," I said. "Your investigator doesn't miss a trick. I guess I'll have to drive down there to meet in person."

"Not necessarily. I gather Father O'Keefe is in charge of Rex and Mimi's funeral arrangements and should arrive in Teresienstadt tomorrow."

"I'd still like to talk to his mom," I said and looked at Laurel, who nodded vigorously.

"Mommas know the shit," she said.

To Deuce, I asked, "Is she in fair health? Do you think she can talk on the phone or, I hope, by web chat?"

Shrugging, he gave me her number in the Midland, Texas, area and the number for Our Lady of Guadalupe Catholic Church in Northeast Houston. My advocate asked me to try to get him on the call with Mrs. Vega, if possible. He also wanted to be at the priest interview; I said I'd try.

"Rex had several laptop computers, but the one he used the most has a password the cops have been unable to decipher," Deuce said.

"We gotta get into that one," I said, "but I think figuring out a password with so little insight into Rex's story might make that damn near impossible."

It was approaching 5 pm. Laurel handles significant emotional trauma such as Juanda's death through what she calls "shopping therapy." That's probably not healthy, but as she would say, "It is what it is." Teresienstadt has some nifty leather goods and silver jewelry stores. Deuce called Yvonne, who agreed to meet us at the Hofbrau at 6-ish. Drinking and dancing tend to elevate Laurel's mood, as well. Her Royal Highness' moods require a deft touch, and her appetites must be satisfied.

The Montecarlo-Traeger couple went out for a nice walk in the late afternoon sunshine on the wide, live-oak-shaded sidewalks of downtown Teresienstadt.

#

25

A Nubian Queen on leather

Monday, Oct. 10, 2022, 5 p.m.

A white and black couple walking arm in arm down a small Texas town's street remained unusual, even well into the 21st Century, and we attracted eyes as we walked. When we passed such folks, Laurel smiled and said, "Hey, how you doin'? Good?" and kept on walking. This was her way of making sure people knew she had noticed their stares and would stop it.

After a few minutes, we found a leather goods store Laurel wanted to explore — another place of pleasant scents for me. Laurel used to trail ride. That means she would ride with wagons and horses from some prearranged location a long distance to an important rodeo or stock show, such as the Houston Fat Livestock Show and Rodeo or the San Antonio Livestock Show and Rodeo.

She wanted to do that again, and I was interested, but with the money she was falling into, she'd be doing it whether I liked it or not. That meant I would be doing it. Don't want some other cowboy carrying my Nubian Queen off with his Mustang, do I?

With the name *"Die Koenigin des Leders"* ("The Queen of Leather") this English Leather-scented store contained the remains of hundreds of dead cows and other vertebrates converted into boots, chaps, dresses, shirts, coats, purses, saddles, gun belts, bull whips. Not vegan friendly.

"Oh lawd," I said, when I saw the whips.

"Exactly," Laurel replied.

A petite, buxom lady with tight black leather pants and a tight black cotton western shirt — with pearl buttons and a pattern of silver and turquoise in all the right places -- stepped toward us, smiling under what might have been a Dolly Parton wig.

"You must be Mr. Montecarlo!" she said, extending her pale, manicured hand. "We saw you on the tee-vee last night."

In some parts of Texas, they pronounce those two letters with equal emphasis on each syllable.

"How kind of you to remember," I said, grinning, eying her over my wire-rimmed sunglasses and holding her hand a little longer than necessary. "One's fame often dims fast in this media-rich 21st century. And you are?"

"Kristina Koenig, but people call me Kricket, starting with a 'K,'" she said, turning to Laurel. "And you are?"

Laurel smiled back and purred in her Eartha Kitt voice, "I'm his Nubian Queen."

Kricket's laughter tinkled like the bell that had rung as

we entered the immaculate brick building built in the 1850s. "How lovely! I've never been in the presence of royalty."

"Oh, she's the highest royalty you're likely to meet," I said. "But aren't you *Die Koenigin des Leders?*"

More of the tinkling. "You got me," she said.

I bowed before Kricket and said, "Your Highness, may I present my Nubian Queen Laurel von Traeger."

More tinkling, and she reached for Laurel's hand. Laurel had a couple of things she wanted to try on, but she first wanted to price some of the cool saddles. We have no horses, but now that she was a landowner, she said as we drove into town, she wanted to correct that unfortunate circumstance.

"You never know," she had said as the wind buffeted us in the open Corvette on the way over. "We may want to offer nude horseback riding as a special treat."

"Might be fun," I had replied. "I've never done that. Not sure the *cojones* could take it, but maybe somebody has found a solution for that particular problem – short of castration, of course."

Die Koenigin des Leders displayed four basic western models: ranch, barrel racing, youth and pleasure/trail saddles, plus an English-style dressage saddle and an English-style polo saddle. The pleasure/trail saddle had the lightest color and the most intricate patterns. The barrel-racing and English saddles had the least adornment, and the other two were darker and had modest patterns carved, inked or sewn into the leather.

The brands included Martin, Cashel, Cavalga, Mustang, Collegiate and Wintec. I couldn't help noticing the prices ranged from about $750 to about $3,300.

"Could I sit on one or two?" Laurel asked Kricket.

"Of course," she responded. "You understand, these are just display models. If you want something specific, we'll show you an online catalog. You could even customize so you have a totally unique seat, but that would be pretty pricey."

Laurel looked over her over-sized sunglasses at Kricket. "Not a problem."

I cocked my head and looked over my sunglasses. "May I add that she already has a totally unique seat, but we can always use another, if I'm not being too subtle," I said.

Kricket giggled.

As Her Royal Soon-to-be Highness swung a booted foot over the back end of the ranch saddle, I couldn't miss a lovely glimpse of my darling's pooty-tang. My eyebrows raised of their own accord. Behind me, someone gasped, "Oh!"

I glanced back and spied the buxom "Karen," the lady who wanted to shoot us at the gate to NTOR, wearing a tan pant-suit, heavy brown leather shoulder bag and a white button-collar Oxford shirt. I wondered what weapon she had in the bag this time.

"I can't believe you let her do that!" she scolded Kricket. "She's not wearing any you-know-what."

"Is that a fact?" Kricket said. "Well, we keep these things pretty clean and polished, so I'm sure there won't be any problem."

Good answer, I thought. I wondered if "Karen" knew we could fire back, if a gunfight broke out at *Die Koenigin des Leders* (there's a movie title for you).

"But children get on those saddles all the time!"

"And sometimes those little darlin's got full diapers," Kricket said. "We clean them between riders."

"Oh!" the indignant woman said, and she stalked out of the store, muttering, "I'll never come back here again!"

One of the blond, teenage girls from the cheerleading squad in front of the NTOR gate followed reluctantly, silently mouthing "I'm sorry" at Laurel and myself.

"That woman is such a pain in my back pocket," Kricket said to me.

"You may have just made a sale – perhaps several saddles," I said. "Your Highness, how many horses do you think you want at NTOR?"

"I figure four to start," Laurel said. "We might want to start a trail ride from there to a stock show, maybe more than one."

"Damn, you are thinking big," I said, chuckling. "I'm sure it would be a big hit. We could call it the Lady Godiva trail ride."

"Hooo-ey!" Laurel said, standing in the stirrups and bumping around on it like a bucking bronco. "Ride'em, cowgirl!"

Other people in the store started clapping and laughing. You don't often see a pink-haired beautiful black woman in a sun dress bumping and grinding on a saddle, at least outside Las Vegas.

We went back to Kricket's office, looked at the online catalog and picked out four saddles at a price of $750 for three and $3,000 for the fourth. Guess who gets the fourth? Each will also have the diamond-shaped NTOR logo stamped into the rear seat padding (i.e.,"skirt") behind the main seat (i.e., "cantle") on either side. We gave Kricket a $2,000 deposit and exchanged contact information.

"You know, I've been out there to NTOR," Kricket said as we got up to leave. "My ex and I had a good time out there – well, at least I did."

"I'll bet you did," I said, raising my eyebrows like Groucho Marx. "If you want to come again … give us a tingle. I've grown partial to listening to the chirping of satisfied crickets."

She chuckled, but hugged my neck and kissed my cheek before we left, leaving her Johnson Baby Shampoo scent on me. Not a wig, I guess. To be fair, Kricket also hugged Laurel and kissed her cheek. When we exited the front door of *Die Koenigin des Leders*, Laurel spanked my left buttock.

"You don't have to flirt with all of them, do you?" she asked.

I ignored the impudent question.

"I have an idea," I said. "The night you unleash this trail ride proposal on the staff and residents, we should show the Agatha Christie/Margaret Rutherford movie, *Murder at the Gallop*, where the mystery happens at a horse-riding hotel/resort. Robert Morley is one of the suspects. Great fun. G-rated."

"We could follow it up with *Rancho Deluxe*," Laurel said. "And, of course –"

"*Blazing Saddles!*" we chorused and fell on each other's necks, giggling.

At that moment, I tripped, and as we fell onto a sandstone sidewalk bench under a hipster-tourist dive bar's awning, I heard a "pop" and window breaking at the same time, and a car rushing away from the scene. I jumped up, grabbed my pistol out of my pocket holster and trotted out into the road, where I saw a gray car disappearing around a corner.

It might have been a Kia Soul.

#

26

Basket case

Monday, Oct. 10, 2022, 6:15 p.m.

"Really, Peter Paul Montecarlo, the twice-cursed?" learned counsel said after we explained to Yvonne and him at the Hofbrau bar and grill about the most recent violence to crash our buzz. "Does disaster have to follow you everywhere?"

Laurel had eased her jangled nerves and the discomfort of a skinned knee from the limestone bench by finishing her first double Tito's Tart without pausing to breathe after we entered the Hofbrau. We had given the dive bar's bearded manager $200 to fix the window and leave us out of it, if he wanted to call the cops. He saw no reason to do so.

Feeling a bit jittery, I had taken a shot of Don Patron myself with the traditional salt and lime as soon as we sat down at the beer-and-bratwurst smelling Hofbrau. I nursed a Robert Earl Keen Honey Pils. Local boy done good.

"Point taken," I said. A buxom young blond waitress (was everybody blond in Teresienstadt?) wearing a low-cut traditional dirndl dress walked up and took our food orders, including a replacement double Tito's Tart for Laurel.

Three unkempt-but-clean white men in their 20s and 30s started setting up a drum kit, guitars, amplifiers and microphones on a stage nearby, while one of Laurel's favorite country singers, Kane Brown, crooned "Homesick" from the juke box.

"On the way over here, I called the rectory of Our Lady of Guadalupe Catholic Church in Houston," I said. "They said Father O'Keefe was driving up here tonight, and they would ask him to give me a call."

I turned to Yvonne and asked how her daughters were doing, one in college, the other a senior in high school. Yvonne was in her mid-40s, about 5'10," slim, an auburn-haired beauty with a nice tan that could turn pale in winter.

In my dotage, I remained a proud admirer of fine feminine taste. Maybe I just miss my mother, who could have given Audrey Hepburn competition in the beauty and class department. Whatever the reason, I noticed Yvonne's fashionable grayish-green dress and waistcoat combination in light wool that left her collarbones exposed and extended to mid-calf. Her Dolce & Gabbana's Light Blue cologne penetrated my senses, more tightly tuned by the recent homicide attempt.

I'm no fashionista, but I found her appearance well matched to Deuce's, now that he had buttoned his collar, straightened his tie, unrolled his sleeves, donned his gray herringbone tweed jacket and refreshed his British Sterling aftershave.

Bless their bougie little hearts.

Yvonne explained her elder daughter's decision to attend

Sam Houston State University on a full soccer scholarship rather than the University of Texas with a partial. She straightened Deuce's not-quite-combed hair with her right hand. Youngish, devoted mothers are so cute.

We continued to discuss their daughters' activities, triumphs and disappointments over salads as Laurel and I finished our drinks. The band started tuning instruments with the help of a technician holding some kind of electronic sound mixer as he walked around the room testing acoustics. Deuce nursed a Michelob Ultra and Yvonne sipped Liebfraumilch.

Laurel had her back to the musical trio, but when the singer tested his mike, she turned and squealed in delight. "Dusty! Yay!" She jumped up and gave him a quick half-hug as he and his two colleagues smiled back.

"Those are The Weak Knights," I said, reaching for my wallet. "We didn't realize they'd be playing this far from Austin. The fun is about to ramp up exponentially."

"We haven't been here in a while," Yvonne said. "Fact is, we don't get out much."

"You know me, man," Deuce said, his lips pursed. "I dig my jazz, New Wave and punk rock. Country music ain't my scene."

"Well, The Weak Knights have a little punk in them and no country at all."

When Laurel returned, I handed her $20 and asked her to request Green Day and whatever song she wanted.

The waitress had replaced our salads with entrées by the time Dusty had introduced the band (bushy brown-bearded Austin on drums, clean-cut, porn-stached Brent on bass). With a close-cropped beard, million-dollar smile and grunge-rock-style shirt and jeans, Dusty drew the attention of the 20-person audience to Laurel as "a special friend of the band" and the requester of the first song, a version of Blackstreet and Dr. Dre's "No Diggity."

"Our food's gonna get cold," I said, as I stood up with Laurel and bebopped over to the dance floor with her. Deuce looked at Yvonne and cocked his head. They joined us. Laurel, of course, was the grooviest dancer, but Yvonne wasn't far behind. Three other couples joined us, including two women who kept cheering Her Royal (quickly getting) Highness. One of them looked familiar, and I realized it was Joanna Metzger, the TV journalist.

The band played four more songs while we finished our meals. Ah, *jaegerschnitzel* and *rotkohl* are among my favorites. Deuce and I ordered coffees and liqueurs – Amaretto for me, Galiano for him.

The next song was Green Day's "Basket Case," during which Deuce and I did our best to pogo as Laurel and Yvonne laughed and shook their heads. That's a song and a dance that encourages a certain amount of random physical contact. I bumped into the back of a big, balding redneck with a cowboy hat, plaid shirt, jeans and boots, standing near the dance floor.

I apologized in an exaggerated manner, sort of going with the song's flamboyant flow, and resumed my ridiculous impersonation of a Masai warrior. The redneck regarded us without a smile.

I turned to Laurel and made a face like the comedian Steve Martin saying, "Well, excuuuuuuse meee!"

Deuce, the poor, desk-chained professional slave that he

is, made it through about two-thirds of the song before he waved Yvonne over and leaned exaggeratedly on her as they walked back to the table for him to catch his breath.

At the end of the song, I did the same act with Laurel, which drew applause and cheers from a couple of tables.

"Please give it up for The Weak Knights dancers!" Dusty said, laughing.

"Yeow!" I howled back. I looked around for the redneck, hoping to give him a friendly, apologetic smile, but he had disappeared.

While I took a swig of the honey pils, Joanna, in a black t-shirt, denim jacket and jeans, joined us with her friend, Adriana, a voluptuous Latina with blond streaks in her hair, wearing an off-the-shoulder white cotton top, tight ripped jeans and stillettos.

"You're quite amazing, you know that?" Joanna told me and turned to Laurel. "Both of you."

"First off, young lady, let's make it clear that this conversation is off the record, OK?" I said. Grabbing Deuce's now sweaty forearm, I said, "I got my lawyer right here, so no funny business."

She bobbed her head and chuckled. I caught the vanilla scent of her shampoo. "What happens in the Hofbrau stays in the Hofbrau," she said.

I looked at Adriana, who appeared confused, but nodded. "I'm not in journalism," Adriana said. "I'm a paralegal."

"No kidding?" my solicitor said. "Great people, paralegals. We couldn't get shit done without them."

"We heard at the station about the death last night at NTOR, and we reported it, but we're not talking about that here," Joanna said. "Our understanding is it was natural causes, and that's not exactly 'man bites dog' news."

"Agreed," Deuce said.

#

27

St. Thomas the Fulsome of Ulster redux

Monday, Oct. 10, 2022, 7 p.m.

We strolled onto the enclosed patio, sat on some padded wicker chairs and chatted about The Weak Knights and other bands Laurel and I follow: Zach Tate and Goldie Locke out of Houston, Sonny Wolf out of Austin. Laurel talked about her favorite recording artists: Kane Brown and Luke Combs in country, Keith Frank in Zydeco, Tucka in modern soul. She then started mocking my love for Latin jazz and '60s jazz pop, which most people would call "easy listening." What can I say? Love my Mancini.

"I gotta admit that in my busy work life – tonight's a rare night off – I spend little time listening or thinking about music," Joanna said.

"Same here," Deuce said. "Yvonne will tell you I often work 50 to 60 hours a week."

"That's why you get the big bucks," I said.

He punched my shoulder and said, "You'll find out why I get the big bucks, if I can keep you two out of prison."

"You two?" Joanna said, her eyebrows raised as she looked at Laurel. "I thought the cops were only gossiping about Mr. Montecarlo here."

"Pepe," I corrected, "and we're trying not to talk about anything serious like that tonight."

"OK-OK-OK," Joanna said, but added, "Pepe, yes, we agreed to that. I don't want to violate that trust and what I hope …" she looked at Adriana with raised eyebrows "… will be an ongoing friendship."

Laurel looked askance at me with pursed lips, and I read her mind: "Swingers?" When she says it, it sounds like "swing-grrrs."

My beloved had a strong appeal for both sexes. I was a little envious of how easily she attracts potential lovers.

"However –"

"Here it comes," Deuce said.

Joanna looked at my attorney, then at Laurel and me. "You may not be keeping up with the local social media, and you may be surprised to learn that you're a big topic among congregants at Reverend Philo Lenfant's First Hill Country Bible Baptist Church."

The Nubian Queen released an ignoble, contemptuous, "Huh."

"Interesting," I said, looking at my advocate. "You know about this?"

"It's a 24-hour job keeping up with you, Pepe," he said. "No. I hope it will remain a low priority, but if they start to libel or slander you, I will make sure you get possession of their building and all their property."

"What the hell am I going to do with a church, for God's sake?" I asked, shaking my head in wonder. I turned to Joanna and Adriana. "I'm Catholic, by the way, and a good one, albeit a sinner."

"Like all of us," Laurel said.

"Same here," Joanna and Adriana said at almost the same time.

"What exactly are they saying about me?" I asked, tapping my fingers on the wooden armrest of my chair. "Not that I care."

"On the church's local Facebook page, they posted several unflattering photos of you and some old newspaper opinion pieces blaming you for the Great Recession," Joanna said.

"That was debunked at the time, total horseshit," I said. "While I benefited from the crash, it was going to come, and I had nothing to do with bringing it on. My work did augur that the bubble was near bursting, but so did other people's reporting and analysis."

"One point these church people are making is that while others were writing about the situation, they weren't investing in a way to benefit from the crash," Joanna said.

"We're still off the record, but the situation is somewhat different for me," I said. "I was not affiliated with any news organization with rules against investments in areas of coverage. Also, every one of my pieces had disclaimers about my investments and a link to my personal portfolio."

Joanna nodded, looked away, sipped her wine.

"The more substantive criticism has provided tinder for the flame that has been nursed by the First Hill Country Bible Baptist Church – that's a mouthful, isn't it? – for some time," Joanna said, looking at Adriana, who, by the way, smelled of Gucci's Guilty perfume.

What can I say? This beak is sensitive, and I've spent some lovely hours buying expensive perfumes for the women in my life.

"Some of my coworkers attend that church, which has been growing fast since Lenfant came here and put it on the tee-vee," said Adriana, giving it that equal emphasis on both letters. "They say some of their rougher members – former drug addicts and drunks, I guess – have threatened to go out there and burn NTOR down."

"No shit?" I said. "It wouldn't be the first time people preaching fire and brimstone brought some of it up to the earth's surface."

Adriana looked sideways at me.

"My coworkers are not the ones advocating that at all," she said. "In fact, they have urged against it, but they, too, don't like what happens at NTOR."

"Why?" Laurel said, waving her hand in exasperation. "What happens there is not happening to them. If they don't like it, don't go."

Adriana shrugged.

"No offense," Yvonne said. "It's hard for parents to explain why they can't go to Nut Tree Orchard Resort. The name makes it seem like a fun place –"

"Which it is," Laurel said.

"I'm sure it is, but it's not for kids," Yvonne said. "So, that forces parents – who may have a lot of other pressures in their lives such as rent, lousy jobs, etc. – to communicate about something that's difficult to describe to kids, much less to teenagers."

"Indeed," I said, turning to Deuce. "How did you handle that with your daughters?"

He turned to the mother of his children, who chuckled and said, "I started to describe how it was a place were a lot of grownups – a lot of them grandma and grandpa's age – party naked and have sex."

"Honesty," I said. "Wow. And the reaction?"

Yvonne stuck her fingers in her ears and said, "LALALALALA! I'M NOT LISTENING!"

We all laughed.

"I wonder how difficult it is to keep teenage boys and girls out of there," Joanna said.

"Not sure," I said, raising my eyebrows like a certain Marx brother. "I'll ask and ring your bell, if I can."

Turning serious, I said, "Obviously, if it's not happening, we don't want to instigate it by having the subject raised on local TV. I can tell you we've never seen anybody that young, and nobody has ever alerted us that a trespasser is on the property."

I hesitated, thinking about the man who carried Juanda back to the hot-tub. "I suspect it happens," I said, looking at Deuce and Laurel.

"We're gonna beef up security," Laurel said.

Joanna cocked her head and looked at Laurel. "We?"

I knocked over Laurel's drink on the table between us, and she squealed in surprise.

"Sorry, babe, let me wipe this up. Go get some more napkins?"

When she came back, I was on my knees next to her chair, wiping up the vodka with a sopping paper napkin.

"Oh, thank you," I said, looking up at my beloved. "You're like the answer to St. Thomas the Fulsome of Ulster's prayer."

"Huh?"

Deuce cackled. Joanna pursed her lips and squinted her lovely eyes at me.

"Did you ever study about St. Thomas the Fulsome of Ulster? He was always spilling things." I looked at Laurel with my head cocked.

"Oooooh, really?" she said. "Well, I'm Methodist, so I never learned all the ins and outs of your obscure Catholic saints."

"Obscure doesn't begin to describe it," Joanna chuckled.

I finished wiping up the drink.

Yvonne murmured something in her husband's ear. "Ah, you're right," he said, as they both started to rise. "I have an early court appearance tomorrow – nothing related to you."

It was about 9 pm, and I figured Laurel was just getting started with the dancing, so we hugged the Joneses and let them exit. Laurel, Joanna, Adriana and I re-entered the main dance floor area, where the band was finishing its second set.

I looked around for the redneck I'd bumped and decided he went home. The jukebox played Coolio's Gangsta Walk, another line dance, and Laurel brought Joanna and Adriana out to the dance floor to show them how sexy quasi-sexagenarians do it. I checked my email and found out my portfolio had grown by 5% over the previous month. Wouldn't last.

When they returned, Laurel was hugging the young women by the shoulders, talking intently and smiling at me like the Cheshire Cat.

"What new fine mess are you getting us into, Laurel?" I muttered to myself.

#

28

Regarding a Corvette, teeth, static

Monday, Oct. 10, 2022, 9:30 p.m.

The young ladies agreed to meet us at the gate to NTOR at 10 pm, so we could wave them in. I called Jonquil to let her know we would have two guests, and she had no problem with it. I texted Jesse and Grace, who were staying all week at their campsite, and they hoped to play with the four of us. Jesse said he would check if any of the permanent guests were free, focusing on males because we had two extra females.

The Playhouse might get a workout, I thought. DJ Ted's Clubhouse only operates Fridays through Sundays, plus occasional holidays, but we could play elsewhere. Because of Juanda's death, the hot tub was off limits.

Joanna and Adriana left right after The Weak Knights'

first song of their last set. I bought the band a round of their favorite shots, carried the drinks over to set them down within reach, gave them another $20 tip and settled the bill.

We had parked the Corvette around the corner, and that's where the trouble began. The redneck I had bumped sat on the hood of my car, now dented – an expensive fix on a fiberglass classic. A couple of his buddies stood nearby, each with a foot atop a burnt-orange rear fender, which I had scrupulously polished to a mirror shine. Each wore Pecan County Sheriff's Office reserve deputy uniforms, but they weren't the same reserve deputies Jesse and I had encountered at NTOR.

Difficult to smile under these circumstances, but I did so.

"Hi, how's it going?" I asked. "How's your insurance coverage?"

The redneck looked around like he had no idea what I was talking about.

I stood on the curb next to the passenger side and gestured to the dent visible under his right buttock.

"Did I do that?" he asked, looking at his buddies, who shook their heads.

"Really, boys?" Laurel said. She had her right hand inside her purse, about which I was ambivalent. In the right circumstances, she could start shooting any minute, with a variety of positive consequences (e.g., keeping me alive). On the other hand, she could start shooting any minute, with a different set of consequences, maybe not positive at all.

"Really, ma'am," said the clean-shaven Latino deputy with his foot on the driver-side rear fender. "It was like that when we got here."

"Was he on it when you got here?" I said, still smiling.

"I believe he was," said the Anglo deputy on the curb, close to me, whose name tag said, "W.O. Wright." His smirk resembled Sgt. Wright.

"Bwah-ha-ha-ha!" I said, unable to restrain the Montecarlo Cackle.

"I get it now, bow-wow," I said, continuing to giggle. "B.O.W. and W.O.W. Your dad must be a real character."

W.O. Wright's face blushed and presented a dead-eye cold stare.

Laurel was behind me to my left, away from the street, where I want her in dodgy situations, which happened more than once during our recent around-the-world tour. It was fun, but what's fun without a little risk?

The big redneck moved his legs over the passenger-side front fender, like he was about to get off that way.

"May I suggest you slide off the front, the way you got on?" I said, continuing the forced grin, gesturing toward the front grill, where a modest chrome longhorn-skull ornamented the usual prominent grille teeth. "You might cause more damage – obviously not what happened before – to the car by moving off via the fender."

He continued sliding via the passenger side front fender so as to stand over me on the curb. The sound of rivets from his jeans scratching the paint caused a little part inside of me to weep.

Trying to minimize my nasal consumption of this particular douchebag's Old Spice aftershave and Lone Star beer, I told myself, *It's only stuff. It's replaceable, and Deuce will likely get this ass-hole to pay for it.* So I kept grinning up at him.

"You got some nice teeth, Mr. Montecarlo," the redneck said. "Want to give me some?"

"I'm kind of attached to these –" I said, and the screen in my head went blank.

Nothing but static.

#

29

A perfectly competent woman

Monday, Oct. 10, 2022, 9:50 p.m.

The rush of the cool September night wind on my face quieted the static and awakened me. I was in the passenger seat of the Corvette, and Laurel was speeding back to NTOR.

"I think we lost them," she said, more to herself than me.

I moved my head a millimeter. "OUCH!" I said and regretted saying it, because that meant moving my head a little more.

"Don't move, you fool," she said. "Let me get you back to NTOR, and somebody there can fix you up. Tuffy's on her way. I texted Joanna and Adriana to head home. No playing tonight."

Being careful not to move my head off the rear cushion, I asked, "Who turned out the lights?"

"Wow."

"Wow, I'm surprised to be alive, too."

"No, WOW got you with a blackjack,"- Laurel said. "W.O. Wright. Right after he did that, I put my Beretta to his neck and persuaded them all to put you gently in the passenger seat and let us alone."

I started to giggle at the "who's on first" turn our conversation had taken, but decided it wasn't quite that funny.

"How did you persuade them -- two, probably three heavily armed men — with your little Beretta Tomcat?"

"I turned on the video on my phone to look through the mesh part of my purse when I saw them sitting on your car," Laurel said. "Thought it would be prudent. I keep telling you I'm a perfectly competent woman."

"You don't have to tell me," I said. "Everybody else does. Deuce, for example. Please go gently off the shoulder into the drive."

"I know how to drive you into this place as gently as this fancy sports car will do it," Laurel said, pursing her lips and giving me a sidelong glance.

"Sorry," I said. "Brain damage, I guess. What's your name again?"

"You makin' jokes, you're gonna be ah-ight," she said, turning slowly onto the driveway of the camp.

In my peripheral vision, I saw a small sport-utility vehicle parked across the highway with the lights off, but I didn't want to examine it, because that would entail moving my head.

As we were starting to pull through the gate, a police vehicle turned on its flashing lights behind us.

"Oh lawd," we said in unison. Laurel looked in the mirror,

and I looked in the passenger-side mirror, but couldn't see anything.

"Laurel! It's me, Tuffy! Let me in!"

The next bit is quite blurry. I blacked out.

———————

Tuesday, Oct. 11, 2022, 11 a.m.

I opened my bloodshot eyes the next morning alone in the bed of our rented RV with a bandage on my head. The RV was empty, and the air conditioning was a bit noisy, but some murmuring voices outside penetrated the white noise. The delicious odor of fresh coffee had awakened me.

I started to move to sit up quick, with momentum, like they taught us in *aiki-jiu-jitsu*, but that was not happening. "Hey!" I called out. "A little help in here, please?"

The door popped open, and Jesse, nude as usual, looked in and smiled. "It's ALIVE!" he said, doing a passable impersonation of Colin Clive in the original *Frankenstein* movie with Boris Karloff.

I started to chuckle, which hurt, so I stopped. "Ass-hole," I said. "Made me laugh. Help me get to that coffee."

"Doc said take it easy, stay in bed," Jesse said, coming in and standing over me as I moved toward the edge of the bed. Doc was a retired Air Force ear-nose-and-throat physician, about 70, with a droll sense of humor, who happened to reside at NTOR.

"Fuck Doc."

"Not me, but Grace probably will, if you ask nicely."

"Stop making me laugh, dammit."

"It's hard."

"You're doing it again."

Jesse, emitting a scent of chlorine from his morning swim, mimed zipping his mouth closed and helped me get to my feet. I was wearing some dark-gray running shorts and a light gray University of Memphis t-shirt. He moved some flip-flops near my feet, and I slid them on. I shuffled to the door, opened it and stepped gingerly down to the grass with him supporting some of my weight under my left arm. No running for me today, I thought.

"Coffee," I said. "But first –"

I shuffled over to the grass behind a tree and took a three-minute leak. Yes, I timed it.

"Evacuation … complete," Jesse said, impersonating the computer voice in the first Austin Powers movie, when he is unfrozen to fight Dr. Evil.

"You just don't quit, do you?" I said, starting to chuckle again. In slow motion, I pulled my shorts up and turned around.

"You don't, either, buddy," Deuce said from a latticed folding chair. I hadn't realized he was in the neighborhood.

"Aren't you missing court?"

"I made it to court. It's about 11 am, bud. You're turning into a full-time job."

"Anything to help that darling daughter get through college."

"She's on full scholarship, remember?" he said. "It's the one in high school you'll be putting through college."

"That's what I meant."

"Sit your ass down before I knock you down," Laurel said. She stood with a steaming mug next to the University of Texas folding director's chair where I drank coffee, booze and protein shakes, usually at different times.

"Yes, ma'am."

In compromised deference to the balmy weather and to the Puritan sensibilities of Deuce, who was in red-and-blue Tejas Club tie, white shirt with rolled up sleeves and navy pin-striped suit pants, Laurel wore shorts, a low-cut knit shirt and flip-flops. My solicitor's suit jacket laid over the back of another folding chair. Jesse sat at the picnic table, sipping coffee.

Her Royal not-so Highness was enthroned in a Texas Southern University chair like mine. She produced a notepad and pen. I noticed she had not started drinking yet. I started to cock my head in surprise, but that hurt, so I stopped.

#

30

Wouldn't it be nice?

Tuesday, Oct. 11, 2022, 11:15 a.m.

"I made a list of things we need to do, in no particular order," Laurel said, looking over her reading glasses at Deuce and me. She ticked off each item as she went through them. "One, talk to Rex's mom. Two, talk to Tuffy, now that you're awake. Three, decide what to do about the Juanda video. Four, talk to Father O'Keefe. By the way, he called while you were sleeping. He said he could talk to us over dinner, if you're feeling up for it, outside the camp."

"Am I feeling up for it?" I asked, curious. "What did Doc think?"

"Doc thinks you're an idiot for whom a brain injury would be an improvement."

"Funny. What did he want to me to do, and what are the consequences if I don't?"

My lawyer looked up at the sky and muttered to himself, "What now, Lord?"

"He said, 'I think he's going to be ah-ight,'" Laurel said. "It's a minor concussion, he thought. Nothing looks or feels broken, but he wants us to go in and have it X-rayed today. If it shows up with no cranium cracks, you may have some swelling. You for sure should take it easy. It should heal on its own -- but!"

"Here it comes," I said.

"But, if you don't take it easy, or if there are cracks in the skull, you could die."

"Lovely."

"Exactly."

Jesse chimed in. "So, buddy, if you leave the premises, I'm sticking with you as your bodyguard."

"Nah," I said.

"Yup," Laurel said. "I don't want a vegetable lover – or a dead one. We three will go to the hospital for the X-ray, and if you're clear, we'll also go see Father O'Keefe. I set the X-ray appointment for 2 pm."

"And it's pretty clear somebody out there doesn't like you," Deuce said. "This ass-hole you bumped into at the Hofbrau, one John Bauer, according to Laurel's sister, is close to that ass-hole preacher, Philo Lenfant."

"That's the Right Reverend Theophilus Lenfant, and don't you forget it!" I said, trying to mimic the Karen again, but it was a painful impersonation.

Deuce didn't get it. Laurel snorted, pursed her lips and rolled her eyes.

"Bauer is in the wind," Deuce said. "The guy who sapped you with a blackjack had a sudden urge to join his National Guard unit on maneuvers out on Fort Cavazos and can't be found. The third guy, a Mario Guadalupe, was suspended as a reserve deputy, but he ain't talking. He's unemployed, but not a flight risk. He can't afford to go anywhere, I gather."

I looked at Jesse. "Think he's related to the deputy that was guarding the crime scene?"

Jesse shrugged. "I didn't look at the names."

"He has an older brother who is also a deputy named Virgilio Guadalupe," Deuce said. "These people around here can be pretty cruel in what they name their kids. You think he got called 'Virgin' in high school?"

Virgilio is Spanish for Virgil, related to the Latin meaning of "flourishing" but also "virgin." Texas teens being what they are, I thought it likely this kid was called "Virgin" if he had a brother named Mario.

"Probably why he became a cop – or a wannabe cop," Laurel said. "I hope those Guadalupe boys don't get into too much trouble. It was Bauer and Wright who were at fault. Mario looked shocked when you got hit, and he was the most helpful and gentle in getting you into the car."

"I wonder why Lenfant is so interested in us," I said. "We need to do some digging on good ol' Philo."

"My guy is working on it," Deuce said. "You got any ideas about what direction to take it?"

"Juanda said she received a hefty sum to shut up about something Lenfant did at Sol Rosensteen's East Mount Houston Church," I said. "I also find it unusually coincidental that Rex and Mimi attended that church a few years back while Lenfant was there. We know Mimi was no good, so if she went there religiously, as it were, there was devilry afoot."

Jesse chuckled.

"I called Rex's mom, got her home-health aide," Laurel said. "She's in her late 80s and has congestive heart failure, so she has 24-hour care, but she is lucid and willing to talk to us. The aide said Mrs. Vega often feels pretty spry right after lunch, so why don't we give her a call at 1 pm?"

"Sounds good," I looked at Deuce, who shook his head.

"I can't do it then, but go ahead and record the conference, so I can look at it later," he said.

"Do you think we'd learn anything from talking to Iris Comemos?" I asked.

"Who dat?" Laurel said, who was texting someone on her phone.

"Mimi's mother."

The solicitor shook his head again. "Probably not, but let's hear what Rex's mom says, and if she offers something we want to check with Iris about, we can dig her up without too much trouble. Whether she'll talk is another matter. My experience with the spouses of criminals has indicated probably … not."

"True dat," Laurel said, as her phone pinged with a text response, and she checked it. When I looked at her with my head tilted, wondering how she would know about the spouses of criminals, she said, "Remember my cousin in L.A. who died last year? He was a big-time gangbanger – a good man, but you didn't mess with him, and nobody ever ratted on him."

"Good to know," I said.

"He was indeed," Laurel said, and tears welled up in her eyes. She wiped them away and said, "Anyway, that brings us to the Juanda video. I want to give it to Tuffy, who says just now that she's on her way, now you're awake."

"No," Deuce said. "I want to hold it back as an ace in the hole, in case the cops decide her death was a homicide and want to prosecute one or both of you."

My noggin suddenly pounding with outrage. I was incredulous. "What possible motive could we have? We loved her."

Deuce stood up, walked to his jacket and pulled out a thick envelope.

"I have here in my formerly ganja-stained hands a little thing known as a life insurance policy," he said.

"Whuh?" Laurel asked.

"Guess who are the beneficiaries."

"Surely not us," I said.

"Yes, but don't call me Shirley." Deuce, bless his heart, enjoys his Leslie Nielsen movies. "Each of you benefit from a $250,000 policy with double-indemnity attached, if the death is accidental or otherwise not natural, which is arguable, if she drowned," he said with a grin more similar to a grimace.

"I understand about Laurel, but why me?" I asked. "She knew I had no need of that sum."

"Well, you guys were her secondary beneficiaries, like Rex and Mimi," he said. "But her father died last spring, and she hadn't changed it afterward. She added a note to the policy, asking you two, together, to look after her little dog, Houston, as long as the dog is in good health."

"Houston, we have a problem," Laurel said.

Deuce looked down at her, a frown on his face.

I had heard the emotion in her voice, building toward tears, and tried to lighten the mood.

"You'll have the beginnings of a petting zoo here before long, between the four horses you're talking about buying and now a little dog," I said, reaching out a hand to her shoulder.

"That dawg is ours, not just mine," Laurel said, shaking her head, drying her eyes and looking askance at me. "You get to walk it, I get to carry it around and make it look cute."

"Houston, you have a problem," I said, rolling my eyes.

Deuce shook his head in frustration. "That's assuming you can stay out of jail long enough."

Looking up at the sky, he sighed. "It was not a good optic, as the politicos say, for you to be seen out partying last night, inasmuch as three of your closest associates — people from whom you inherit — recently died, possibly all three from unnatural causes."

"Oy," I said, rubbing the temples of my throbbing head-ache.

"Oh lawd," Laurel said, her voice breaking with emotion. She dabbed her eyes with a napkin.

"Staying above ground would be a worse look, and that's not a dead certainty," Jesse interjected.

"Oh yeah," I said. "There's that mere bagatelle."

Deuce put on his jacket in preparation to leave.

"If Lt. Traeger is on her way, I realize she doesn't want me here," he said, looking at Laurel. "If it were any other person than your sister, I'd insist on being here, but you trust her, which makes sense to me. I've had some dealings with her in court in the past, and I know she's an honorable, straight cop."

"Exactly," Laurel said, smiling up at Deuce through watery eyes.

"If I were you, I'd worry about her future after all this is over," he said. "She had to recuse herself from the Rex and Mimi and Juanda cases. It is only because of the assault on Pepe, here, that she may communicate with you, and that's only supposed to be about the assault. If she shares something with you about the killings, you need to inform me immediately, understand?"

"*Por supuesto,*" I said.

"What he said," Laurel said.

"I would be surprised if they let Sgt. Bend Wright continue to work with Sgt. North on the killings, but Sheriff Augie Oberst has surprised me before," he said. "I imagine the fact your sister was enjoying the camp's more interesting amenities at the time of the killings is something Augie would like to keep out of the evening news."

Deuce started walking back to his dusty silver Lincoln Navigator.

"True dat," Laurel said. "It would be so nice if we all could sit back and let each other live our private lives the way we want to."

Singing in a fair imitation of The Beach Boys, Deuce said, "Wouldn't it be nice?" He hopped into his car, waved and drove away.

#

31

A dangerous sine wave

Tuesday, Oct. 11, 2022, 11:45 a.m.

"Want something to eat, baby?" Laurel asked, looking at me.

"Depends on what's on offer," Jesse said, "as Pepe would say, 'if I'm not being too subtle.'"

"If I'm not intruding," I said, giving him a mock glare, "I would like a couple of naproxen, two eggs scrambled, two slices of bacon, one slice of toast and a small glass of orange juice. I know it's lunchtime, but I want breakfast food."

Laurel and Jesse stood, and Jesse started walking toward the pool with a towel over his shoulder.

"I believe I'll see if somebody yummy can be had at the pool," he said. He glanced back at me and added, "Don't wander off the reservation without me, Pepe."

"Aye-aye, captain."

I was sopping up the egg with the toast and paying much less attention to my throbbing skull as Tuffy's official vehicle stopped in front of our RV. She stepped out of the car with a beautiful grin on her handsome dark brown face.

"You look a lot better than you did last night," she said, approaching me and giving me a half hug with her left arm. She was careful to avoid bumping my head and set my SIG Sauer pistol on the table with her right hand. She smelled like coconut oil. Gesturing to the gun, she said, "They decided this wasn't evidence."

"I certainly feel better, but we'll see what the docs say after my X-ray," I responded. "I suspect the infamous hard-headedness of *la familia* Montecarla will have won the day."

"Exactly," Laurel said, picking up my plate and refilling my coffee cup.

Tuffy pulled the chair Deuce had occupied, sat down and looked me square in the face with full attention.

"I've seen the video and heard Laurel's version of the story," she said. "Tell me yours."

So, I did.

At the end, she said, "Well, that's very un-fucking-fortunate."

"Exactly," Laurel said.

"We have two angles on this situation that appear to be feeding on each other, like sine waves with one frequency exactly double the other, you follow me?" Tuffy said, waving her hand up and down and horizontally, like a sine wave.

Tuffy originally majored in engineering at Texas Southern University, but switched to criminal justice. Not sure why, but it turned out to be a good fit for a woman with a low tolerance for foolishness and a high sense of justice.

"Not exactly," Laurel said.

"She means when those two angles – whatever they are – coincide, the impact is exponentially greater," I said.

"More or less," Tuffy said, chuckling. "I guess you didn't get too much brain damage, at that."

"What is your assessment of those two forces?" I said. "I have an idea about one of them – the Right Reverend Theophilus Lenfant. Where is the other antagonism coming from?"

"I think it's Sgt. Bend Wright," she said. "I think he sees this situation as an opportunity to oust me so he can get promoted. He may not realize Augie Oberst despises him, but maybe he has a way of getting around that. I don't know."

"Good to know," I said.

"Bad to know," Laurel said.

"Do we need to worry about Sgt. North?" I asked.

"Monster?" When I looked confused and surprised, she chuckled. "His full given name is Muenster Truman North, but we call him Monster, since he's such a big ol' hunk o'meat."

"Where do these people get these names?" I asked, shaking my head -- slowly to avoid seeing stars -- and looking at Laurel, who rolled her eyes.

"I had to ask," Tuffy said. "He said his dad had his life saved in Vietnam by somebody named Muenster, and his granddad thinks Truman saved his life by dropping the A-bomb on the Japanese so he didn't have to participate in an invasion.

Monster's cool with it. I gather nobody messed with him in school, since he was so big."

"But do we need to worry about him?" Laurel asked.

"I don't think so," Tuffy said. "He may be big, but he ain't dumb. He's also a straight arrow. I'm thinking of changing his nickname to 'Tru,' so people would call him Tru North."

I like people who have a "straight arrow" reputation, but sometimes those folks can get persuaded to do some hateful things. Pick any war with a religious element, and I can find folks who otherwise might have been humane, but in the wrong situation became egregiously cruel.

"Since one set of antagonists includes Philo Lenfant and his minions, I gotta ask: Do either North or Wright attend his church?"

"Monster and Bend both attend the First Hill Country Bible Baptist Church," Tuffy said. "Monster has since he was a kid, from what I understand, but Wright is a more recent convert."

"Hmm," Laurel said with more than a hint of skepticism.

"I wonder why the right reverend is so hot to fry my ass," I said.

"My first thought is that it's a way to rile up his congregation to get NTOR shut down somehow," Tuffy said.

"That's one explanation," I said. "Juanda, before she died, told us she had attended Sol Rosensteen's East Mount Houston Church back when Lenfant was a minister there, and she got a hefty settlement to keep quiet about something involving Lenfant."

"That's Wright and North's case," Tuffy said. "By the way, the coroner's report says Juanda was murdered."

Laurel and I looked at each other but kept silent.

"You're not surprised," Tuffy said, shaking her head. "That, in itself, surprises me."

"How did the coroner reach that conclusion, if it's permitted for you to say," I asked.

"I can only tell you what has gone out to the media on the subject," Tuffy said. "The statement is, I quote: 'The condition of the body indicated foul play.'"

"Jesus have mercy," Laurel said, shaking her head and looking down.

"You guys know something, you need to tell us," Tuffy said.

"We were asleep when she died," I said. "I swear to you."

"True dat," Laurel said.

Tuffy squinted her eyes and looked askance at both of us. I looked up at the trees. Laurel stood up to take my coffee cup inside for a refill.

"That's some mo' shiggedy," Tuffy said. "I hope you know what you're doing."

"Upon the advice of counsel, I cannot be more forthcoming at this time," I said.

"Now I absolutely know you know something you're not telling me."

As Laurel went inside the RV for the coffee pot, I gave Tuffy an exaggerated nod and said, "I have no idea what you're talking about." Without making a noise, I mouthed the words, "Trust me."

In a whisper, I asked "What's good for the sub is good for the dom, isn't it, Lt. Chocolock?"

Tuffy's mouth dropped open.

#

32

Shades of blue

Sunday, Oct. 9, 2022, 11 p.m.

I should explain.

After Dean Franco dropped that napkin in front of us at DJ Ted's Clubhouse, I spent about two hours exploring 13D5M.com on my smartphone.

I started with LtChocolock's profile. Laurel, not wanting to look, continued her dancing-and-drinking lessons for the remaining, quickly disrobing playmates.

To gain access to the site, I had to create and pay for a profile, which wasn't too difficult, and I didn't have to submit photos. You're welcome.

Tuffy had been a discreet little dominatrix. In her photos, at least her eyes and often her whole face were indecipherable, which, as counterintuitive as it might seem, would tend to endear her to prospective playmates. The dominatrix/subservient relationship is all about trust, and a kinkster's willingness to be identifiable in a widely available website would

196

tend to diminish trust in that particular sphere. Most people want to keep their involvement in BDSM on the down low.

This particular "social media" portal was about as dark and kinky as one might expect.

Clever, too, in a way.

Fake profiles are ubiquitous in sex-oriented websites. One way to ensure people accept your profile as genuine (not a bot) is to have other real people "certify" or "validate" it. On 13D5M.com, getting certified is getting "spanked" by someone.

Another way to make connections is to do something like Facebook's "friending" a person. On 13D5M.com, that's called being a "cell-mate."

LtChocolock was a popular young dominatrix. Her "cell-mates" included, in addition to Dean and Rose Franco, one "FiddyShadesofBloo," which stirred my curiosity, so I looked at his profile.

The eyes were blacked out, but the perfect brushed-back hair, the build, the porn-stache and the ears (about as unique as fingerprints) left no question. It was Bend Wright. He had photos and videos of Tuffy and himself, plus others, all with him in the dominant role.

One recording was quite disturbing, but also had several thousand "likes" from fellow 13D5M.com enthusiasts -- disturbing in itself. LtChocolock was bound, blindfolded and ball-gagged. It appeared she was being gang-raped not only by Wright, but by three other white guys, all masked: one big balding man, one man who likely was Bend's brother and another tall skinny dude who kept looking off-camera as if checking whether another person off-camera approved his performance.

Some women claim to dig this kind of thing. LtChocolock dug it not. She kept moaning "S-O-S" in Morse code, as tears rolled down her cheeks. I assume that was supposed to be her "safe" signal.

Watching this, I must confess I felt a thorough-going desire to find FiddyShadesofBloo and kick 51 shades of feces out of his creepy ass. Then I looked away from the screen and paused the recording.

Not 10 yards away, a delightful mix of sexiness, rhythm and laughter — not just Laurel but all the people falling in love with her as I did — proved how much joy the world could provide. I took a deep breath of that joy. I recognized the dark, sick shit I had been viewing was in the past and immutable. I realized witnessing it might help me learn how to prevent further, similar atrocities. I allowed the video to continue.

As the scene reached climax, with all three men exploding semen on her face and buttocks, I heard a giggle from off camera, and I turned the phone face down on the table.

I recognized that giggle. I started to gag at the realization, and tears welled up in my eyes. I finished my beer and took a deep breath, recalling how I used to cause that giggle myself. How could I? I looked again as Laurel led yet another line dance, and my love for her girded my courage for another peek into the dark side. I flipped the phone back over.

The giggle prompted me to look at LtChocolock's other "cell-mates," and who did I find? Mistress Mimi.

After such an ordeal, I would have thought LtChocolock

wanted to no longer "spank" or be a "cell-mate" of Fiddy-ShadesofBloo. I assume 13D5M.com offered no way to do that.

MistressMimi surprised me by having no cell-mates. She did have interesting photos and videos, some involving FiddyShadesofBloo, his brother and the other two gang-rapists. I couldn't identify them, all with faces obscured. Some of those recordings involved homosexual acts. Most involved something called "edging," bringing a person to the very precipice of orgasm, but then doing something (e.g., dousing the genitals with cold water) to prevent the climax.

What can I say? A libertine such as myself stumbles across this kind of trivia.

———————

Tuesday, Oct. 11, 2022, noon

Now, in front of my rented RV, sitting before me with tears in her eyes, Tuffy whispered in a stammer, "I-I-I have no idea what you're talking about, Pepe."

"Really, Tuffy?" I whispered with genuine compassion. "You don't have to dissemble with me. I don't judge."

"You can't tell Laurel," she said, her voice quavering.

I mimed zipping my lips closed.

"I need to know, though, so I can keep her safe," I whispered, looking back to hear Laurel doing dishes in the RV. "I suspect Mimi's kinky friends are in this mess."

"Does Laurel have access to your messages?" Tuffy asked.

"I don't think so, but as she told me last night, she's a perfectly competent woman," I responded. "We can talk on Kik or WhatsApp, if you want."

My beautiful darling had stepped to the door with another

cup of coffee for me, but hadn't yet exited, looking at her own phone.

"Kik me, same profile, tell me it's Boo-Thang," Tuffy whispered.

Raising my voice for Laurel's benefit, I told Tuffy, "We would never do anything to betray your trust, Lt. Traeger."

Tuffy rolled her eyes and breathed easier.

"I got my eyes on you two!" she said loud enough for Laurel to hear, but her voice still quavered. She took my paper napkin to blow her nose and surreptitiously wipe away her tears. She then cleared her throat and spit toward the fire pit.

"I got my own reserve deputy out there watching the entrance," she said, clearing her throat again. "If you two troublemakers leave, he will be an open tail on you wherever you go, so if you make any trouble or get into any, at least we'll have our own witness."

"That is very kind of you," I said, reaching out to cover her hand, which was shaking, on the armrest of her chair. "I promise to do my best to be on my best behavior and stay out of trouble."

"You, too," Tuffy told Laurel as she exited the RV with my steaming cup. "If you don't, I'll tell mama."

"You my little sister, so don't tell me what to do," Laurel said. "But, to keep my Boo Thang in one piece, I promise to be good."

Tuffy snorted in disbelief.

"Famous last words," she said, standing up. "Like 'Hold my beer!' or 'Watch this!'"

\#

33

Gone a long time ago

Tuesday, Oct. 11, 2022, 1 p.m.

After Tuffy left and I had laid down for about 30 minutes to let some pain pills kick in, we reached Mrs. Vega's home health care nurse and set up a video call between her laptop computer and ours at the RV's dining table. We dressed for the occasion, out of respect for the bereaved.

Mrs. Vega must have been a lovely young woman – light brown graying hair done up in a short bun, good bone structure on her clear pale face, a slight overbite and only the hint of a double-chin. On the screen, she wore a collared knit shirt and thick gold-rimmed bifocals.

"Goodness, what happened to you?" she asked, her eyebrows going up in surprise at the sight of my bandage.

"The result of a slight fracas in the mess, ma'am, with regard to the quality of the pudding known as spotted dick,"

I said. I enjoyed Sir John Gielgud's performance in *Murder on the Orient Express.*

She giggled. *Hey, she got it!* I thought. This was going to go all right. Laurel rolled her eyes and shook her head.

"It wasn't very important, ma'am, in the context of your loss," I said. "And I speak for both of us when I say we are truly sorry for your loss."

Mrs. Vega's slight grin went away, and her red-rimmed eyes pulled up a lump in my throat.

"We thought the world of Rex," I said.

Laurel said, "We're terribly sorry he is gone."

"He was gone to me a long time ago," Mrs. Vega said. "So long ago."

She looked down for a few seconds, then looked up with her bloodshot eyes blazing fury. "That bitch!"

One does not expect such language from what appears to be a nice, polite, gentle octogenarian. Our eyebrows jumped.

"Umm, who would that bitch be, ma'am?" I asked.

"Mimi, of course," she said. "Mimi, that was the perfect name for her. To that creature, the world was all about me, me, me, ME, ME!"

"Since the tragedy, we have learned about the various … shall we say 'issues'? … the various issues in Mimi's life, but we haven't learned so much as we would like about poor Rex," I said.

"He wasn't so poor," Mrs. Vega said. "We had a good business, his Papa Enrique and me. While we weren't oil-patch rich, we were on solid financial footing. And, from what I gather, those two got rich, somehow."

"He does have the two printing businesses, one in Houston and another in Miami," I said.

"There's more, but you might have to look into some offshore accounts," Mrs. Vega said.

Offshore accounts? Mrs. Vega remained a sharp cookie for being in her 80s.

"Interesting," I said, and Laurel made a note.

"What was he like, growing up?" I asked. I had asked the same question about subjects of my news reports hundreds of times in my 35-year journalism career.

"He was smart, strong, a good boy, kinda shy," she responded. "Papa Enrique was too hard on him, gave him an inferiority complex, if you ask me."

"What was Mr. Vega like?" Laurel asked.

"Enrique was a hard worker, a proud man, retired from the Air Force as a senior master sergeant when Rex was 12," said the woman, obviously proud of her late husband. "About then, my stepfather died and left me some money, so we bought a gas station and convenience store here in Midland, and it did well."

"How did Mr. Vega die?" I asked.

"Enrique fell off a garden tractor as he was mowing the grass on the property, and it ran over him," she said. "The machine was faulty, and the manufacturer settled with me for a million dollars. The lawyer took half. This was after Rex chose Mimi over us, and we hadn't seen or heard from him for two years before that."

I sighed. Wow. Does this family have shitty luck or what?

"What was Rex like in high school and college?" Laurel

asked. She wrote out a note to me: "When puberty strikes, things happen." I nodded.

"Well, he got that girl pregnant."

"He never told us about that," I said.

"I'm not surprised," Mrs. Vega said. "Shameful. Paid for an abortion. He shed a few tears over that, but I had no idea what to do for him. *Su padre fue furioso.*"

"How old was he?" Laurel asked.

"Oh, he was just a sophomore," she said.

"At San Angelo State?" I asked.

"In high school. Bunny Sue Bishop, her name was – oops!" Mrs. Vega looked around her to see where her home health aide was. "I shouldn't have said that. She's still here in town, married now of course. She was a preacher's kid. Wild, like preacher's kids can be."

Laurel nodded.

"As far as I know, he didn't date much in college," Mrs. Vega said. "After he injured his knee, he must have fallen out of the social swing there. He got into computers, which I thought was a good fit for a quiet, smart young man like him. I thought he'd get on with some big oil company out here, doing seismic analysis and stuff, settle down, have a family. But then the oil glut hit just as he graduated, and he went to Houston, where he got a job with a big copier company, doing maintenance and repairs.

"Kind of embarrassing for his father, who had always wanted Rex not to have to work with his hands," Mrs. Vega said, and then she sobbed. "His hands! If only he had stuck to that, he would still have both of them, and he'd still be alive!"

The home health aide – Terri, according to the name

tag – appeared and put a comforting arm around Mrs. Vega. Laurel's eyes were streaming also, and I'll admit I was also a bit choked up at the grief of the mother of a man we had known as a friend.

"We need to wrap this up," said Terri, a slim redhead with light green scrubs and calloused hands.

After we rang off, I held Laurel in my arms, her body wracked with sobs.

#

34

A date with the devil

Tuesday, Oct. 11, 2022, 2 p.m.

Jesse and Grace drove us in their Cadillac Escalade to Pecan County Memorial Hospital. After a couple of hours of intense antiseptic odor, I learned I would in fact live, the Montecarlo hardheadedness having defeated yet another challenger. However, I remained at risk of a stroke if I took any further blows to the head before it finished healing.

"You know, old farts shouldn't get in bar fights," said Dr. Rodell, the general practitioner who viewed the images – still and moving – of my unfortunate melon. Rodell's russet-brown melon was shaved, but he wore a short graying goatee.

"That's what I tell him," Laurel said. "He keeps telling me he's going to kick somebody's ass, and this is what happens."

Keep it up, I thought, cocking my head sideways to look at her from the examination table. *Keep making me look like an idiot. You'll get the tongue lashing that's coming to you. Yum.*

"Are you people stalking me?" A voice came from the hall.

I turned my head to look into the hallway beyond the exam bay curtain a little too fast and immediately regretted it, partly because of what I had seen and partly because my brain was sloshing around inside my half-empty ice-bucket of a head, causing a mixture of dizziness and nausea.

It was "Karen," of course. I decided we needed to at least find out her name, so I gingerly slid my khaki-clad buns off the exam table and approached her with a smile and an outstretched hand. I sensed, rather than saw, Laurel's eyes rolling and her brain thinking, *He thinks he can flirt this bitch into submission.*

"L. Lenfant" was on her name tag on her generous left breast, clad in gray scrubs. So, I could no longer think of her as "Karen."

"You must be Mrs. Lenfant," I said, still holding out my hand, despite her looking at it with disgust. "Somehow, we got off on the wrong foot. Can we be friends – or at least not enemies?"

"I will always be an enemy to the devil and his minions," she said.

"That's pretty harsh, Louise," Dr. Rodell said, stepping into the hall before heading to his next patient. "Mr. Montecarlo has had enough hard knocks lately. How about we offer him a little milk of human kindness?"

Given the robustness of the udders staring out at me, I thought that was the least she could do. I was wrong.

"Please find him a wheelchair and take these nice people to the checkout counter," he said, and ducked behind a curtain into the next patient exam area.

Louise gave him a dirty look, turned away from Laurel and me and muttered, "Just a sec."

She strode to the nearby emergency room entrance area where several wheelchairs were parked and returned with a squeaky one.

"This isn't really necessary," I said.

"Doctor's orders," she said, rolling the thing up behind me, setting the brakes and moving in front. "Don't make me push you into it."

"You bett' not!" Laurel growled. I glanced over at my Nubian Queen with her tie-dyed, skin-tight, red-and-white jeans, her red Converse trainers, tight red sleeveless knit top with the straps crisscrossed across her décolletage and red-framed sunglasses. I thought Louise indeed "bett' not."

I eased into the chair, and Louise arranged the footrests under my huarache-clad feet. I don't think she saw the imprint of the pistol in my cargo pants, but maybe it would have been good for her to be forewarned.

I must admit to a little piloerection on my neck, realizing right behind my white knit shirt's shoulders were hands likely to take great delight in wringing aforementioned neck.

"May I ask why you dislike me so much?" I asked as she rolled me at three-quarters ramming speed down the first leg of the Cretan labyrinth reconstructed in your typical hospital. Ah, the scent of disinfectant. She didn't respond.

"I love the smell of hospitals, don't you?" I asked.

More silence. The hallway took a dip. Laurel's shoes

slapped the tile behind us. I wondered if she had her hand in her purse, and if she did, was it on the pepper spray or the Beretta? I was hoping it was the former, but thought the latter was more likely. We passed a hallway.

"Hey!" I said, pointing down the hallway. We stopped. "Is that Matthew McConaughey?"

She looked down the hall and saw a large, heavy black man wearing greasy overalls and a Texas Rangers baseball cap sitting in a chair outside a patient's room and staring surprised back at us.

"I guess not."

Laurel had caught up with us, looked down at me, offered a small grin and shook her head. I responded with a toothy smile.

"I understand why you wouldn't want to talk to me about your beef with me here at work," I said to Louise as she resumed marching to greet the point-of-sale Minotaur. "What time do you get off?"

"I'm not about to make a date with the devil," she muttered, and glanced aside at Laurel as she continued walking toward the main lobby adjacent to the checkout area. "Or his minions."

"Some mo' shiggedy," Laurel muttered, but she waved and smiled at Jesse and Grace sitting in the lobby.

"No, I'm just trying to learn how we can somehow fit in here in Teresienstadt," I said. "You never know. You might convert me. We're meeting a priest at the Farmer's Rest Café this evening. All this excitement has been a bit much."

We stopped in front of a miniature office with beige desks and solid-looking wooden divider walls labeled "Billing and Statements," and Louise set the brakes on the chair. She walked around until she found a white-haired, harried, bespectacled woman to sit on the other side of the desk from me. Louise looked down at me with a scowl. "I'll talk to my husband," she said. "If he says we can talk, then we'll talk."

"That would be lovely," I said, as she stepped around, undid the brakes and rolled me into the little cubicle. I smiled at her again. Never underestimate the value of fine teeth. They cost me a bundle. "Thanks for the delightful ride."

She gave a silent snort and shook her head as she stomped away, looking much like the bull that gave up fighting Bugs Bunny at the end of one of those Looney Tunes cartoons.

#

35

Fiat tenebrae (Let there be darkness)

Tuesday, Oct. 11, 2022, 6 p.m.

After meeting Deuce — and Adriana, coincidentally — at the office of the Cenas' lawyer and signing some papers, Jesse, Grace, Laurel and I decided to spend the time before meeting Father O'Keefe doing some touristy shopping. Grace and Laurel went into a Christmas store. It was October, so of course there was a Christmas store. Jesse and I wandered around a huge used bookstore resembling, in my mind, The Old Curiosity Shop, only without the English Victorian charm.

I love old children's adventure/mystery books from the early 20th Century (e.g., *The Boy Scouts' Victory*, the Hardy Boys in *The Sign of the Crooked Arrow*). I was looking at similar tomes when Laurel, Jesse and Grace dragged me kicking and screaming to the restaurant to meet Father O'Keefe.

Farmer's Rest Café is one of those quaint, well-lit, no-nonsense Hill Country restaurants. You get the German food *mit bier aber ohne Polkamusik* (with beer but without polka music).

Father O'Keefe was what American Catholics call FBI – foreign-born Irish. He was the only man in a Roman collar at the entrance, so easy to spot: a pale, wiry, clean-shaven man with short gray hair, horn-rimmed glasses, about 5'8," about 70 years old. He greeted us with a sad smile but a firm, warm handshake. He carried an odor of incense. A Manila envelope was in his left hand as we went to a six-person table.

"That bandage looks interesting," he said, gesturing toward my unfortunate top noodle.

Laurel snorted derisively and looked around for a waitress to take our drink orders. Jesse chuckled, and Grace gave me a sincere look of concern, bless her heart.

"Not all that much, really," I said, slowly shaking the noggin to minimize the ongoing throb. "You could call it a bar fight, although I didn't get to do any punching."

He raised an eyebrow. "You have about as many of those here as we did back in Derry," he said. "Back there, it was all about the football – soccer you call it. Here, it's as likely to be about politics or music."

Laurel pursed her lips. "Huh," she said. "Mostly about some smart-ass bitch where I drink."

Jesse's eyebrows rose, clearly wondering about my Nubian Queen's history of violence.

"You could say it was about a car," I said. I squinted at

Laurel for a moment, then shook my head to dismiss the subject. I regretted the painful move immediately. "Not important. How are you doing, Father? I gather you and Rex were good friends."

"Yes, we were," the priest said, a pained expression on his face. "You can call me Dan, if you like. Your name is Pepe?"

"Peter Paul Montecarlo, but everybody calls me Pepe," I said.

"Ah, twice blessed you are."

"Huh," Laurel scoffed and rolled her eyes. "Or cursed."

"Sure, and he's blessed to have you in his life," Dan said. "Laurel, is it?"

"Exactly," she said. "I keep telling him he's lucky to have me."

"And I keep agreeing with her," I said.

Jesse and Grace introduced themselves, said they were Catholic, too, and had attended Our Lady of Guadalupe Church a few times over the years.

"You have a 7 pm Sunday mass, and sometimes we can't get to church earlier than that if we've been traveling," Grace said.

"Bless you, child, for making the effort," Dan said, sighing and shaking his head. "During the pandemic, it got a mite lonely for us at Our Lady of Guadalupe."

The waitress – a thick twenty-something pale woman with brown hair in another traditional German dirndl, like those worn at the Hofbrau – stepped forward and took our orders.

"OK, give me your wurst," I joked. Grace laughed. Laurel rolled her eyes.

"I'll bet you never heard that before, right?" Jesse said.

She shook her unsmiling head and walked away.

"I can see why Rex liked you," Dan said, chuckling. "He gave me something for you, an envelope to give you in the event of his death."

I was gob-smacked, as the Brits would say. I suppose after watching Rex kill Mimi and himself and learning he left all that money to Laurel, I should not have been surprised. In death Rex had an amazing capacity to flummox me.

He handed me the Manila envelope, labeled, "For Pepe Montecarlo in the event of my death." I opened it and extracted a piece of parchment emblazoned with the words, "*Fiat Voluntas Tua,*" in Gothic script and illuminated in red and gold, as if by a Medieval scribe.

Flummoxed again.

"How nice," I said.

"Thy will be done," Dan said.

"I have studied Latin, but I am unclear why he would have you give me this," I said. "When did he do that? Did he say why he wanted me to have it?"

"In June it was, Corpus Christi weekend," Dan said. "I remember thinking it odd he didn't take the host that Sunday."

If he was a good Catholic, failing to take communion might mean consciousness of mortal sin.

Something happened around then, but I couldn't immediately put my mental finger on it.

"Did he talk to you about this or about me?"

"Or me?" Laurel asked, her gaze intent on his answer.

Looking at Laurel, O'Keefe smiled and cocked his head.

"He said you were a lovely person, and he wished he had

met you as a young man," Dan said and turned to me. "He said you were a smart investigative journalist, who some say broke the global economy in 2008."

"Dang, you got me," I said deadpan, with the tiniest hint of sarcasm.

O'Keefe chuckled and shook his head.

"He said you and he used to talk about computers a bit, and he enjoyed that. There's a handwritten note in there, but I don't know if it's important."

I dug out a three-by-five neon green sheet of notepaper with the Vega Printing logo centered at the top of one of the short edges. "Dear Father Dan: If something happens to me, leet Pepe Montecarlo have this, will you? Love, Rex," it said in typed letters.

I began to get an inkling of Rex's intentions, but it would take some doing to check it out. The food came. We didn't talk about Rex during the meal, turning our attention to how the Houston economy fared during the pandemic and how the hurricane season had been tame that year, so far.

As Laurel and I shared a piece of blackberry pie ala mode and coffee, our attention returned to the man who brought us together. Rex also had a life insurance policy naming Father Dan as a beneficiary. Who was selling him all this life insurance?

"I'm not sure what I'm going to do with $150,000, but sure, a decent funeral I can give poor Rex and Mimi," Dan said. "Took a vow of poverty, don't you know. Might endow a scholarship for the school."

"Couldn't name it for Rex, though, given how he died," Jesse said.

"Sure, and the man was not of sound mind, but no, that would not do," Dan nodded. "We might put it in his mother's name. I spoke to her, as I gather you did today."

Laurel and I put down our forks at that statement. Laurel sniffed, stood, held a napkin to her face and headed to the ladies' room, with Grace in tow. "Oh Lord," she muttered as she walked away.

As we exited the restaurant around 8 pm, the sky had streaks of red in the west at the end of the wide main street. I was a bit jumpy, given our recent drive-by shooting in what was touted as one of Texas' safest, most conservative, pleasant little towns. For me, Teresienstadt was beginning to acquire the malevolent ambience of J.B. Fletcher's Cabot Cove.

We waited outside the front door of the two-story restaurant for Laurel and Grace to come from the ladies' room. Father O'Keefe's Chrysler Town & Country minivan stood in the diagonal handicapped spot in front. Two other handicapped spaces remained open. Dan stood next to the open front door of his vehicle, and chatted with Jesse and me about the weather forecast and his plans for the next day, which included finalizing arrangements for transportation of the bodies and returning to Houston in the afternoon. I said the next time Laurel and I were in Houston we'd plan to attend mass there.

The restaurant door opened. Laurel and Grace emerged, with a long trail of toilet paper adhering to Her Royal Highness' right shoe. I pointed and laughed.

A car pulled into the two clear handicapped spots for a split second as Laurel bent over to remove the toilet paper and gum adhering to her shoe. Three champagne corks popped in quick succession. The car drove away with a squeal of tires.

Three holes appeared on the wall next to the front door, and Laurel fell to the ground bleeding.

#

36

Some asses need whippin'

Tuesday, Oct. 11, 2022, 9:30 p.m.

Standing in the hospital emergency department hallway, Tuffy's right leg kept bouncing like a karate combatant waiting for the referee to start an Ultimate Fighting Championship bout. Her fists kept opening and closing, as if trying to keep a grip on her anger, as her eyes blazed fury at the reserve deputy standing guard in the hallway. Yes, Tuffy was perturbed.

She was not alone.

Laurel was in pain but had a smoldering rage in her eyes with which Huntsville Unit Prisoner No. 02264085 no doubt became all too familiar in a certain courtroom back in the day, if I'm not being too subtle.

My beloved lay half-reclining on the emergency room bed while Dr. Rodell briefed her on her injury. A bullet pierced her left trapezius muscle, missing her clavicle and major neck arteries by a whole centimeter or two.

I get sympathy pains when I see people with grievous injuries. A rusty needle twists in the vagus nerve in my groin and gives me stomach cramps. Weird, right? I felt that point now, hunched over, pacing back and forth at the foot of her bed, trying not to look at Laurel but listening intently.

"We'd like to keep you at least overnight, because you're going to be in some pain, and we want you to sleep and not move around," Rodell said.

"Nuh-unh," Laurel said. "I'm gonna cut me a bitch."

"No, you're not," Tuffy said with quiet, patient intensity. "You're going to stay here with a guard on your room, and you're not going to give me any shit about it."

"Bullshit."

"I'll tell Momma," Tuffy said.

"You'd tell Momma?" Laurel said. "You realize that'd kill her? You bett' not tell Momma."

"You bett' not get out of the bed they assign you."

"Sheeutt."

"Dr. Rodell, would you mind letting me talk to Laurel alone for a few minutes?" I asked. "Tuffy? Give us the room?"

"I've instructed the nurse on what to give her as soon as you get done here," Rodell said. "It'll put her down for the count, and she'll feel better in the morning."

"Outstanding. Thanks."

After they left, I could no longer hold the tears back. "Baby, if you hadn't bent over to get that toilet paper off your shoe, the bullet would have gone through your heart."

I kissed her right ear and held her gingerly on the bed,

trying not to cause her any more pain, and smiled through my sadness.

"We don't need no impatient patients here," I said. "You know how I lost my first wife. Please don't make me go through that again."

She grunted in pain as she bent to kiss my lips. "Yes, you're right."

"You mean the world to me, woman. You think I'm going to let the SOB who shot you get away? Tuffy and I – hell, Jesse, too, come to that – plan to get medieval on somebody's ass, if not tonight, damn soon."

"You'd better. God will not deny me."

"Speaking of God, Father Dan is sitting outside, and he wants to sit with you tonight."

"That's very sweet of him."

"Indeed. He gave us a good lead, by the way."

"Yeah? What?"

"*Fiat Voluntas Tua.*"

"So?"

"During the slow period at one of my lifestyle birthday parties, Rex and I got to talking about his work, and he wanted to know how I prevented hackers from downloading my research in the period leading up to the Great Recession. I mentioned making passwords based on known phrases, translated into Latin and then converted into leet."

"Leet?"

"You know, a code converting certain letters in the western alphabet to numbers or symbols resembling those letters," I said. "An 'E' becomes the numeral '3,' an 'A' becomes the numeral '4' and so on." Laurel nodded in sudden recognition.

"It's simple, but combining a common phrase – or prayer, in this case – gives you a hard-to-crack password. The 'leet Pepe Montecarlo have this' was the key to Rex's Latin password puzzle."

"So now you need to get into Rex's computer."

"I think Tuffy will make that happen, although it's not completely kosher."

"She'd better." Laurel started to chuckle but winced in pain. "I'll tell Momma."

I smiled down at her and kissed her eyes, the tip of her little button nose and her full lips.

"You rest easy, now, baby," I said. "We got you."

"Yes, you do. You bett' not forget it."

I stepped out the door and let the nurse (not Louise, thank you, Jesus) know Ms. Traeger would stay the night without any trouble now.

Tuffy was conveying intense, whispered, angry words to the reserve deputy who had been watching my back. He was a white young man of about 22 years of age, standing a foot taller than Tuffy and weighing probably twice as much, but I could see my Nubian Queen's little sister had him cowed.

Gotta love a kick-ass Texas woman.

The reserve deputy, F. Johnson, according to his name tag, gave a short, sharp nod at the end of each sentence, punctuated by a little poke in the chest with Tuffy's right index finger. He wore a bulletproof vest under his uniform, so he was not hurt, but he flinched at each touch. Tuffy's nickname fitted her well.

He stood next to the door to Laurel's room and stared ahead as Tuffy approached me, shaking her head.

"He'll stay with her until she gets into her overnight room, and another deputy will relieve him around midnight," Tuffy said. "I'm keeping an eye on you myself, and I have the office locating another deputy to stake out the camp's gate overnight."

We started walking back through the labyrinth to the emergency room lobby to meet Jesse and Grace, worrying and waiting.

"We need to send these folks on home, and I'll ride with you," I said. "We got a lead to talk about."

"Do we? Hmm."

Grace was still shaken the shooting, so I gave her a brotherly hug. I explained that Laurel would stay overnight and suggested they return to NTOR, as Tuffy and I had some work to do.

"If there's some asses need kicking, I'd like to help," Jesse said.

"There are, but we're not to that point yet," I said.

"You gave your statement to my deputy, right?" Tuffy asked

"Of course," Jesse said. "We both did. I think it was a late-model silver Dodge Charger, but I didn't catch the plate."

"There were at least two people in the car, but I couldn't describe anyone in the evening shadows," Grace said, her arm still around my waist. "I just saw what looked like a long, thin dark tube come out of the car's half-open, darkened passenger-side front window, three puffs of smoke, and it raced off toward the sunset."

"Right," Tuffy said. "I heard that part before. Well, we got a deputy watching her here, and another one relieves him at midnight. We'll have a deputy parked outside the camp by the time Pepe and I get over there, so you guys need not worry."

"This place has always been so peaceful – quaint, even," Grace said.

"It still is, but we got some trouble brewing right now that we need to cool off," Tuffy said.

#

37

LtChocolock's bitter tears

Tuesday, Oct. 11, 2022, 10 p.m.

When we sat in Tuffy's cruiser and closed the doors, I said, "We're alone now. I need you to talk to me, Lt. Chocolock."

Tuffy left her hands at 10 and 2 on the steering wheel and bowed her head. For the next two minutes of silence, I looked outside to verify no one was watching. Hearing her sniffle and gag, I glanced toward my dear friend, sister of my beloved, almost family to me, and my composure crumbled. Hot tears rolled down my blushing cheeks and into my mustache.

"I'm sure you don't want to talk about it," I croaked through the phlegm in my throat. "I hope you have talked to someone."

Tuffy kept her head bowed and shook it without looking up. "How can I in this little piss-ant town?" she said, her voice also choking with emotion. "If I do, everyone in town will know about it within 24 hours."

I sniffed, wiped my eyes and nose with my shirt sleeve, looked out the window again at the shadows of the live oak trees next to the hospital.

"I understand," I said. "We're not too far from Austin or San Antonio. Go find a therapist there to discuss it with."

Tuffy snorted and looked sideways at me.

"You think any counselor is going to say anything constructive, when he or she finds out what the circumstances were?" she asked, and looked out the window on her side of the cruiser.

I cocked my head and looked at her.

"I like to think my late wife would have listened and understood and helped you," I said. "She was a clinical psychologist who worked with women and children in battered women's shelters in Houston. She had seen and heard it all, and she never judged."

"It's not just that," Tuffy said. "If I go through my health benefits, my 'brother officers' — HA! — will find out, figure it out and drive me out."

"Sister, sister, sister," I responded. "You have but to ask, and I will pay. In fact, you don't have to ask. Have your therapist call me while you're there, and I will pay."

She turned to me and grabbed my neck in her calloused hands and pulled me in for a hug. Her tears fell to my shoulder.

"You're a good man, Charlie Brown," she whispered and then chuckled.

I chuckled, too, but stiffened a little, thinking about Carlos

Marron. We broke the clench and looked out our side windows again, a little self-conscious, lest any non-filial sentiment be misconstrued. Tuffy grabbed facial tissue from a box at my feet and blew her nose. I did the same.

I took a deep breath and said, "I still need to find out about Mimi's role in that scene."

She cocked her head and looked at me sideways.

"What are you talking about?" she said.

"Why lie?" I said. "I saw the video of your gang bang, which looked like a gang rape, to me by the way."

"Which it was, but Mimi had nothing to do with it," she said, but then looked out the window, frowning in thought.

"I heard that giggle she does — did -- when she was having an orgasm," I said. "Who do you think recorded the atrocity?"

"One of the men, I assumed. Once I saw what it was, I stopped watching."

"Who were the men? Aside from Sgt. Wright, I mean — whose nose, by the way, I intend to punch at the first opportunity."

"I don't know. Bend kept the blindfold on me the whole time they were there, and they didn't say much. I did not recognize them. I blacked out at one point, and they were gone when I woke up."

"Uff da," I said, a Norwegian word my Minnesota relatives use. No idea what it means, but it conveys the idea of getting hit with something bad.

"Tell me about it," Tuffy said, her head bowed, and a tear dropped off her nose and into the tissue on her lap.

She sniffed, wiped her nose and raised her head to look straight at me.

"Leave Bend alone. Right now, it's a case of mutual assured destruction. If I don't rat him out, he won't rat me out. I've got more to lose. If Sheriff Oberst and my colleagues learn how I let myself get into that mess, they'll drive me out. I like being a cop."

I gave a heavy sigh.

"Bastards like that got no business being cops," I said. "You realize that, right? He's a sadist -- and narcissist, or he would not have shot that video and had it posted."

She looked out the window again, her face and eyes showing deep thought.

"He's a sadist, sure, and most men I've met have some significant narcissistic tendencies —"

"Ahem."

"Present company excepted, of course," she said, giving me a small grin. "Sort of. Anyway, when I asked him to take the recording down, he said he can't. When I asked him why he put it up, he said he had to, as if he had no choice."

"Interesting, verrrry interrrresting," I said with an absent-minded allusion to an old TV comedy German character. "But not funny." Inappropriate, I know. I blame my wobbly brain.

"Yeah, well, after that happened, we broke up. It was fun for a while because we had to sneak around. Deputies are not supposed to be bumping uglies with each other. Once we broke up, we stopped being friendly at work. People noticed, but at some point, they gave up trying to get in our business."

"Good fences make good neighbors."

"True dat."

#

38

ReadMeFirst.txt

Tuesday, Oct. 11, 2022, 10:30 p.m.

I wiped my nose and eyes again and said, "You got access to Rex's laptop?"

"Yeeesss?" Tuffy said. "It's not my case, but I could take a look at it. Wright and North poked around in there and came across some files they couldn't open because they couldn't crack the password. We have a computer program trying to compose the right one, but I understand it could take years."

"Not surprised," I said. "Rex was a smart guy. I think he gave me the key to unlock it."

I handed her the envelope Father O'Keefe had given me. Tuffy looked at the parchment, cocked her head, looked at the note, smiled and nodded.

"Looks like it," she said. "Let's go."

Dang, Tuffy was a sharp cookie. The *"Fiat Voluntas Tua"*

was incongruous to us both, but the "typo" of "leet Pepe Montecarlo have this" cleared our clouded minds.

The Pecan County Sheriff's Office was in a former funeral home, refurbished and expanded with holding cells in the back and some space for gunmetal gray desks in an area beyond the claustrophobic front lobby. Bullet-proof glass protected the desk deputy from ill-tempered visitors.

Alongside the open area, still reeking of disinfectant some trusty jailbird had liberally applied at the end of the previous shift, were a series of offices and interview rooms. In one of the latter, Tuffy met me with Rex's laptop, adorned with a shiny picture of a pineapple on the cover over a little map of Jamaica highlighting the location of the Hedo II "sex positive" lifestyle resort with the intertwined medical symbols for males and females, two of each. I chuckled at the sight, and Tuffy looked at it, and rolled her eyes. Swingers will have their secret little jokes. Sorta like Freemasons, but without the fezzes and tiny clown cars.

Once we booted up the computer, it took us a few minutes to find the file the sheriff's password-decipher program found so hard to crack. I entered the following symbols: F14tV0lunt4$tu4.

"*Voila,*" I said, and found a series of files, one labeled "ReadMeFirst.txt." I opened that one, which contained a link to a video file.

"If you're seeing this, you are probably Pepe Montecarlo," Rex said to the camera. He sat in a computer cold room in front of several racks of servers intertwined with wires. "I hope you are. If not, I hope you are police or somebody with some authority who can handle what I have to say.

"May God have mercy on my soul and Mimi's," Rex said, his face flushed with emotion. "I love her so much. I can't quit her. But I can't let what she's done – what we've done – go on."

He looked away from the camera for a minute, wiped a tear from his right eye, and released a rueful chuckle.

"She's so fucking smart. If I were to give her the slightest hint I was trying to stop her, she would kill me and find someone else to help her – maybe you, Pepe."

"Scary thought," I said. Tuffy kept staring at the screen.

"You may wonder why I'm even going to try to stop her. The reason is Frank and Ruby Dahl – poor Ruby."

"I thought that might have something to do with it," I said. "Now I remember why it was important that Rex didn't take communion on the Feast of Corpus Christi."

Tuffy stopped the recording.

"What you talkin' about, Willis?" Tuffy asked. Given Tuffy's vague resemblance to the adult Gary Coleman, Arnold of the TV situation comedy *Different Strokes*, I gave a soft snort in amusement but cleared my throat and frowned to explain.

"Frank and Ruby Dahl disappeared on the Intracoastal Waterway south of Port Aransas on Memorial Day weekend," I said. "I don't think you had met them, but Laurel, Frank, Ruby, Rex, Mimi and I would occasionally hook up at larger house or hotel parties in the Houston area. In the Catholic liturgical calendar this year, the Feast of Corpus Christi is the weekend after Memorial Day. Corpus Christi is an important holiday when good Catholics try to be ready for communion – i.e., not conscious of any unconfessed mortal sin. Father Dan said tonight Rex went to Our Lady of Guadalupe Catholic Church that weekend but did not take communion."

"Ah," Tuffy said. "Maybe that means he knew something about the fate of Frank and Ruby."

"I think we're about to find out."

Tuffy restarted the video.

"You may not realize, just as I didn't, at first, that Ruby and Mimi had been friends since middle school, back in Miami," Rex continued. "Her maiden name was Rubia Trevino, and she was Mimi's closest friend, lover and biggest … I guess you could say, henchman? … back in the day. They did some sick shit back then, but when Mimi went away to college – just ghosted Ruby and barely spoke to her when they met in the years after – Ruby was devastated.

"I know all this because when we got together for house parties, Ruby and I would play, and she would chat with me as we cuddled afterward, or at other times separate from Mimi and Frank.

"Ruby was a clinical psychologist. The pain she experienced after the breakup with Mimi prompted Ruby's intense interest in the field. She had learned back in school that the shrinks, counselors and priests had done some tests and learned Mimi was, in effect, a budding psychopath, although they refused to use that word. She had what they called 'Type 1 antisocial personality disorder.'"

Rex provided air quotes around the last five words with his one remaining hand.

"But Ruby didn't understand at the time what that meant, not fully. It was only after the breakup and she started on her psych degree that she understood Mimi could not help but act how she did – manipulative, selfish, amoral. Back then, they didn't do brain scans, but Ruby said some researchers think people with this particular disorder have a malformation in their brain structure. Whether it is hereditary or a function of experience is not determined yet, she said, probably a combination of the two."

Rex took a sip of coffee from a mug bearing the slogan, "Don't mess with Texas women." I snorted in amusement. Laurel had one like it sitting in a cabinet in our Houston condo.

"Now that I understand who her father was – did you know Mimi's father was Jim Bob Kefauver, the guy who stole all that money from Dullestown Bank? I don't think Ruby did. I think she thought Mimi was just another Marielita from Cuba. Now that I know about her dad, I think heredity played a big part in her personality disorder.

"Ruby spent much of her career counseling veterans and active-duty military personnel at bases in San Antonio. After 9/11, her clinic became involved with various programs to help soldiers and first-responders with post-traumatic stress disorder. That was a big focus of Sol Rosensteen's East Mount Houston Baptist Church's post-9/11 veterans outreach program. As a life coach, Mimi thought she could pursue that to her own ends. She found a willing stooge in Reverend Theophilus Lenfant, one of the assistant pastors."

"Now it's coming together," I said.

#

39

PTSD Sunday drama

Tuesday, Oct. 11, 2022, 11 p.m.

"How did that happen?" Rex continued. "You might well wonder how a sexy psychopath like Mimi might ensnare a fine, upstanding, born-again Christian like Reverend Philo Lenfant in a sordid business like ripping off veterans. Well, as it turns out, Lenfant worked with church youth."

Rex bent forward, as if he were explaining rudimentary mathematics to a seven-year-old.

"And, oddly enough, Philo really likes teenage girls, and the girls could be seduced into thinking they really liked him back. Mimi facilitated that, although without my knowledge at the time.

"The church raised money for the PTSD program for clinics serving San Antonio military facilities with big, popular campaigns on their TV broadcasts. You may remember."

"Never watched it," I said.

"I did, and I donated," Tuffy said.

"They raked in about $5 million for that purpose from 2001 through 2004, but only about $1 million made it to services provided for veterans," Rex continued.

"Late in 2003, Ruby realized her clinic needed many more people to help with all the veterans coming back from Iraq and Afghanistan, but no money was available. When she asked Veterans Administration folks about private contributions, she learned how little was received, so she wrote a letter to Rosensteen.

"The letter went through Lenfant, first, and he consulted with Mimi about how to respond. Ruby had married Frank Dahl by this time and went by the name Dr. Ruby Dahl, so Mimi did not realize she already knew Dr. Dahl.

"That letter, by the way, is in one of the password-protected files in this computer. It's also in the cloud."

I looked at Tuffy. "See? Smart guy."

"Between the two of them, Mimi and Lenfant," Rex continued, "they persuaded me to construct an electronic trail leading to a dummy veteran service organization, headed by Mimi, which provided fictitious services to a variety of Houston-based veterans, including two guys named John Bauer and William Wright. Write down those names, because they're important."

Tuffy did so as she muttered, "Shit."

"Most of the other veterans' names on the list either did not exist or received very little service, for which Mimi's 'organization' was paid millions."

Again with the air quotes. That could get annoying.

"Meanwhile, back at the 'religion ranch,' both Lenfant and

Mimi were *baisaient les beaux enfants* on overnight church youth camp-outs and lock-ins."

I'm not great at French, but I guess Rex had learned enough to translate "fucking the beautiful children."

Rex chuckled, looked down and shook his head. When he looked in the camera again, tears filled his eyes.

"The irony," Rex said. "Those events were to keep kids out of trouble. Fool that I am, I assumed Mimi was chaperoning Lenfant, keeping the girls safe. Little did I know, she was using both them and the boys for sex. How do I know? Well, she gave one of the boys gonorrhea, and the boy told his mom, and she told – wait for it – Lenfant.

"The boy shot himself with his dad's pistol the following week. At least, I think that's what happened. Given what's happened since, who knows? Maybe Mimi, maybe Lenfant, maybe one of their teenage lovers did it. Somehow, it got hushed up. No idea how.

"The 'good news' is –"

Again with the air quotes. I was beginning to dislike Rex. I think Tuffy was, too.

"—Everybody got treated for gonorrhea, and Mimi has since been very good about getting tested and using protection."

"Lenfant, however, was not using protection, and as such things happen, teenage girls get pregnant," Rex said, again leaning in like he was teaching a child.

"More than one did. All but one had an abortion with the help of Lenfant and Mimi. But one of those pregnant girls didn't tell anybody until she was showing, and may not have understood she was pregnant. About then, Juanda had been managing the church's food programs – food for the poor, church potlucks, and so on – and the pregnant girl had been helping Juanda, in whom she confided.

"As all this happened, Ruby persisted in trying to find out where the veteran PTSD donations went. This was late 2004. Juanda approached Mimi about what was happening on the camp-outs and lock-ins. Mimi consulted Lenfant, and together they decided Juanda had to go. With the help of John Bauer, a former military policeman who worked as a private detective, they concocted evidence Juanda had not only been embezzling money from the PTSD program, but also from the food program, which never missed a dime.

"When this situation came to a head between Christmas and New Year's, Rosensteen, his wife, the chairman of the church board of directors, Lenfant and Mimi confronted Juanda, who brought the hugely pregnant girl to the meeting, thinking it was about Lenfant's pedophilia.

"How do I know this stuff? At Mimi's insistence, I bugged the church offices and conference rooms. It was easy, because she volunteered my services as the church's chief technology officer.

"What Mimi did with those recordings, she never said. I suspect people got blackmailed, because I often encountered people friendly to us one day who despised us the next. The relevant conversation I'm talking about here, with Juanda, is in one of the password-encrypted audio files on this laptop. It is also in the cloud."

Rex took another sip of coffee, which made me wish I had some — even that I could be sharing this conversation in person. Rex was a fun conversationalist when he wasn't shooting people.

"Rosensteen and the board chairman, Humbert Smith, found themselves in a quandary. On the one hand, they had documents indicating Juanda was culpable for millions in embezzled funds. On the other, they had no proof Juanda had access to so much money, and they had the testimony of a young girl whose story was backed up by, guess what? DNA evidence.

"Juanda was a little smarter than either Lenfant or Mimi realized. Juanda had persuaded the girl, by the name of De-lilah Samson, to have a test of the amniotic fluid compared with the DNA of Theophilus Lenfant. I've no idea how she got it, but it wouldn't have been difficult, given her access to things he had put his fluids on, such as napkins and cups."

The name of the girl had struck some chime in my head, so I stopped the video. I looked up and tried to recall where I'd heard a similar name, but it was gone. Could it be because of the cleaning my clock had taken at the hands of Reserve Deputy W.O.W. the evening before? Maybe.

"What?" Tuffy asked. "You know something?"

I tried ten seconds more but finally shook my head. "Let me sleep on it. Maybe it will come to me in the night. That often happens." I resumed the video.

"Rosensteen and Smith were in a tight spot. They needed to keep the donations flowing, which would dry up if a scandal broke over Christmas. They needed to stop the hemorrhaging of funds from the veterans organization and get it moving into Ruby's programs. Remember, Mimi and Ruby hadn't seen each other yet. The church needed to find a way to deal with the pregnant girl. They needed to get rid of Juanda somehow.

"What did they do? They threw money at the problem. They ceased all relationships with the relevant parties. Lenfant was out. Mimi was out. I was out. Juanda was out. Delilah Samson would go to a remote location where she could have the baby and have it adopted. In exchange for significant funds, each of us would sign a nondisclosure agreement. By the way, I was in the purge because I was Mimi's husband.

"Each of us got $250,000 to pledge never to discuss this matter again. Since you're seeing this, I assume neither Mimi nor I will worry about that. Delilah's parents got $500,000 – I assume half was for the baby, half for Delilah. Her parents, by the way, were just fine with that. They thought she was a little tramp. Not nice people."

Feeling nauseous, I stopped the video.

#

40

A sexy beast of the Apocalypse

Tuesday, Oct. 12, 2022, 11:45 p.m.

I went to the men's room, vomited, washed my face and exited to find Tuffy staring at the door with the folded laptop computer under her arm.

"Some grim shit," I said.

"True dat," Tuffy said, and looked up at me sideways. "You gonna be all right?" I nodded and started toward the interview room we had been using.

She looked at her watch. The place was quiet except for occasional static and incomprehensible conversation beyond a steel door labeled "Communications."

"I know you're sick, but if you can handle it, we should continue," Tuffy said. "I don't want a lot of people thinking about the fact I'm spending so much time with evidence in a case I have recused myself from."

But she stopped, sniffed, and bent over to look at the crack beneath the steel door next to the interview room where she and I had been viewing the video recording. There was no light under the door. "Speaking of which ..." She snapped open the door and found the room empty. She went to the intercom next to the two-way mirror through which officers could view witness or suspect interviews. The switch was off. She sniffed the switch. She frowned and looked at me for a moment.

"Stay in this room," she said. "Don't let anyone near that switch. If somebody does, raise hell and I'll be back before you can say Nolan Ryan."

OK, I've known women who can detect a scent much better than men, especially if they smell the scent of a romantic rival on their man. That was spooky. How did she even think to look in there? Oh, yeah, FiddyShades of bullshit works there. That's a reasonable level of paranoia, I guess.

I waited in the room with the door open. A minute later, she strode into the area and gestured for me to exit. She handed me the computer, went to an office and came back with tape stating "POLICE LINE – DO NOT CROSS," which she taped across the door frame, covering but not touching the doorknob. "Son of a bitch," she muttered. "I'll have that son of a bitch's badge for this."

She opened the interview room where we sat before, gestured for me to sit down and closed the door behind her.

"Sgt. Wright has been here, and I'm positive he was in that room," she said. "I smelled him. He still wears an expensive men's cologne I used to like. Just before we stepped out, he flew out of that room and out the front door past the desk sergeant, telling Sgt. Schultz not to say he'd been there. I had to threaten her to make her tell me, and I reminded her his picture would be on the surveillance video of the lobby."

"Can't he claim he was watching you because you have a personal interest in his case – your sister?" I asked, a little concerned that Tuffy may get pulled into taffy by her boss — or by a smart lawyer like Deuce.

"You were a witness to a case that dropped in my lap tonight, with Laurel's shooting," Tuffy said. "There can be no question of her being a perpetrator, since she was the victim according to all witnesses. I had — have — hopes that this evidence will be relevant both to her shooting and your attack by Bauer and Wright, witnessed by Guadalupe last night. And I still think it's going to be relevant, because both Wright and Bauer are mentioned in it. So, no, I don't think Sgt. Wright would win a fight about me horning in on his case."

I nodded and asked for coffee. She said the machine sludge resembles in sight and smell what the jailbirds leave in their communal toilet, so we settled on a Diet Coke for me, water for her. Before resuming the video, she asked why I got sick when I did. I explained that I get nauseated by human behavior sometimes, particularly when it involves maltreatment of children.

"I can't watch *Law & Order: SVU* because kids are so often the victims," I said.

Tuffy rolled her eyes and resumed the video. We could tell we were about ten minutes into it, and it had another 50 minutes before the end.

"So you have an idea of what went down involving Theophilus Lenfant. ... Theophilus! What a name! You couldn't invent a person with more clear contempt for God," Rex said.

Ah. I was beginning to like Rex again. I had been thinking something similar. Tuffy nodded, sipped her water and maintained her unblinking stare at the screen.

"You'll never guess where little Delilah's parents brought her to deliver her baby out of prying eyes, and at what church Lenfant wound up resuming his vocation. Teresienstadt and Hill Country Bible Baptist Church, respectively. Who adopted Delilah's baby girl? Well, Theophilus and Louise Lenfant, of course."

"Whoa," I said.

Tuffy stopped the recording.

"Did not see that coming," I said. "Go on – wait!"

"What?"

"There's a Delilah who works at NTOR," I said. "She would be about the right age. Damn, if so, she was about 13 when she had the baby."

"That's some seriously evil shiggedy, right there."

"And I think I've seen the adopted girl. She's a cheerleader who we saw at the Sunday protest outside NTOR and at a store with Louise yesterday. Nice-looking kid. Hope her dad has kept his hands off her, but I'm pessimistic."

"Sheutt," Tuffy said. "He is not going to enjoy prison, if I can help it."

I nodded for her to resume the video, and I sipped my Diet Coke, which roiled my stomach.

"Mimi still had her bank teller job and her side gig as a life coach," Rex said, and sipped some coffee. "Those poor souls. They never had a chance. She'd manipulate them into thinking whatever she told them to do would restore their lives after Enron or after the Great Recession, and mostly what she told them to do would make her tons of money.

"Part of it was sex. She has used sex like some gangbangers use a Glock."

At the word "gangbanger," I detected a flinch from Tuffy, but she kept watching.

"Mimi and Bauer set up offshore accounts she intended to use when she decided she had enough — never likely to be possible. She must have about $20 million in a Panamanian bank account. I think Bauer thinks he'll get that, that she'll jump from me to him, and then he can have her AND the money all to himself. I'm sure he'd have no compunction about killing me. What a fool."

Rex shook his head and sighed.

"If her hunger for power and money can never be satisfied – and it can't -- does he really think he can help her achieve that better than I can? He's nothing more than a barely competent grifter and thug. I think – hope, I guess – Mimi realizes that.

"But this is where you come in, Pepe."

"Whuh?" I said, my eyebrows crawling up my forehead. I choked on another sip of Diet Coke. I coughed but heard what came next.

"She thinks she can manipulate you into joining her in her quest for – what would you call it? World domination?"

He chuckled, bowed his head, shook it.

"Whoa," I whispered and swallowed Diet Coke-flavored phlegm. Yuck.

"Yes, it's pretty clear what she has been doing in making

sure you and Laurel played with us often enough for her to sink her teeth into you and suck you in."

"Mercy," Tuffy said, shaking her head. "Good thing Laurel ain't hearing this while Mimi was alive, or she really would have killed the bitch."

"Ya think?" I said, stopping the recording. "And who would be fool enough to think they could lure me away from Laurel? I mean, has Mimi not even looked at her? She's like Halle Berry's prettier, sexier sister."

Tuffy rolled her eyes and resumed the video.

"Your work on the Great Recession impressed her. She realized you could see several steps beyond the chess pieces on the board toward the ultimate end of the game. She said she likes that about you, as well as your prowess in bed."

I blushed prettily.

#

41

A biting commentary

Wednesday, Oct. 12, 2022, 12:30 a.m.

"Laurel's days are, at the moment, numbered," Rex said.

"Bett' not be," Tuffy said.

"That sort of brings us back to Ruby. Ruby wasn't bought off by the funds starting to flow into the PTSD program in San Antonio," Rex continued. "But, with the inflow of funds, she was too busy at first, hiring staff and expanding space, to spend any time in finding out where the previously donated funds landed.

"A few months later, she was dealing with more clients – people who not only had to cope with the war but also the Great Recession. A lot of veterans retired or left the service and tried to start businesses on credit, and the crash halted cash flow, and those businesses went under."

I nodded and sighed. I knew people in that situation.

"By early 2009, Ruby and Frank had decided to embrace the swing lifestyle, and we stumbled across them during a Valentine's Day party at another lifestyle-oriented nudist camp, Lost Maples and Cypresses Resort."

I was familiar with this place. Known among the hipster swingers as "Lost My Clothes," the semi-secluded spot lay about halfway between Houston and San Antonio.

"Mimi was excited about the opportunity to play with Ruby all these years later, but Ruby wasn't having any of it," Rex continued. "Instead, she wanted to play with me. Mimi shrugged, said she was happy with Frank.

"That was when I started learning about Mimi's history before I met her -- her junior high and high school extra-curricular activities. We'd play in bed, and then we'd talk. As couples, we made dates to attend parties together, and Ruby and I would talk and play some more. I think Mimi hoped to lure Frank away as some sort of revenge for Ruby not playing with her.

"But Frank, God bless him, was older and craftier than any of us. He was just using Mimi as a sexual plaything, since Ruby kept reminding him of how twisted Mimi's mind was.

"At first, when Ruby started telling me this high school stuff, I denied it. This could not be the sexy angel who lit up my life, the loving nurse who helped me recover from the loss of my hand, the poor victim of abuse by priest and nun alike, the unfortunate fatherless child."

I shook my head in sympathy. I had not seen her true character myself. Little Pepe often leads Big Pepe astray, and damn the consequences.

"When I told Ruby about our involvement with the scam

at East Mount Houston Church, a light went on in Ruby's head," Rex said. "She knew what had happened, and she wormed out of me what I had helped Mimi do. Little did I know, she was recording our pillow talk with a plan to expose and imprison Mimi, if necessary."

"Huh," Tuffy grunted as Rex sipped his coffee. "Serves her right."

"About a year later," Rex continued, "a year in which Ruby and I played and talked a half-dozen times, she and Frank made a special double date. Before, our rendezvous had been at house or hotel parties with other people. This time, the plan was to meet at a Galveston restaurant and go from there to a hotel.

"The meal was pleasant enough, at Gaidos, an upscale seafood restaurant on the beach. You may know it. We all had some wine. Frank was friendly, chatting about the Houston Rockets and San Antonio Spurs and their respective stars. I realized Mimi was rubbing Frank's crotch under the table's white linen, and I think Ruby realized it, too.

"Ruby flirted with both Mimi and me, which was unusual. Most times, she expressed no sexual interest at all in Mimi. When we went out to the car to move to the hotel, Mimi was quivering with excitement.

"When we got to the room with two beds, Ruby said she and Mimi want to play, and we could watch, and start playing once they were ready for us. Frank and I stripped down and set up chairs to watch the fun.

"Ruby insisted on going down on Mimi first, and after Mimi started giggling – you know she's orgasmic when she's giggling –"

"Oh lawd," Tuffy said.

"—Ruby bit her clitoris, which made her howl.

"'You bit me!' she said. 'What the fuck?'

"'Just a little taste of the pain you caused me, *mi querida*,' Ruby said.

"Thus ended the 'fun weekend,'" Rex said, again with the air quotes. Oy. "Ruby laid it all out: She knew about the embezzlement. She knew about the underage sex with Philo Lenfant. She knew everything, and she was ready to expose Mimi to her bank employers and her life coach clients, and put both Mimi and me in prison.

"But Ruby cared about me, and she thought I was a dupe in the whole scheme, and she didn't want me to suffer. She also cared about Mimi, and she understood Mimi's disability, as she called her psychopathy, was at least a contributing factor to her crimes.

"So, Ruby was willing to let Mimi remain free and keep her out of jail, if Mimi would stop victimizing people. She had enough money she could live off the interest of her ill-gotten gains. She had the pick of any man she wanted. She could continue to play with Frank all she wanted, but she must forget about trying to take Frank.

"If anything happened to Frank, Ruby or me, Ruby said, Mimi's crimes would come out, because Ruby's evidence was in a safe place, and it would go to the proper authorities if anything ever did happen.

"Mimi's eyes turned colder than I'd ever seen them before. She was caught, and she was furious. She looked at me, and I shrugged. Ruby said I was 'not the source of the evidence. It was the only lie I ever heard her tell.

"Mimi started dressing and told me to get dressed. As I was dressing – not easy with one hand, by the way – Ruby asked Mimi to promise to stop.

"'What does it matter what I say?' Mimi said. 'You won't believe me. But, I can tell you that you will never hear or see of me victimizing, as you call it, anyone ever again. You and Frank and Rex are all safe from me. In fact, I will do all I can to make sure you stay safe from other people.'

"And that was that. We never played with them again. If we showed up some place where Frank and Ruby were, we left. But ..."

"Here it comes," Tuffy said.

#

42

The Cena scenario

Wednesday, Oct. 12, 2022, 1 a.m.

"Mimi was a leopard, and she couldn't change her spots. She did, however, keep me out of her schemes for the most part. She started spending more time with Bauer. She kept wanting to visit Teresianstadt and NTOR. She would disappear for hours, sometimes overnight. I think she suspected me, so I started using her phone to spy on her. It's not difficult.

"When she was away, I could track her location, and if she spent much time in one place, I'd turn on the sound and start recording. Bauer was trying to backtrack where Ruby might have left her evidence. It took a lot of work -- part of which he used William Wright for, by the way – and the better part of ten years, but eventually he tracked it down to someone at NTOR.

"We started spending a lot of time at NTOR, making friends with the regulars and the residents, playing with anybody and everybody. Mimi never met a cock or clit she couldn't lick. The gossip flowed, and we discovered the Cenas were Frank and Ruby's special friends.

"So, we bugged their RV and listened to hours and hours of mundane small talk, punctuated by some hot sex sessions, including you and Laurel, by the way. Good for you."

Tuffy paused the picture just as Rex blinked. She rolled her eyes and squeezed them shut, as if trying to block out a mental vision from her mind.

With a twinkle in my eye, I shrugged and said, "Mongo just pawn in game of life."

She sipped her water and resumed the video. I drank my Diet Coke.

"Bauer did a lot of the listening, and he was the one who caught the exchange between Dave and Maeve, when Maeve asked about an envelope in their RV safe, and Dave reminded her it was the envelope Ruby wanted them to hold in the event of her death. That was last December, the day after Christmas, because he was putting away a new pistol he had given Maeve.

"We came to NTOR New Year's Eve. You were missed, but we understood with the pandemic you couldn't get back to the US from your Korean ski trip. We made a special effort to use the Playhouse. Mimi wanted Dave to make her cum on the swing, and he was delighted to comply."

"This is making me just a little nauseated," Tuffy said, looked away and finished her water. She had known the old man but had not found him attractive.

"We stayed there about an hour," Rex continued. "Mimi, who was for once wearing her smart watch, received a beep toward the end, and she suddenly decided she was tired, so we left the party. Dave was a little disappointed. I know I was.

"The next day, Mimi made some excuse to go into town, and I turned on her phone to listen what she was doing. She was meeting Bauer, who had burglarized the Cenas gun safe, removed the evidence from the envelope, replaced it with documents and an empty thumb drive like what had been in there before, closed it up and left. They were certain the Cenas knew nothing had happened.

"Six weeks later, Mimi and I spent another weekend at NTOR, not realizing it was going to be hellishly cold – snow, for Christ's sake! – and on Sunday, no power for about a week in most of Texas.

"We didn't party much that weekend, just enjoyed the hot tub and sauna. We played with Ron and Petra in their RV, which you may know is near Dave and Maeve's. We dressed warm to leave Ron and Petra's place, and as we were walking back toward our own, Mimi said she wanted to look in on Dave and Maeve. They always kept their door unlocked. Mimi said she didn't want me to go in with her.

"She came back and told me they were fine. A few minutes later, I heard that giggle, the one indicating she's reaching orgasm. I couldn't figure it out at the time, but it was late, and I was tired, so I didn't think anything of it.

"Later in the week, as the snow started to melt and the power came back on, somebody at NTOR thought to look in on the Cenas, who had been dead since Saturday night of carbon monoxide poisoning.

"I'm certain Mimi did it, not sure how. She may have slipped something in their drinks at DJ Ted's Clubhouse or in the sauna, so they would be asleep when she looked in on them and closed the ventilator. If you can, another autopsy might reveal what kind of drugs were in their system.

"Bauer may have had something to do with it, too, but I had not tried to listen in on her conversations with him in the next week, because I was busy with my own work to keep our pipes from freezing up and my business from imploding because of the pandemic and the freeze.

"Another aspect of the situation, by the way, is Philo Lenfant."

BANG! BANG! BANG! The door. I jumped, spilling some of my drink. Tuffy stopped the video and snapped the laptop shut.

#

43

Memorial Day

Wednesday, Oct. 12, 2022, 1:30 a.m.

"Lt. Traeger, what's going on?" said Sgt. North, who looked like he had thrown on a windbreaker over a thin, sleeveless undershirt and some gym shorts.

"Monster, I'm interviewing a witness in my sister's shooting," Tuffy said.

"May I ask why you're looking at evidence in the case Sgt. Wright and I are pursuing, in which your witness is a suspect?"

"You may," Traeger said with a quick exhale through her nose. "He had an idea about how to crack the password-encoded files in Mr. Vega's laptop computer. He was correct. We have been hearing information involving the man who was with Sgt. Wright's brother when WOW assaulted this witness. You may remember that assault is also my case."

North, still standing and occupying 90% of the doorway, frowned.

"May I ask you a question?" Tuffy said.

"Of course."

"Who told you I was here, doing this?"

"Bend."

"I'll have his badge," Tuffy said with soft intensity. "I'm convinced he is trying to interfere in my case. I don't know why, but I'll find out, and when I do, look out. Do not let loyalty to a brother officer ruin your career, as well."

North looked worried and shook his head.

"Two more questions," he said. "May I listen to this, too? And how did Mr. Montecarlo crack the password?"

Tuffy agreed to let him stay. He pulled up a chair as I wiped up my spill, tossed the can in the trash and explained how Father O'Keefe had given me the parchment with the words "*Fiat Voluntas Tua*" and the "leet" code clue.

We resumed the video.

"By now, I decided I needed to listen in on Bauer's phone, as well. It took some doing, but I figured out a way, and I learned he had begun to spend a lot of time with Lenfant, and Lenfant was very interested in NTOR.

"Dave Cena had an estranged older sister, Marta, who condemned the swinger lifestyle body and soul. As sort of a joke, I think, Cena left NTOR to Marta as a tertiary legatee, if something happened so Maeve could not keep it and Laurel, for example, had died before taking ownership. Guess where Marta attends church and to whom she plans to leave her estate? Hill Country Bible Baptist Church and the Right Reverend Theophilus Lenfant.

"When the Cenas died – innocently, as far as Lenfant knew – the preacher hired Bauer to track down Laurel and prevent her from taking ownership of the camp. Marta, by the way, has fourth-stage pancreatic cancer and, as far as we know, has less than six months to live. So, you better keep Laurel safe."

"Fuckedy-fuck-fuck-fuck," Tuffy said as she stopped the video and strode out of the room.

North and I looked at each other. I smiled and gave him my "'sup?" nod with raised eyebrows – the full charm offensive.

"I've heard good things about you," I said.

"All I can say at the moment is what I've heard about you has been interesting," North said. "You have some *aiki-jiu-jitsu* training?"

The question surprised me. I thought my name had been kept out of Mr. Cole's visit to the emergency room.

"Yes," I said. "Just enough to either get me out of trouble or into trouble, depending on how sound my judgment is at the moment. Drinking, too vigorous lovemaking and emotional trauma tend to diminish one's judgment."

"Good to know."

"I try to be. What do you think about Philo Lenfant?"

"I like how he has brought our church into the 21st Century and attracted more attention to our Lord Jesus Christ," North said and sighed through his nose. "He's just a man, though, which means he's a sinner like the rest of us."

"Not so sure he's like the rest of us," I said. "You need to listen to this from the beginning."

Tuffy stepped back into the room. "I sent another reserve deputy and a patrol deputy over to the hospital to keep an eye on Laurel. The patrol deputy – Corporal Singer – is there to supervise."

Tuffy paced back and forth. "Dang!" she shouted. "Momma'll kill me if I let anything happen to Laurel."

I looked at North. "Don't mess with Momma."

Tuffy plopped down in front of the laptop and resumed the video.

"You and Laurel were sure hard to locate for over a year since the pandemic started, traveling around the world to all those places, getting quarantined, where Bauer had no way to travel. Lenfant was getting worried, but he didn't have unlimited funds to hire international hitmen, for example, during the pandemic."

"Who knew the silver lining of a pandemic killing millions would be a recession for assassins?" I asked and shook my head. "Not on my COVID-19 bingo card. Damn."

Tuffy rolled her eyes and shook her head, too. North chuckled.

"Bauer, who continued to play with Mimi, by the way, from time to time, confided Lenfant's interest in Laurel to her, and she came up with a scheme to benefit them all. She would compose a fake will for Laurel, leaving Laurel's property to you, Pepe, who would be her new chief henchman, replacing me, and together you would turn NTOR into a church camp and life-coaching retreat run by her, where she could exploit people *ad infinitum.* I tell you, the woman's ego, chutzpah and hunger know no bounds.

"However, she had a problem: the larger role she and Lenfant would play in his new Hill Country Bible Baptist Church empire – I think of it as Fort God – would draw attention to both of them, and they needed to dispose of Frank, Ruby and Juanda. Delilah was not a problem, as I'll explain later.

"So, we come to Memorial Day weekend, and Frank and Ruby planned to party with a couple they never met on a boat out of Port Aransas. They met and communicated on a swinger website and set the date. Of course, the couple was in fact four people: Mimi, Bauer, Wright and me. Quite the sausage-fest."

"Oy," I said, shaking my head.

"Sausage fest?" North asked.

I paused the recording. "A swinger party with a lot of dudes and not enough women. Too many wieners."

"Ooooh," North said, and made a squeamish face.

I resumed the video.

"Wright got the drop on them as they exited their car, and forced them out to the boat, which Bauer had rented in Frank's name with fake ID and Frank's own credit card. How he got it, I've no clue. That may be why there was a months-long hiatus between the Cenas' death and the Port Aransas trip. Bauer's not as dumb as he looks."

Rex's voice had reached a synthetic-voice-like monotone at this point.

"They wanted me along to drive the boat needed for the return after disposing of the bodies. We went out into the Gulf. The seas were calm. Bauer and Wright tied cinder blocks to their legs, shot them both in the head and dropped them overboard. They ran aground on the landward side of the barrier island. I picked them up, and we returned to a different marina where we had picked up the getaway boat.

"It goes without saying, I'm ashamed of my role in this. I'm not ashamed to say those guys scared me. I knew Mimi was willing to have me dropped over the side with a hole in my head, as well. It was a pleasant evening, weather-wise, and the breeze cooled the sweat on us, but the most chilling thing was hearing Mimi's giggle much of the way back to port.

"Since then, I have avoided sex with Mimi as much as possible, and I didn't want to be around when she was having sex, because I didn't want to hear the giggle."

#

44

Burning questions

Wednesday, Oct. 12, 2022, 2 a.m.

I paused the video and looked at North. "That explains why he came and shot Mimi at that exact moment. I was giving her an orgasm, and she started giggling. The next thing I knew, he was behind me blowing a hole in her face."

North cocked an eyebrow and nodded side to side, as if to say, "Sounds plausible."

Three firm knocks — not the earlier pounding — drew our attention to the door. Tuffy opened it to reveal two men. The man in the rear, barely visible, was Sgt. Wright. The man in front was about 60 years old, wearing a light gray Stetson hat, a light-blue-and-navy PCSO uniform with a star on each collar point, a badge, a heavy gun belt and what appeared to be a .45 1911 Colt with pecan hand-grip inserts and expensive-looking snakeskin cowboy boots. His name tag said Oberst.

"*Mierda,*" I muttered.

"Sgt. North, please take possession of the evidence and return it to the evidence room," Oberst said. "Lt. Traeger, please join me in my office. Mr. Montecarlo, you may go. Sgt. North, you will join us in my office as soon as you have returned the evidence to its cabinet."

I looked at Tuffy and shrugged. She looked at me and moved her head two millimeters sideways in either direction.

I wasn't sure how to return to NTOR. Ride-sharing service was limited — and expensive — at that time of night so far out into the Hill Country. I exited the building and started walking. It was about 2 am, and I despaired of finding a taxi or an Uber, for example. I had no deputy escort as bodyguard. I guess Tuffy concluded I faced little risk. Maybe she was just busy.

The air was fresh and cool, so I wasn't bitter about the hike ahead of me. I had walked about a mile of the five miles I estimated it would take to reach the entrance to the camp when a car blew by me at about 60 mph in a 45 mph zone, then came to a screeching halt. It was a late-model Jaguar F-Type convertible, British Racing Green. I had my arms folded with my hand inside my shirt, gripping my pistol in a shoulder holster as the car spun tires in reverse to stop beside me.

"Blimey, Pepe, don't you ever quit partying?" said Shawn-from-Manchester, a big grin on his face, and a light scent of mint on his breath. "Escaping from some angry husband, no doubt."

"Not exactly," I said, releasing the gun grip and leaning on the passenger-side door. "Would you mind dropping me off at the camp?"

"No problem at all, mate. Just heading home myself from a little *rendezvous au trois*, and that's on the way."

I hopped in the car and said, "*Laissez les Bontemps roulez!*"

I didn't feel like explaining everything, just said the Corvette was out of commission and I found myself downtown without a return ride. The lady I was with had to stay, I explained, and it wasn't Laurel. I didn't say it was Tuffy, no sex involved.

"Got a hall pass, eh? Good on ya, mate. Does your Nubian Queen get those?"

"She's got a permanent hall pass, but she doesn't use them often." I cocked an eye at him, thinking he might not meet Laurel's standards. "I'll let her know you're interested."

"Abso-fucking-lutely, mate," Shawn said, his grin broadening.

Shawn-from-Manchester was a quick, competent driver with no extraneous moves, and I admired how the Jaguar handled and accelerated along *El Camino Real*, a.k.a., Texas Highway 27. For about five seconds, I pondered moving my transportation into the 21st Century. Naaah.

He stopped in front of the NTOR driveway, let me out, and sped away without much tire spin. No PCSO cruiser sat stakeout on the shoulder nearby. I guessed Oberst assumed Laurel was the main target. However, I saw just over the hill the roof of a small vehicle parked on the opposite side of the road, facing the camp entrance driveway.

I entered the gate and ambled toward our rented RV near the rear of the property. I passed by DJ Ted's Clubhouse and the adjacent office and smelled smoke. I thought someone might have lit the fireplace there. It was a little early in the season to be lighting fires in the Texas Hill Country, but not outside the realm of possibility.

The smoke wasn't so much woodsy as it was chemical. In my early days as a journalist, I covered quite a few house fires, which have an unmistakable odor. I looked around and saw smoke billowing from a cracked window in the office area at the back, Jonquil Clarke's office.

"FIRE! FIRE!" I yelled, wondering why the alarm was not sounding as I ran toward the building, hoping nobody was inside. I ran into the clubhouse, which was open, pulled the fire alarm and found an extinguisher. I doused my shirt with water from the bar sink and wound the back of my shirt over my shoulders to cover my face as a makeshift air filter so I could start to attack the flames in the office.

I saw out of the corner of my eye several nude people coming with extinguishers from their RVs. I felt the glass front door of the building. It was warm but not yet hot. I opened the door, propped it with a folding chair and started toward Quil's office. I thought it possible somebody wanted to destroy the digital record of Juanda's killing.

Quil's wooden door was hot, but I had to make sure she wasn't in there. I doused the door with the extinguisher, kicked it open and crouched down as I entered and shot fire retardant all around while holding my breath and squinting through thick smoke. The blaze was centered on her desk and a computer underneath.

Feeling and smelling the hair on my head and arms start to smolder, I crouched lower. As I rounded a chair at the corner of the desk, I saw Quil on the ground with her feet toward me. I grabbed an ankle and began pulling her out of the room while shooting the extinguisher as best I could around her and me.

I got her into the front reception area. Jesse and Dean saw me through the front door. They rushed in shooting their extinguishers and helped carry Jonquil and myself out of the building.

Doc and Grace administered first aid to Quil, as Dean and Jesse did their best with extinguishers to keep the blaze contained. DJ Ted and Sven arrived. Ted turned off the power to the office, while Sven hooked up a garden hose to shoot into the building.

In about three minutes, a fire engine and an emergency medical service ambulance arrived, and the blaze was soon out. About fifteen minutes later, as the EMS unit carrying Quil sped out of the gate, Sheriff Oberst, Tuffy, North and Wright drove in with several deputies, who kept various nude onlookers at bay. A second EMS unit arrived.

"This is Pecan County Sheriff Oberst," Oberst announced via his in-car loudspeaker. "Would those of you who are not now involved in helping one of the victims or the fire department please go put on some clothes? We don't mean to impinge on your clothing optionality, but it would help us with our work if you made that little sacrifice until the situation is under control. Also, please do not leave the property until we have collected your contact information."

After setting the microphone back into his official sport-utility vehicle, Oberst took off his hat to reveal a bald head and wiped it with a bandana from his back pocket. "This is starting to be a long day," said Herr Oberst, *der meister des minimierens* (master of understatement).

At the time, I sat on the side platform of the fire engine, inhaling oxygen at the insistence of Ben, my new best friend. Lovely stuff, oxygen.

Jesse and Dean talked to North and Wright, and my fellow nudists pointed at me and smiled. North's face was noncommittal, but Wright looked suspicious.

"Oh lawd," I muttered.

Tuffy walked toward me. "What?"

"Already I can see your colleague thinks I had something to do with starting the fire, not putting it out," I said.

"Hmm," she said. "He does seem to have it in for you."

"How'd it go with your boss?" I asked.

"Unresolved at the moment," she said. "I'm not doing you any favors by standing here jawing with you. I do believe I'll mosey on into the building and see what I can see."

"Mosey on, dudette."

As she left, North and Wright approached and asked if I could give them an account of what happened. I said the last time I did so, my lawyer threatened to quit, so if they wanted to bring me in for questioning, I won't resist, but I'll wait for my lawyer before I do any talking.

They started to reach out to my arms to lead me back to the car, but I stepped back. "Before you do that, I should mention I have a concealed pistol in a shoulder holster," I said.

They asked me to hand it over, which I did verrrry carefully. Wright unloaded the weapon and stuck it in his pocket with the grip sticking out. "I see you got your gun back," Wright said with a thick layer of sarcasm.

As they led me away with no handcuffs but a hand on each arm, Jesse's face turned red, and he grimaced with suppressed rage.

"What the hell do you think you people are doing with a man who just risked his own life to save Jonquil Clarke's life?" he said, standing in our path, the red of his face flashing darker from the police emergency lights. Even naked, he had the commanding presence of a Navy captain and pilot. "You should be pinning a hero's medal on him, rather than dragging him away to jail."

Oberst stepped in. "They're not dragging him. They're helping him."

"Bullshit," Jesse said.

"Sir, I'm going to ask you to step aside," Wright said.

Out of the corner of my eye, I saw Wright's right hand slip to the side where he kept both his 9 mm Glock semiautomatic and his Taser. I didn't want either of those deployed.

"Jesse, it's OK," I said with my "What's up?" grin. "They want a statement, and I don't want to give them one without my attorney present, and it will be more convenient for everybody for us to do so at the Sheriff's Office. You have my permission to break me out – or pick me up, as the case may be – if you don't hear from me by noon … today is it? Yes, I do believe I spy rosy-fingered Dawn in the east."

I gave him a two-handed hand-clasp to show how much I appreciated his heartfelt emotion and to signal the conversation's end.

He stepped aside, and I stepped into the back of a Sheriff's Office cruiser for the second time that week, this time with the pungent aroma of some drunk's vomit greeting my nostrils. If it weren't for the honor of the thing, I'd have just as soon skipped it. I fell asleep on the way.

#

45

A stray ace up Deuce's sleeve

Wednesday, Oct. 12, 2022, 8 a.m.

"Wakey, wakey, bud," Deuce said, shaking my shoulder. I looked up and realized I was on a cot in a holding cell. The door was open, but this was the most comfortable accommodation they could offer me until my attorney/best friend showed up.

I swung my legs over the side of the cot and shook my head to my immediate regret. My previous head injury had resurrected as a throbbing headache, but the brain fog began to dissipate. "Got any naproxen or ibuprofen?" I asked. "Coffee would be nice, too."

In a dark brown pinstripe suit, tan shirt and red-and-blue Tejas Club tie, Deuce reached into his leather satchel and extracted a small bottle of naproxen.

"Bless you, my child," I said. "Now, for coffee."

268

"It's in the interview room," he said. "I want to have your attention while we chat off the record before those guys get a crack at us. You OK to walk? I know you've been through the wringer the past few days."

I shook my head dismissively but slowly, in deference to my lingering headache. "A mere bagatelle," I muttered as I stood, swaying for a half-minute as the blood pressure equalized around the old edifice. "Lead on, Macduff."

He narrowed his eyes and looked askance at me as he sidled out of the doorway and walked toward the middle of the building. "Don't talk about what happened until we get there. I have confidence in privacy there, but not out here."

I mimed zipping my mouth shut, looking at my fingers and tossing away the invisible key.

"You'd joke as they were putting the pentobarbital needle in your arm."

I shrugged and mimed an inability to open my mouth to respond.

Once we were in the interview room with the door closed, I told Deuce what happened when I got to NTOR, between slurps of robusto coffee smelling a bit more delicious than it tasted. Deuce said Quil had some small second-degree burns, but they were likely to heal. More important, she had been conked on the head and was comatose. That might kill her, if the swelling and/or bleeding did not stop.

I explained what happened at the Farmer's Rest Café, the hospital and back at the police station with Tuffy and North. It took about a half-hour. The 13D5m.com profile of LtChocolock did not appear in the conversation.

"I want to hear what Rex said all the way through ASAP,

but we got another problem: the video of the night Juanda died," Deuce said. "If Ms. Clarke dies, how will we get access to it, if we need it? Do we need to bring the recording up in talking about the fire?"

"I think we do," I said. "You may already know the coroner determined Juanda's death was a murder, so we're withholding relevant evidence now, but damned if I can figure out how to access it with Quil unconscious. I speculate the killer attacked her and set the fire to destroy evidence, but she told us it was also on the cloud. How we get to it? Haven't a clue."

My solicitor stopped taking notes, frowned at the page, looked up at me and paused about 20 seconds.

"I'm thinking like them – or at least like somebody convinced you're a bad guy," he said, and hesitated 10 seconds more. "If I thought you had killed Juanda, I might think you tried to destroy evidence and even kill the woman who knew about it to make sure nobody talks about it."

"Okily-dokily. That's some mo' shiggedy."

"Mo' shiggedy, indeed," Deuce said. "So, if we bring it up now, we can say all we want that it supports your innocence, but they can just as easily claim you were destroying the evidence, and Ms. Clarke happened to be in the way."

"How would they explain me saving her life and risking mine?"

"Showboating, not expecting her to survive."

"Glad you're on my side."

"I guess as a gesture of good faith, the thing to do is tell them about the video and what we think might have been happening when you showed up – i.e., somebody was trying to destroy evidence," Deuce said. "You ready to face their questions?"

I swallowed the dregs of my Dunkin Donuts coffee. "As I'll ever be," I said. "Thanks for the coffee, by the way." He stood up to go to the door. "You can be my office boy any time."

"Fuck you," learned counsel said as he stepped out.

Oberst, Wright, North and Tuffy returned with Deuce.

"Mr. Montecarlo –" Oberst began.

"You can call me Pepe." I gave him my dazzling smile and raised eyebrows, like we were old pals.

Through a wide grin that would put Captain Hook's crocodile nemesis to shame, Oberst said, "OK, Pepe. It's a bit cramped for all of us in here, but be warned: It's not just Wright and North observing your interrogation. Lt. Traeger and I will be on the other side of the two-way mirror, listening."

I have never been a fan of the word "interrogation." It calls to mind the phrase "enhanced interrogation techniques," which inevitably end in tears and too often in outright lies.

"Okily-dokily." I smiled again as they left and gave Deuce a nod, who placed a phone on the table and punched a button.

"You should know we're recording this *interview* –" the corners of my mouth rose at Deuce's emphasis on the last word "– which my client offers of his own free will in an effort, as a good citizen and taxpayer, to see justice done."

Wright and North looked in the mirror, expecting a knock? None came. North's eyebrows raised and he said, "OK."

In a quick, flat voice, my attorney described for the recording the time, date and individuals present.

"Of course, we are recording this, as well. You just can't see the microphone or camera," Wright said.

"Good fences make good neighbors," I said. "Nice to know the boundaries."

#

46

Where there's smoke

Wednesday, Oct. 12, 2022, 9 a.m.

"So, you want to tell us what happened?" Wright asked.

I went through the story again, repeating what I'd said to Deuce.

"So, how did you get to the resort again?" North asked. "An Uber?"

"No, it's a guy I met who I think of as Shawn-from-Manchester," I said, smiling. "He's a Brit who must live not far from here, because he was driving by, recognized me and gave me a ride."

"Shawn Manchester is his name?" Wright asked.

My advocate moved closer and whispered, "They're trying to confuse you. Just be patient and make sure they get it right."

"I don't know his last name," I said, smiling a bit sheepishly.

"He goes by Shawn, and when we met, he said, 'Just call me Shawn-from-Manchester.'"

"To be clear, you're all fucking each other, and you don't know last names?" Wright said. "Or even if you're sure of their first names?"

Embarrassed and blushing, I bent forward and smiled. "I'll let you in on swinging's dirty little secret. We often have no idea with whom we are making whoopee. For some of us, it's part of the fun. It's also a running joke between Laurel and myself. And, for the record, Shawn-from-Manchester and I did not fuck each other or anything else. We might have been on either end of the same woman or two over the past few days. I'm not sure."

North, also blushing, nodded, wrote that down, shook his head with a small grin on his pursed lips.

"But, I've been around enough to recognize a fake British accent when I hear it," I said. "I'm sure Shawn-from-Manchester is from the U.K., although maybe not from inside the Manchester city limits. I can't imagine Pecan County or the greater Pecan County metropolitan area has many genuine British residents. By the way, you might ask Laurel if she has his number, because he does want to play with her again. He loves him some Laurel."

North and Wright looked at each other, then at their watches. A full minute later, North asked, "Exactly when did you arrive at the camp?"

"It would have been no more than three minutes before I pulled the fire alarm in the building," I said. "Perhaps the Fire Department will have a record."

"Could it have been, say, 15 minutes before? Ten minutes?" Wright asked.

"No, three minutes is a good estimate of the time," I said. "If you want, I can re-enact my walk into the camp, my run into the clubhouse and then to the office. I'm a fair runner, it might have been less time, and I was excited. A re-enactment should give you a good time estimate."

Deuce caught my eye and gave me a confidence-building nod and microscopic grin. My willingness to help scored a brownie point.

"Did anybody leave the premises?" North asked.

"Which premises?"

"Either one," Wright said. "We'll put it another way: Did you see anybody else walking or driving when you entered the campground and went to the clubhouse and office?"

"No, sir."

"So, you were just walking along and all of a sudden you realize there's a fire in the building, and you call out 'FIRE! FIRE!' and you saw nobody respond?"

"I take that back. After I called out and just as I was entering the office building itself, I saw people approaching with fire extinguishers," I said. "I didn't see anyone before I shouted fire."

"Interesting you noticed the fire at all, when you think about it," Wright said, his head cocked to one side. "Have you set fires before?"

"HA!" my barrister barked. "The question presupposes he set this one. Reframe your question, please."

"Is there any special reason you noticed the fire?" Wright

said, frowning at my zealous advocate. "It was a cool night. People might have fires at their camps."

"I used to be a newspaper reporter," I said, continuing the helpful smile, but recalling the acrid odor of burning plastic, wood, gasoline and paint. "I have covered my share of house fires. They smell different – more chemical than woodsy — toxic, when you get right down to it."

"I agree," Wright said. "Very dangerous, yet you went in knowing how you might get killed. Why? I don't think many people would do it."

"You may have noticed I'm a bit weird," I said, bringing on the pearly whites with more gusto. "I once did a story where I trained as a volunteer firefighter and even got certified. I thought it more likely I would get out alive than anyone else nearby, and I wanted to make sure no one in there died – and…"

I looked at my attorney, and he nodded.

"I thought it likely some evidence about Juanda Falcon's death was in there," I said.

North's eyebrows raised as he took notes, but Wright's dead sardonic stare never wavered.

"Really," Wright said with palpable sarcasm. "What evidence would that be?"

"Video of the area around the hot tub where she died," I said, giving my grin a sheepish quality. "We just learned the coroner had determined her death to be a homicide. We intended to present the digital recording when we had the chance. We've been … busy."

"Counselor, did you know about this?" Wright said.

"Yes, I did, but I only discovered this morning Ms.

Falcon's death was a homicide," my solicitor said. "A judge would consider this a timely presentation of evidence."

"Actually, it's no evidence at all," Wright said. "If there's video in that room, it's the digital equivalent of *chicharrones* now."

I nodded and sighed, my eyebrows raised in acknowledgment of the Tex-Mex-fried truth of the comment.

North said, "Want to go ahead and tell us what you saw on the recording?"

I described what I'd seen. At the end, North said, "We're going to want to talk to that female resort worker again. We talked the day Ms. Falcon's body was discovered, but this sequence of events was not mentioned. What was her name again?"

"She may not have seen any connection to the death," I said. "After all, it was the previous day, and she was delivering barbecue to a different location. Delilah. Not sure of her last name."

Grinning, I added, "No, I did not knock boots with her. Hard as it may be to believe, lots of women's names I don't know have successfully resisted the urge to dance the horizontal mambo with me, if I'm not being too subtle."

Wright and North looked at each other and stepped out of the room. Deuce and I looked at each other. I folded up a sheet of his legal pad into a little triangular football, and we played table-top football until they returned about 10 minutes later.

"Damn!" I said, as they re-entered. "My attorney is 12 points ahead! He's not only gouging me with his horrendous legal fees, but also embarrassing me at tabletop football. Life's not fair."

"Glad you can maintain your sense of humor," Wright said, ladling on more sarcasm and sprawling in the chair across from me.

"Here's my theory of the crime," Wright said, speaking in the menacing monotone he had used the first time I met him. "You arrive when you say you did, only you go straight to the office, conk Ms. Clarke in the head, set the blaze, step outside and yell 'Fire! Fire!' Then you run into the clubhouse, grab the extinguisher and re-enter the office lobby, knowing full well the fire wouldn't have time to get to the lobby door. You pound Ms. Clarke's head once more for good measure and drag her out, thinking she's done for. That way, you get credit for trying to save someone's life, but you have also destroyed evidence pointing straight at … you."

Wright and North looked at each other, then looked at their watches for a full minute.

Waiting patiently to satisfy their need to follow the silent-treatment routine in trying to make me crack, I finally gave him my mock-shocked look. "My goodness, what you must think of me," I said, shaking my head in disappointment.

"Passable theory, short on evidence," Deuce said. "Assuming Ms. Clarke survives, there's at least one way we can back up our story."

"Really?" asked North, sitting across from me. He raised an eyebrow, shifted forward and stared into my eyes. He was beginning to like me. Surprising. Wright frowned at him.

"Yes," Deuce continued. "The digital record we're discussing was saved, by her, to the cloud. So, when she reawakens, we should be able to access it using her password."

"Not great chain-of-evidence," Wright said. "Who's to say you didn't doctor it?"

"She may give you credible testimony on that," Deuce responded.

"Assuming she lives," Wright said.

"I'm sure we'll all be praying for her," I said. "If you have her phone, you might find something in in it leading to her cloud storage and whatever her password is."

A knock-knock-knock focused our eyes for a moment on the two-way mirror. The deputy sergeants scraped their metal chairs back and left again. I picked up the paper football. "Who's turn was it?" I asked.

Learned counsel shook his head and made the goalposts with his index fingers. I'd made up six points of my loss by the time everybody – Oberst, Wright, North and Tuffy – returned, which was about 15 minutes.

Oberst looked at the football and chuckled.

"Anybody who likes football can't be all bad," he said. "Counselor, please get your client out of my Sheriff's Office. If you encounter any more evidence, please do inform us at your earliest – and I do mean earliest – convenience."

"Of course," my solicitor said, helping me to my feet.

I resisted his pull to the door. "May I please have my pistol back? It has not been used in any crime this week."

"Tuffy, give him his pistol back."

She walked away muttering, "Getting to be a habit."

#

47

Wanted: old farts

Wednesday, Oct. 12, 2022, 10 a.m.

"Lt. Traeger went to bat for you," Deuce said, as he pulled out of the driveway, heading toward NTOR. "You got people who believe in you. You might just need all of them before this is over."

I was still a bit groggy from lack of sleep, and my head was pounding again.

"Good to know," I said. "I never want to let anybody down, goes without saying."

"Wouldn't hurt to slow down a tad," he said. "You drive an old Corvette, not a Bugatti Veyron."

"True dat," I said. "Got a feeling my git-along will have been long-gone today, at least. I am spent."

My phone rang. Joanna Metzger. "Okily-dokily," I muttered with a hint of sarcasm.

Putting a smile on my face, I answered, "How's my favorite TV reporter today?"

She wanted an interview about the fire. I told her to stop by around 1 p.m., and I would determine if she and her crew can enter and we can talk about the fire. If so, the camera could only be rolling inside the office building or out next to the road, and I'd hold her responsible to ensure nobody's nude body showed up in any TV reports.

"Would I do that?" Joanna said.

"As Laurel would say, 'You bett' not!'"

"How is Laurel? We heard about the shooting at the Farmer's Rest Café."

"Fine, I think. She will be coming back to camp later today. The doctor wanted to keep her overnight."

After I rang off, Mr. Bill-'em-by-the-hour said, "I'm sure you know what you're doing, but what is it exactly you're doing?"

Expending a dwindling modicum of energy, I giggled.

"I see us as held hostage by this story, hounded by a public whose hostility has been whipped up by the Right Reverend Theophilus Lenfant. My hope is by presenting an affable – avuncular even – image to the public, they will see us not as monsters, which we're not, but as humans, which we are."

"Makes sense. It would be a big help if you could stop being at the center of some violent news event every couple of days."

"True dat," I said. "Somebody has set this situation up so we are in the bull's eye. I'm just trying to make the best of a bad situation."

Looking at my friend, I said, "It could get worse before it gets better."

Turning into the NTOR drive, Deuce said, "I got you, my brother."

I'm such a softy. I choked up a bit.

I exited the car, waved goodbye, let myself in the gate and started walking to our rented RV for the second time in 12 hours, where I slept for two. When Joanna showed up in a fashionable Stewart plaid skirt and jacket over a light-blue, button-collar Oxford shirt and string tie, she and her denim-overall-clad cameraman with a backward Texas A&M University baseball cap entered the property and shot video inside the smoky office building, per Sven's orders. Sven was second in command when Quil was away.

In denim shorts, loose chambray Guayabera leisure shirt with my SIG Sauer in a shoulder holster underneath, I explained what I had done, but did not explain about the recording of Juanda's death or give the details of where I had been for the hours leading up to my arrival at the camp.

"I was helping the Pecan County Sheriff's Office with their enquiries, as they say on the British detective shows," I explained. "I don't think Sheriff Oberst would like me to release details. If you want to ask him, I can't stop you."

I listened as Joanna provided the closing for the segment in which she painted me as a hero. I had no expectations that particular angle would survive without a shaker of salt.

"Doing anything this evening?" she asked, as her cameraman walked ahead and packed his camera in the van in the dry, pine-scented air.

I cocked my head, which kinda hurt my sore noggin, and sniffed her Chanel No. 5. "Not as far as I know. Laurel will be feeling pretty shitty when she gets here, I imagine. Want to come over and hang out naked for a while, with the understanding neither of us will likely do anything strenuous?"

"I'll ask Adriana," Joanna said, smiling. Ah, she likes us, I thought. Lovely. Nice for old farts to be wanted, right?

To cope with trauma such as the death of lovers and people shooting at my Nubian Queen, I have a different kind of therapy than Laurel's, and Little Pepe, the mindless little social worker, was holding office hours.

As the TV van rolled out the driveway, I started unbuttoning my shirt and walking to the pool, where I saw Jesse, Grace, Doc and his lovely ginger-haired wife, Tricia, about 40, standing neck-deep in one end.

I removed my shirt, shoulder holster, shorts and flip-flops, and stepped with care into the pool. I realized the bandage on my head might not benefit from exposure to chlorine -- and who knows how many fascinating body fluids.

"Expecting trouble, Pepe?" Doc asked, his widow's peak flat-top pointing toward the shoulder holster.

"Hasn't done me much good, so far," I said. "But, the one time you don't have it is when you'll wish you had it."

"So I hear," Doc said, the zinc oxide on his nose providing a comical contrast with his black Wayfarer horn-rimmed sunglasses and age-spotted, smiling face.

"How long have you been living here, Doc?" I asked.

"About five years, isn't that right honey?" he asked Tricia, who nodded her cute little freckled nose.

"You know Delilah?" I asked.

"Of course," Doc said. "I know everybody who works here, but I haven't poked many of them, and Delilah is one such unfortunate missed opportunity."

Tricia giggled.

"How charmingly you put it," Grace said, starting toward the ladder.

"Facts is facts," Doc said. "How's the noggin?"

"It's healing," I said. "Need more sleep, but I'm curious about why we didn't see her when we were fighting the fire. We saw everybody else who works here, I guess."

"Some people don't dig living in the clothing-optional lifestyle full time," Doc said. "Delilah lives off-campus – no idea where."

"Do you know her last name?"

"Why? Jesus, Mary and Joseph, Pepe, haven't you had enough sex over the past five days?" Jesse laughed.

"Mmmmmmaybe," I said, trying to channel Bugs Bunny. "Not sure yet. Last name?"

"Samson," Doc said.

"Uff da," I said, and Jesse cackled.

"Delilah Samson," I said. Doc nodded. "Where do these people get these names? Do these parents, in fact, want their kids to get into fights every day they're in school? We got a couple of brothers named BOW and WOW, more brothers named Virgilio and Mario Guadalupe, and now Delilah Samson."

"I don't know, but I do know she came here from Houston," Doc said. "So, it's not just the Hill Country with goofy names."

"Yeah, Pepe, you do realize your name is a little odd, right?" Jesse said, watching his lovely wife's tushy getting toweled off next to a reclining beach chair.

"I always thought it would make a good name for a porn

star," I said. "Can't you see it on the marquee of some sperm-soaked triple-X theater back in the '70s? Pepe Montecarlo and Linda Lovelace go all the way in 'In so Deep'?"

Jesse, Doc and Tricia chuckled. Grace looked over her shoulder at me and cocked an eyebrow.

Mercy, I thought.

But ... I saw Sven and DJ Ted carrying a ladder from the back of the clubhouse to the office, and thought to give them a hand while learning more about Delilah. My thinking: She might – just might -- give me a clue about who set the fire.

I started to put the shorts and shoulder holster on my wet body, but Grace, bless her, insisted on drying me off a bit first. Little Pepe showed his appreciation, so she gave the little pecker a peck.

"Hey!" Doc said in mock consternation. "No sex in the pool area."

"Spoil sport," Grace said.

I continued dressing.

#

A Nubian Queen awaits

Wednesday, Oct. 12, 2022, 2 p.m.

Sven and DJ Ted were ripping down the charred ceiling tiles over the remains of Quil's desk as I walked in. When I asked if I could help, they put me off, but I pointed out Laurel had an interest in getting the resort back on its feet. They allowed me to do some sweeping and shoveling of tiles and Sheetrock, and hauling a wheelbarrow back and forth to an open construction dumpster delivered that morning.

These guys like to work, I thought. Good for them.

"All your computer systems down?" I asked, looking at the point-of-sale system and computer monitor at the front counter. The fire had been centered in the office with a few signs of charring on the otherwise white wall above the doorway to Quil's office.

"No, *gracias a dios*," said Sven, wearing a medical protective mask and work clothes. "We can still conduct business. The computer in the burnt room had a lot of records, but all the transactions happen via a remote off-site server farm in town."

"Pretty sophisticated for a rural resort," I said, shoveling more Sheetrock into the wheel barrow.

"My sister balked at first at the expense," DJ Ted said, standing halfway up the ladder, also masked, but shirtless with cut-off shorts, combat boots and a "Keep Austin Weird" baseball cap. "That's one argument I'm glad I won, given all the natural disasters hitting Texas – hurricanes, tornadoes, the Longhorns –"

"Hey!" I said in mock indignation. "We ain't in the Big 12 cellar yet. Football season's not over."

"Yeah, right," Ted said with a heavy scoop of of sarcasm. "Anyway, it's a good thing she agreed, for sure. She's ..." He stopped pulling down ceiling tile for a minute, leaned on the top of the ladder and looked at his gloved hands.

"*Una mujer excelente, seguro*, and she's going to be fine," Sven said.

"Damn right," I said, although I wasn't feeling quite so certain.

"Gotta keep workin'," DJ Ted said. "It's worse if I'm not busy."

"I hear and agree," I said, remembering when my wife died, but not wanting to raise the specter of death.

"I'm not complaining, but where's Delilah?" I asked. "Shouldn't she be here, helping out?"

Sven pulled some charred Sheetrock off the wall with a

little more force than necessary. "It's her day off," he said. "We offered to pay her overtime, but she said she had a prior commitment."

"Looks like an all-hands-on-deck kinda thing," DJ Ted said, looking around at the interior ceiling. "But waddayagonnado?"

"I wanted to ask her about something that happened the day before Juanda Falcon died," I said. "Would you mind giving me her address or phone number?"

"Sorry," Sven said. "Against policy to give out personal information of employees. I'll call her this evening and ask her to give you a call, OK?"

I told him I understood. Laurel rang my phone.

"So, you been fucking all those hoes at NTOR, too busy to come visit your Nubian Queen?" she said.

"Giving you time to rest, baby," I said. "And I've needed some rest, myself. Little Pepe's hangin' low."

I told Ted and Sven I needed to chat with Laurel, so I went outside as Jesse and Grace, dressed for hard work, walked in. "We kinda renovate houses as a sideline," Jesse said. "This is like a busman's holiday for us."

"Yeah, you won't play, so I gotta work off this sexual energy somehow," Grace said.

I pointed to the phone and said, "Would you repeat that for Laurel's benefit?"

"Your man ain't making it easy for us hoes!" Grace said, as Jesse shook his head, laughed, walked into Quil's office and asked how he could help.

"You give him a good whippin', girl!" Laurel shouted back at her.

"All of a sudden, I'm sorry I allowed this conversation to proceed in this direction," I said, turning out the door of the lobby.

I explained what Jesse and Grace were doing, then started to explain about the fire, and what Tuffy and I did at the sheriff's office.

"Yeah, yeah, yeah, Tuffy told me when she stopped by earlier," Laurel said. "When you gonna get your ass over here and take me away from this place? I've seen Louise a couple of times, and it's more gruesome each time."

"OK, I'm heading to the RV now to get dressed and get the Corvette, such as it is," I said, thinking about the Bauer-butt-sized dent in the hood. "Listen, Joanna Metzger might want to stop by and sit around naked with us for a little while this evening."

"Huh," Laurel said. "That woman's got something for you, I think."

"For me? I think she's got something for you," I said. "She said she was gonna ask Adriana."

"Well, get on over here and pick me up," Laurel said. "Tuffy says we'll have an escort back to the campground. How's my investment going over there?"

"Just a reminder: You own the land, not the business on it, but your tenant has some good workers, at least two, in Sven and DJ Ted," I said, explaining what they were doing in Quil's office, and how the computer system had remote backup.

"Good to know," Laurel said. "Let's check on Quil while you're here."

"We can try," I said. "We're not relatives, but we can look in on her, at least. I have a little experience with comatose women, you may recall, and I'll be able to get some idea of how she's doing by looking at the instruments. A decent heart beat and blood pressure, good color in her urine, and we'll have reason for hope."

"It's what I'm praying for."

"Your Highness, I'm at the RV, so let me get dressed, and the magic coach, slightly worse for wear, will arrive for you in about 30 minutes."

#

49

A familiar scene

Wednesday, Oct. 12, 2022, 3 p.m.

As I walked into the disinfected, quiet lobby of the hospital, I saw Louise, who strode toward me, handed me a slip of paper.

"I don't have much time, but my husband said we could chat at this address tomorrow at 8 pm. Come alone." She almost trotted in her escape.

At the front desk, I learned where Her Royal Highness spent the night and took the elevator to the top – third – floor and followed the labyrinth tour to my darling.

A reserve deputy and a regular deputy, the former Virgilio Guadalupe and the latter a 6'3," muscular bronze African American named Corporal W. Keogh sat in chairs in Laurel's room, chatting. Everyone was smiling, of course. Laurel can be charming, even in clothes.

"Here's my boo-thang," she said as I walked in and kissed her cheek. "He's the sexiest man I know."

"And you're the most delusional Nubian Queen I ever met," I said, sniffing her honey-scented, spikey hair. "Are you keeping these gentlemen entertained?"

"She's amazing," Virgilio said, a big grin on his swarthy face. "You're a lucky man."

"True dat," Laurel said.

"And she's so modest," I said. "Let's go check on Ms. Clarke."

The four of us went down to the intensive care unit and inquired about her. The emergency room nurse who treated both Laurel and me recognized us and pointed out the room.

Quil had a bandage around her head, a bruise on her left cheek and bandages around her neck, left shoulder and arm, and on her right hand.

"Shit," my sad darling said, tears welling up in her eyes. "Dammit. Somebody's in for some serious beat-down."

"True dat," I said, looking up at the screen for heart rate, blood pressure and temperature.

The scene had become too damn familiar for me. My aforementioned late wife, Frankie, died when a blood vessel in her skull burst out of the blue. She had suffered no blow, unlike Jonquil, but Jonquil's injury could have similar stroke-like consequences.

The scene of my poor late darling Frankie's deathbed popped unbidden before my eyes and held me transfixed. They had shaved part of my darling's head to install a shunt to relieve swelling pressure inside the skull. Jonquil had nothing like that, which might mean the pressure was not so bad.

Frankie's heart rate was slow like Jonquil's, about 40 beats a minute. Frankie's heart beat had been weak, but Jonquil's heart beat strong and steady.

They had needed to keep Frankie's blood pressure low, to keep from popping the stent they had installed in her cranial artery. Jonquil's blood pressure was in the normal range.

Jonquil's body temperature was low, about 97 degrees F, about the same as Frankie's.

I looked at Jonquil's urine bag, which was clear and light yellowish, same as Frankie's.

I smelled nothing unusual in the room. I looked at the intravenous bags and saw saline solution; I couldn't determine what the other stuff was.

All in all, as we say in my family, *hoc posset esse peius.*

In the case of Frankie and me, it most definitely had been *peius.* I looked at the ceiling and whispered to my late darling Frankie, "Love you and miss you, darlin'."

Laurel cocked her head and looked at me. "I'm right here."

I reached out a reassuring hand to her forearm, smiled and said, "So you are."

I stepped a little closer to Jonquil and watched her chest rise and fall.

"Not too bad, given all she's been through," I said. "I think she's going to make it."

I looked around and realized her lack of protection. "Uh, Corporal Keogh?"

"Sir?"

"Is there no one guarding her?" I asked.

"Should there be?"

I asked Laurel to ask Tuffy to detail somebody to watch

Quil and make sure no one – not a minister, not a nurse – who was not authorized to treat Quil came near her.

Laurel talked to Tuffy, who talked to Keogh, who gave Virgilio explicit instructions about how to watch Quil until his relief arrived.

I took Laurel's hand and said, "Let's go."

"Where to?"

"You eat yet?" I asked. "I could do with a bite."

"Let's not go back to Farmer's Rest Café, if you don't mind. Whataburger? We may be rich, but we ain't stupid."

"Good enough for me," I said.

After checking out, yet again, from Teresienstadt's sole hospital, we filled up on a jalapeño cheeseburger for me, bacon cheeseburger for Corporal Keogh ("Bill," Laurel called him) and half a chicken sandwich for the Nubian Queen. Then we moseyed back to Not-a-Thing-On Resort. Bill met his backup reserve deputy out front.

Driving in the late afternoon sun, I said our investigation was stalled until we could locate Delilah and learn what we can about the delivery man. I had a feeling he was the key to Juanda's death and might even be the killer.

It would also be helpful to have a chat with Bauer or W.O.W., but I was not hopeful of locating either of those fellows soon. KUT-FM, the local public radio station, said Texas' esteemed governor had discovered hordes of angry infants and their mothers overrunning our Rio Grand defenses. He had deployed Wright's National Guard unit to the Rio Grande. What a douche.

As for Bauer, who knows?

Laurel said she had met a black nurse who attended

Lenfant's church and might be able to learn Delilah Samson's address. As usual with my Nubian Queen, she makes confidants faster than most people make TikToks — or munch Tic Tacs, come to think of it..

Back at the RV, we stripped down to our bandages (I also had my Kel-Tec P3AT and phone in a fanny pack) and relaxed by the pool until I got a call from Joanna Metzger.

"Adriana and I would like to come over, OK?" she asked me. I passed the phone to Laurel, and they agreed Joanna and Adriana could bring us some Chinese food around 7 pm. Laurel loves moo goo gai pan. I dig General Tso's Chicken.

They showed up and stripped as Laurel and I laid out the food on the picnic table. Both were lovely, with Adriana a bit more buxom, topped off by cute little nipple piercings. Little Pepe was happy to see them, but not yet giddy.

"How did the news report about the fire go?" I asked. "Haven't had time to look at the news today."

"I'm afraid hardly anybody does any more, but you came across as pretty heroic," Joanna said. "I heard you asked the Sheriff's Office to find somebody to guard Ms. Clarke in the hospital. Why does she need guarding?"

"You gotta admit getting conked on the head and having one's office burned is a mite suspicious," I responded, trying to sound hypothetical and giving a warning glance to Laurel as she munched her savory food. "Herr Oberst *und kinder* likely realized Ms. Clarke may have known something her attackers wanted to remain unknown. If she doesn't reawaken, they may get their wish."

Joanna raised her left eyebrow and looked askance at me. "You playin' me, Mr. Montecarlo?"

"I'd a lot rather be playing with you, Ms. Metzger."

"Huh," Laurel said, and swallowed some food. "I'm sure you would."

Laurel's phone pinged for a text message, and she looked at it. Adriana couldn't help but see it as well, as the phone was between them on the picnic table.

Adriana blushed a moment, giggled and reached out a tanned hand to Laurel's forearm, "I'd like some dessert. You up for that, Ms. Traeger?"

"I'm still a bit hungry, darlin'," Laurel said, smiling at her and giving me a wink. "Let's finish what we're eating, wander over to the pool and see what happens."

"I thought you couldn't get in the pool because of your bandage," Joanna said and nodded at my own *cabeza rota*. "Or should I say 'bandages'?"

"Should be OK if we keep our heads and shoulders above water," I said. "Won't be watching any submarine races this evening, I'm afraid. You know about those?"

"Pay no attention to the old fart," Laurel said, shaking her head and rolling her eyes. "He means he'll try to keep his head above water – something we've pretty much failed to do since Sunday, figuratively speaking."

We continued chatting while my wounded lover, who ate little at the hospital, finished most of her entrée for once. Most times, she eats half and saves the rest for a later lunch. About a third remained, which she put in a container with the leftover shrimp fried rice, and half of my General Tso's chicken. Why do they always give you so much?

We grabbed towels, our guests grabbed cups of Moscato wine and I grabbed a Hopadillo IPA. Laurel brought a bottle of water, saying she could not drink alcohol while on antibiotics from the shooting. It was a sobering thought, a not-so-High Royal Highness. How can one cope? Little Pepe had some ideas.

I also had my trusty fanny pack full o' pistol. If somebody wanted to get to Laurel, they'd have to go through me.

#

50

Borrowed heartbeats

Wednesday, Oct. 12, 2022, 7:45 p.m.

At the pool, each of us went to the restroom, where Laurel tarried as the young'uns joined me at the shower and waded enticingly into the cool, chlorine-smelling water. Another couple I did not recognize were entwined at the other end.

Joanna looked around, seeing the couple in the water, an older nude couple holding hands as they walked along a pine straw path in the cool of the evening, and a fifty-something foursome playing cards next to a complex cab-over camper across the main clearing. "It's like a nice neighborhood pool and common area, except nobody is wearing clothes."

"Most observant," I said. "Of course, you're here midweek, so there's no significant activities planned I know of. That foursome plays every Wednesday evening, I believe. I may hear some very cross words, but it never gets what I would call rowdy."

"What are the stakes?" Adriana said. "Can't be strip poker."

"It's pinochle," I said, moving closer to both of them. "I wonder about that, too. Out of curiosity, are you both only interested in playing with Laurel? Or do I fit into the picture?"

Joanna laughed. "You're pretty direct, aren't you, Pepe?"

"I'm well past the midpoint in my life, and I have much less time than I used to, to practice my wanton, wastrel ways."

Joanna moved closer and started fondling Little Pepe, who liked it.

"Does that answer your question?"

"Mmmmmmaybe," I said, again imitating Bugs Bunny and sniffing her Johnson's Baby Oil. Do they make it out of real babies? Out of the corner of my eye, amid the gathering twilight, I saw Doc and Tricia headed to the showers. "Hey, Doc, aren't you gonna get pretty pruney if you get back in the pool?"

Tricia giggled and called out, "I'll straighten out the wrinkles."

"Oh lawd," Laurel said, as she, too headed to the showers. "Feeling a bit weird, Pepe."

"Either lack of alcohol or lack of semen," I said.

"I recommend an injection of both," Doc said, offering her his Yeti cooler bottle, which I happened to know was full of gin and tonic. "Delighted to offer either or both, my dear."

"As Pepe's lawyer would say, I'll take your recommendation under advisement," Laurel said with a chuckle, but she pushed the drink away. The sound of her running the water to remove the dust from her legs and gingerly wading into the pool came to my ears, but my eyes were closed as Joanna started rubbing her nipples against my chest, nibbling my neck and stroking Little Pepe's ego.

I felt the movement of water as Adriana approached Her Royal Queasiness and led her toward the deeper end of the pool. I opened my eyes and saw Adriana behind Laurel, rubbing her body while reaching around to her vagina.

We were well on the way to violating NTOR's no-sex-in-the-pool-area policy when Laurel groaned and splashed completely underwater.

My attention seized, I pushed Joanna away.

"What's going on?" I asked. Laurel was moving back and forth, grabbing her stomach, but not standing up because she was in too deep. I swam to her, turned her on her side so her face was out of the water and pulled her toward the shallow end.

Adriana looked scared and said, "No idea! She just convulsed and turned head first into the water."

Laurel was groaning and sounded ready to vomit. "Oh, Pepe, it hurts, it hurts!"

I glared at Adriana, because we had warned her about keeping our heads and shoulders above water.

"I'm sorry!" she said, and she waded to the pool steps.

I got Laurel to the shallows and lifted her out of the water and set her on the concrete ledge. Doc was already kneeling next to her, sober as Samuel Alito.

"Dial 911!" he said to Tricia, who did so and recounted Laurel's symptoms to the emergency operator.

"Any idea what the problem is?" I asked, as I pulled myself out of the pool.

"What did she eat for supper?" Doc asked as he checked her pulse and looked down her throat, using his phone flash for light.

"Some Chinese."

"Any left?" He checked her pulse. "Still good heart beat." He turned her on her stomach.

"Yes."

"Hold onto it." He pushed hard repeatedly on her lower back to empty her stomach. "I think she's poisoned."

I looked around. Adriana was back at the RV, quickly donning her clothes. Joanna was still in the water, shocked and staring at Doc working on Laurel. I walked, then jogged toward the RV. Adriana saw me coming, and bolted for her small Honda SUV. I was barefoot, and the stones kept me from catching her before she sped away.

"Dammit," I said, continuing on to the RV. I checked the refrigerator for the leftover moo goo gai pan. It was gone. "*Mierda.*" Thinking we would want samples of what Laurel coughed up, I collected a couple of clear plastic sandwich bags and put on some shorts, a t-shirt and slippers. I ran back to the pool, where Laurel was busy expelling poisons from both ends of her digestive tract. She has looked better, I'll admit.

"She gonna make it, Doc?" I said, as I reached my phone and speed-dialed Tuffy.

"Dunno yet," Doc said, pressing more gently on her lower back now. "Depends on the dose." He looked up at Tricia, who had wrapped herself in a towel. "Where the hell is that ambulance?"

"At the gate."

"I'll let them in," I said. As I ran, I speed-dialed Tuffy,

who answered the phone on the first ring. "Tuffy. It looks like Laurel is poisoned. Ambulance is at the gate. I'll tell the deputies about it when I get over there."

"'Bye," she said, and hung up.

I let the ambulance enter and told the deputies what was going on. One of them drove me back to the pool, while the other kept the gate open for any other arriving emergency vehicles.

We got back to the pool, where Laurel was on her back. Doc listened to her chest, which did not rise and fall as normal. He started cardiopulmonary resuscitation. "Heartbeat stopped," he said.

Sven and DJ Ted arrived, and Jesse and Grace stood nearby. Doc looked at Sven and said, "Get the defibrillator. Ted, Jesse, let's get her to one of the flat lounge chairs and dry her off as much as possible while I keep doing this."

My own heartbeat was beginning to drown out the sound of what was happening. I whispered, "God, You can give my heartbeat to Laurel. I don't need it any more."

So, that's what He did.

As I collapsed, Doc looked over at me and said, "Oh shit, there he goes."

#

51

Lenfant perdu (Lost child)

Wednesday, Oct. 12, 2023, 8:30 p.m.

The jostle of the ambulance as it entered the highway awakened me. I saw Joanna, in clothes of course, and a female emergency medical technician checking my blood pressure.

"Is she?"

"Laurel's heart restarted, and she's in another ambulance ahead of us," Joanna said, smiling down at me. "Doc said he thinks she's got a good chance to make it."

"Thank you, God," I prayed and tried to cross myself, but my hands were bound. "Did anybody think to collect any of her vomit or feces?"

"What an odd question," Joanna said.

"When she recovers, she's gonna wanna cut a bitch, and some evidence would help her decide which bitch," I said. "That's why I brought the sandwich bags."

"Huh," she responded. "I think her sister will have handled it."

"Tuffy arrived before we left?"

"She drove in before the second ambulance – this one. She talked a little to the deputies, pointed out the fluids that came out of Laurel, and got in the other ambulance with Laurel."

The EMT was a stout thirty-something Latina with a short pony tail and a faint scent of isopropyl alcohol. "I need for you to stop talking," she said. "He needs to stay as quiet as possible, let his body recover from the shock. You can hold his hand; that may be calming."

"In his case, it might get him excited," Joanna grinned at the woman, but held my left hand in both of hers. "You're going to be OK, Pepe. Rest."

Rest sounded like a good idea. I closed my eyes, felt the jostling of the ambulance as well as the soft slightly calloused skin of Joanna's delicate, small hands. The swimming pool chlorine scent overpowered Joanna's Johnson's Baby Oil and the isopropyl alcohol from the intravenous drip's injection site. I slid softly into the Land of Nod.

Thursday, Oct. 13, 2022, 9:30 a.m.

"Pepe, you need not go to all this trouble to see me every morning," Deuce said as he patted my hand.

I opened my eyes and realized I was in a hospital room, with sunlight streaming in from a window. Deuce and Tuffy stood on one side of my bed, Wright and North on the other. All were in uniform except my sartorial solicitor in his charcoal pinstripe suit, light gray shirt and dark red tie. I may ask for his tailor. A light hum of bustling activity outside came into the area of my bedside, where the beep from my heart monitor held forth. Old farts get heart monitors, no matter their cardiovascular health status.

"Well, you know how much I love you, man," I said, the words slurring a bit with the lingering mucous of sleep in my mouth.

He looked at the others and blushed. "I'm not sure he's lucid enough for questions."

I chuckled and started to sit up. "Joking, asshole. Help me lift the head of the bed." The scent of coffee wafted from Tuffy's Yeti cup on a nearby mobile table. I felt a sudden pang of caffeine hunger.

He handed me the remote device, and I raised the bed enough and motioned for another pillow so I could look straight at everybody.

"It's a funny thing," I said. "When I wake up, I always need a cup of coffee."

Tuffy stuck her head out the door and dispatched a deputy to retrieve the magic elixir that makes life worth living.

"How's Laurel?" I asked the room in general.

"She's much better, in pain but thoroughly pissed," Tuffy said.

"If she's pissed, she's gonna be ah-ight," I said, flashing a genuine smile. "Did Joanna give you an account of the evening's activities?"

"More or less," Wright said. "I'm interested in what you have to say about it."

I told him what happened, excluding Little Pepe's interest in the proceedings and Adriana's proposal to indulge in the dessert between Laurel's legs.

"We did collect the ... uh, material from the scene next to the pool," North said. "It's being analyzed, but it appears from the symptoms and Ms. Traeger's response to treatment the substances contained arsenic – more than enough to kill a person, if the doctor had not done what he did."

"Don't worry, he'll bill me," I said, not knowing he had no such plans.

"This reinforces the idea somebody is trying to kill Ms. Traeger," Wright said. "But, the previous attempts both on you and she were violent – more canine than feline, as Holmes would say."

"We're dealing with a sophisticated set of perpetrators," Tuffy said after giving Wright a side glance. "If there's a tie to Ms. Falcon's killing and the attempted killing of Ms. Clarke, this asshole or these assholes have a rather wide repertoire of crime. Makes me wonder what else we missed, maybe with a less resilient set of victims."

"Well, from Rex's video, we know about the Cenas and the Dahls," I said. "Mimi Vega directed those, but Bauer and -- forgive me Sgt. Wright -- your brother were involved."

"Assuming Vega wasn't lying."

I shook my head and shrugged. "True enough. When and if Bauer and/or your brother reappear in your jurisdiction, you'll have an opportunity to ask."

"Alright, ass-hole," Wright started toward me, but North imposed his bulk between us.

"You have had ample opportunity to interview a few people other than my client about these events," Deuce said, presenting a hold-your-horses outward palm to Wright.

"Have you, for example, spoken to Theophilus Lenfant? Delilah Samson? Adriana what's her name?"

"Ramirez," North said.

"We were told Reverend Lenfant is at a revival in Lafayette, Louisiana, and Ms. Samson is not at home," Tuffy said. "We have a bulletin outstanding for her and Ms. Ramirez. Ms. Metzger, by the way, reported what happened last night on this morning's news, leaving Ms. Ramirez's name out of the story."

"I wonder why," I said.

"It was our request," North said.

My attorney paused, looked at me and explained, "They don't want to say this, but if they locate her and offer to keep her name out of it, she may be more forthcoming."

"Any idea when Lenfant will return?" I asked.

"They said he would be back Saturday so he can preach Sunday," Tuffy said.

"You're sure he's there?"

"No reason to doubt it, but we can ask the Lafayette police to make sure," North said.

"Old Russian proverb: Trust but verify," I said, doing a passable Ronald Reagan impersonation, including the tremor.

Blank stares from around the room. Crickets at a distance.

"Keep your day job, bro," Deuce said. "These youngsters wouldn't know Reagan if his reanimated zombie corpse bit them on the ass."

Tuffy giggled.

#

52

A review of proctology

Thursday, Oct. 13, 2022, 10 a.m.

"How's Ms. Clarke?" I asked.

"Why do you want to know?" Wright asked. "You want to know whether you're going to get the hot shot once she gives us the password to that video?"

I smiled at him and shook my head as if he were a disappointing child.

"Sort of the same reason as I asked about Laurel," I said. "I care."

"She's still in a coma, and signs show she's getting better," Tuffy said, inclining her head so she did not have to view Wright.

"Every so often, they go in there and pinch her hard, and she responds — a good sign," North said, a look of compassion in his blue eyes.

"I know," I said, thinking of the dark bruises on the shoulder and arm of my late wife in her death bed. "I assume they have to feed her intravenously?"

"They inserted a tube in her stomach, and she is digesting through it OK, also a good sign," North said.

"Poor kid," I said, sighing with frustration and anger. "We gotta get these ass-holes. I'm thinking there's more than one involved at this point."

"Makes sense," Tuffy said.

"Unless you're the ass-hole," said Wright in his monotone as he sat in a chair tilted against the wall.

"Seems like there's enough proctology to go around," my zealous advocate said. As Wright rose to respond with physical intimidation – not advisable with a man Deuce's size – my solicitor changed the subject. "If you don't have any more pertinent questions, I'd like some time alone with my client."

"Bend, Monster, give us the room," Tuffy said.

North guided Wright out the door and closed it.

"What's my prognosis?" I asked her. "How soon can I get out of here?"

"I shouldn't know this, because I'm not a relative, but you can get out of here this afternoon, if you promise to take it easy," Tuffy said. She held up a clipboard. "That reminds me: I need you to sign this release so I can keep up with your medical situation. With Laurel impaired, I'm the closest thing to a relative you got."

"Well, I'm his lawyer, and I already have a power of attorney," Deuce said. "But, I don't object to having somebody else give a shit whether we pull the plug on his sorry ass."

"Some mo' shiggedy," I said, shaking my head and reaching

out with my un-hypo-needled left hand. "Just give me the damned paper."

I glanced through it, gave learned counsel a questioning look. He nodded, and I signed it.

"Do you have any particular reason to suspect Lenfant may not be in Lafayette?" Tuffy asked.

I frowned and looked at my solicitor, who said: "With all due respect, Lt. Traeger, I do need to confer with my client alone. If we have some information pertinent and helpful for you, you will have it."

As Tuffy frowned and headed to the door, I said, "Tuffy, could you hang around a few minutes? When we finish, let's go visit Laurel and Ms. Clarke." She nodded and exited.

"So, why do you think Lenfant is in town?" my attorney asked.

"His wife made an appointment for her, him and me to chat this evening," I said.

"Oh?" he said, his eyebrows raised. "Just a chat? With a murder suspect and his batshit crazy wife? What could possibly go wrong?"

"I take your point," I said. "I'm not out of the hospital yet, but if I do break out, Madame Lenfant specified I should come alone, so I won't abide an escort. They did not say I couldn't bring my trackable cellphone along, and Tuffy – or you, for that matter -- can keep tabs on my location from an unobserved distance."

"Where?"

I shook my head. "I wouldn't want to tempt you either to show up yourself or work with Tuffy to set up an ambush."

"May I ask what's the point of this conversation with the Lenfants?"

"The point is keeping Laurel alive. I must learn what I have to do to accomplish that. If they're not involved in the attempts on her life, which I doubt, they must know more about it than we do."

"What if you show up, they kill you, dump your body, and nobody finds out anything more about them?"

"A reasonable question. I plan on walking in there with a hand on my gun, locked, cocked and loaded. I will not go down without a fight."

"Sounds to me like you're going in half-cocked and fully cracked," learned counsel said, shaking his graying head. "Anything I can do to stop you?"

"No, and don't send your private investigator around to tail me. I would hate to embarrass him or her by executing one of my patented ghosting acts."

"Ass-hole."

"Spoilsport."

My friend approached and put his hand over mine.

"Dude, please be fucking careful," he said, looking solemnly into my eyes. "We're getting to an age when more and more of our friends are in all the wrong places – like six feet under. Since you've been back in the USA, after this goddamn pandemic killed a couple dozen of our relatives and friends, it's been like a breath of fresh air to have you around and so, so ..."

"Annoying?"

"So clearly enjoying life to the last drop," he said, shaking his head, which was blushing. "You've always had that quality

– one of the reasons you used to be late to everything. You'd be late to your own funeral."

"You trying to make me cry? You know how easy that is."

"Just don't make me come back to identify the body. It would be great if we never had to meet in a hospital like this again."

"You'll get no argument from me, counselor."

"OK, ping me your location when you get there." My best pal picked up his satchel and waved as he headed out the door. Yeah, he was choked up. "C-call me when you finish with them."

I waited a moment, trying to calm my emotions, and called out to Tuffy, who rolled in a wheelchair, followed by Dr. Rodell.

#

53

The wisdom of Al Green

Thursday, Oct. 13, 2022, 10:45 a.m.

It turned out I could leave before lunch if I promised to rest, so I asked to stop by Quil's bedside before heading to talk to Laurel. Quil's vital signs were better – stronger blood pressure and heart beat, still clear urine, temperature at 98, the bruise on her cheek uglier than before, as expected.

We got closer – me in a wheel-char, Tuffy pushing – and I put a hand on the cold skin of Quil's one bare forearm. She inhaled a little more deeply then, which made me feel better about her survival.

"By the way, Tuffy, I have an idea about how to access Quil's cloud account," I said. "Try some Leet variation on Laissez les Bontemps roulez. You got some paper?"

She handed me her notepad and a pen, and I

wrote down "L35B0nt3mp5r0ul3$," "L3$B0nt3mp$r0ul3$" and "L3$B0nt3mp5r0ul3$." I handed it back.

"That's the general idea," I said. "Keep replacing 'S's and 'Z's with dollar signs or numeral fives until you exhaust those possibilities. If none of those work, start all over by replacing the 'T' with a plus sign."

"What makes you think this will work?" Tuffy said.

"We were chatting one day, and she used the phrase," I said, and shrugged. "It's just a hunch – might not work."

We started rolling toward the elevator up to Laurel's room.

"Have you heard the rest of Rex's video?" I asked.

"No. Wright is keeping it under wraps."

"Silly rabbit," I said. "Trix are for kids. Rex is – was -- a brilliant information scientist. If he wanted something known, he will have planted, somewhere in the bowels of the Internet, a means of making it known to the people he wanted to know."

On the off-chance, I checked my email on my phone. Nothing from Rex. I checked messages for the profile Laurel and I maintain on a swinger website. Bingo.

"No doubt," she said, as she punched the top-floor button of the elevator. "If something occurs to you, please tell me ASAP. I would dearly love to drop-kick Bend Wright off our payroll."

"I will be most cooperative, Lt. Traeger," I said, looking at the message: *"Pater Noster"* and a link to a Google Cloud account. I had a good idea this was what we were looking for, but I wanted Deuce to see it first and make a copy.

As Tuffy and I exited the elevator, I asked her to wait a

minute while I composed an email containing that information and sent it to my solicitor.

Corporal Keogh sat in a chair next to the bed when we rolled in. He hopped up and moved around the perimeter to avoid bumping into medical equipment. Laurel was asleep, an oxygen tube feeding her nose, a fresh bandage on her shoulder, a pulse and oxygen sensor on a finger, tubes in her arms, a vital signs screen overlooking the bed.

I'd seen this movie before when my wife died, and I didn't want to see it ever again, dammit.

A male Filipino nurse walked in and told Tuffy, "She's not comatose, just tired. She wakes up. We want to keep her calm until the poison is out of her system as much as possible." He left.

"That was for you," Tuffy said. "He told me that a half-hour ago."

I rolled to the side of the bed where Laurel's hand was free. I pulled it to my lips as I had so many times before, and I let the tears flow. Tuffy left.

The movement awakened Laurel, and she looked down at me. "Baby, don't cry," she whispered. "I'll be alright, they said."

"So I heard," I said. "I'm crying because I haven't been good enough for you. You have deserved better. I don't want to waste another moment with you. I want you to know how much I love you. We've talked about getting married but were having too much fun to do anything about it. Let's pull that trigger, OK?"

"If you're sure."

"When your heartbeat stopped, I prayed for God to give mine to you, and maybe that's what He did, for a minute or two," I said. "Dunno how much pull I got with the Big Guy, but here you are."

She chuckled. "Here I am, baby," she whispered the Al Green lyrics. "Come and take me."

#

54

Mann tracht (Man plans)

Thursday, Oct. 13, 2022, noon

Tuffy returned me to the campground – straight to the RV, as a matter of fact. I think she worried I'd get in more trouble. I didn't bother stripping, just crawled into bed and napped most of the afternoon. I did get a call from Father O'Keefe, who was back at his Houston vicarage.

"How is the delightful Ms. Traeger," Dan said.

"She's been better, and she will be better, but she's back in the hospital," I said.

I explained what happened, and he said he would pray for her.

"Thank you, Dan," I said. "There's something else you could do for us. We'd like you to officiate at our wedding."

"Oh?" he said. "Congratulations! We'll need to be

synchronizing our calendars, won't we? Will you be wanting a June wedding? Those weekends tend to fill up first."

"As you may have concluded, this will not be our first rodeo, so having a big wedding is not a priority. In fact, we're both widowed. She is not Catholic, but is Christian."

"Well, there are several options on how we can handle this," he said. "When you have some time, come on down and we can chat about it."

"Given our ages and the fact we have tended to be danger magnets, of late, we want to do this sooner, rather than later."

"Understandable, but you're not talking about eloping, right? It's not something easily done, if you want a Catholic wedding with a non-Catholic."

We set a tentative date to visit the following Wednesday afternoon. I hoped our situation in Teresianstadt would be resolved, one way or another, by then. I was smiling when I hung up, and fell back to sleep.

Deuce called about 5:30 pm.

"Dude, have you seen this video?"

"About an hour of it," I said, yawning. "Pretty fucking dark, right?"

"I've watched it all, and when you meet Delilah, you need to watch out," he said. "She's a diabolical snake on two legs – a virtual clone of Mimi Vega. You ought to think twice about going alone this evening."

"I don't expect her to be there," I said, sitting up and looking with an overwhelming lust at the coffee pot. "I see Lenfant as sort of a free agent in this affair."

"Rex Vega thought Lenfant was as addicted to Delilah as Rex was to Mimi," Deuce said. "Mrs. Lenfant is willfully ignorant about it, Rex said. Lenfant may be pimping out his own daughter to Bauer and/or the Wright brothers at Delilah's insistence."

"Oh lawd." Feeling nauseous again, I stood, swaying as blood flow rebalanced around the ancient corpus.

"It was a repeat of the cycle of abuse and manipulation Rex saw happening with Delilah Samson that prompted this recording," Deuce said.

I hit the speaker button on the phone and started making coffee while I listened.

"Rex said he was going to find a way to stop Mimi from continuing to 'cannibalize people's souls,' as he put it. He feared Juanda and Laurel would be killed, and Mimi would enslave you to feed her all-consuming hunger."

"I realize you're worried about me," I said, pouring water into the coffee maker. "I admit I'm not invincible, but I am pretty smart, and I've had some decent self-defense training. I realize it may be a trap, but they don't realize I'm laying a trap as well. I'm pretty sure I can defeat these schmucks without too much trouble. I'll be well armed, recording sight and sound."

"*Mann tracht, und Gott lacht,*" learned counsel said.

"Excuse me?"

"Old Yiddish saying: Man plans, and God laughs."

"True dat. We'll find out whose plans get Yahweh giggling the hardest."

I asked how Yvonne and the girls were doing, and he made believe this was the end of an ordinary call to one of his closest friends and rang off.

As I stood waiting for the magic elixir to finish brewing,

I sent a text to Joanna. "F U want good story, start recording @ this loc @ 7:30 pm. Keep out of sit. Mak sur u hav plenty of memory and pwr. Use remot mic, f u hav 1."

I inserted the address for the rendezvous with the Lenfants.

Could I trust Joanna? We'll see.

I ate a banana and some yogurt with the coffee, drank a bottle of water, stretched, put on my running shoes. I still wore the shorts and t-shirt I'd put on the night before, so I went to the shower next to the pool. I waved at Jesse and Grace and let them know Laurel was feeling better.

I shaved, showered, brushed my teeth, thinking how my father had once told me what soldiers did before a battle: Get as squared away as possible. I smelled like Old Spice.

Naked back at the RV, I stretched as if going for a run, including some stretching I used to do for *aiki-jiu-jitsu* classes.

I duct-taped a Kel-Tec P3AT pistol and spare magazine to my inner thigh and wore baggy navy cargo shorts over them. In the shorts' back pocket sat another Kel-Tec P3AT. I hoped if they found the outer one, they would give up. The SIG Sauer 9 mm went into a shoulder holster against my skin underneath a loose-fitting, light-blue chambray shirt with the sleeves rolled up to my elbows. I had the SIG Sauer under my left arm and two spare magazines under my right arm. I had no illusions this arrangement would fool someone seriously looking for a weapon. Therefore I had two backups. I also had a couple of three-inch switchblades clipped to my belt, just in case.

In my left shirt pocket was a tiny battery-powered Go-Pro camera with a Bluetooth link to my phone, which would live-stream the meeting to my lawyer, who had no idea that was one of my fail-safes. I checked to make sure the camera could pick up some of the video through the worn, thin cotton shirt. It was dim, but I thought if the light was contrasty enough, it ought to work. The sound was more important, anyway.

I put on my running socks and shoes and made sure I could move around with the pistol on my inner thigh without it becoming obvious.

"Run away," Bob Agnelli, my *aiki-jiu-jitsu* instructor had told us once upon a practice mat. "The best fight is the one you never get into."

Not this time.

#

55

A wanted man

Thursday, Oct. 13, 2022, 7:10 p.m.

The map app on my phone said it would take me about 20 minutes to arrive at the appointed address on the outskirts of Teresienstadt – almost to Luckenbach. I wanted to show up around 7:45 pm.

I drove the open Corvette over those darkening hills with the pleasant cedar-scented wind buffeting my head. A sign pointing to Luckenbach recalled memories of Willie and Waylon and the boys. Those laid back, wacky-tabacky-tokin' days were well behind me now.

Back in the day, as they say, the man who would eventually become my attorney and I would drive back to Austin during those college years thoroughly buzzed. Hunter S. Thompson inspired us to such foolishness. On one such occasion my somewhat erratic driving in the 1976 El Camino drew the attention of an Austin cop, a young Latino not much older than we were. He pulled us over and probably smelled the organic

322

aroma of cheap marijuana when we opened the windows. For some reason, he looked at my driver's license, took down the information about our destination, Jester Dormitory about a half-mile away. He sent us on our way with a warning and a smile. Bless his heart, he did follow us to the dorm. I almost emptied my bowels.

Facing what could well be a much riskier ordeal than a night in jail, I was surprised to be pretty calm. When one has had enough death in one's life – a lot in the past week, for sure, but much more since March 2020 – one tends to greet little things like meeting a batshit crazy nurse (Mrs. Lenfant), an amoral thug (Bauer), a corrupt, perverted preacher (Lenfant) and maybe more, with no more than an elevated pulse.

Such was my story, and I stuck to it. I may have had more brain damage than anyone realized.

At 7:30 pm, I pulled over and parked on the shoulder around the corner and a quarter-mile away from the meeting house, which sat on a large, wooded lot isolated from other smallish houses on large lots set well away from the road. I texted Deuce what I was doing with the livestream and told him not to call or text back. I turned on the Go-Pro, stepped out of the car and tried to sneak up to the house. I kept close to the tree line, so I could see whether anybody else watched the place.

About two blocks away from the meeting house, a newish, bronze Hyundai Tucson SUV sat silent on the shoulder on the opposite side of the road. It had an orange sticker on the back window, a tow-away warning for the owner. It faced away from the house, but the back window with dark tint was half open. If that was Joanna, I silently congratulated her for a providing herself a well camouflaged deer blind from which to watch the snipe hunt.

I approached close enough to see the front of the single-story, smallish ranch-style, tan and rusty-colored, river-rock-sided house's driveway. Aha! That damned gray Kia Soul. I couldn't see the plates, of course, but this mess would be unlikely to feature a different one.

I returned to the Corvette, hopped a nearby barbed-wire fence and walked like an Egyptian burglar through the trees toward the meeting house. I expected to see no one, but I wanted to see what was on the other street parallel to the Corvette's parking space. I'm no Army Ranger, but I was pretty quiet, given the breeze rustling branches overhead and the occasional 18-wheeler barreling by on the highway about a half-mile from the meeting house.

As expected, a silver, late-model Dodge Charger sat nose-out in the driveway of an empty house for rent around the corner and across the street from the meeting house. I saw no one in the vehicle, but it was getting darker, and everybody's car windows have a dark tint these days. Maybe I missed a potential threat in there. I'd have bet this was the car from which Laurel was shot, and my blood was starting to sing an ominous dirge in my veins.

Channeling William Powell's Nick Charles from the Thin Man movies, I muttered, "Quite the gathering of the clans."

Now 7:45 pm, I returned to the Corvette and glanced over it to make sure no one had tampered with it. I decided to leave it where it was. You never know when its unknown location might come in handy. Arriving on foot might pro-vide some small element of surprise. I walked around the Kia

Soul about 7:55 pm, the shadows darkening a house with no lights on.

"I know I'm early, Mrs. Lenfant, but would you mind if we start our chat now?" I called from the driveway toward the front of the house.

No answer. I walked onto the porch and knocked on the door. No answer, but a sort of a muffled, hysterical hum emerged from behind it, so I pulled out my SIG Sauer and tried the door handle. It opened -- never a good sign in the movies. The road to Hell, they say, is wide and easy.

In the middle of an otherwise shadowy, empty front room sat Mrs. Lenfant, taped to a wooden chair, crying and moaning through the duct-tape over her mouth and wrapped around her blond head. From the doorway, I could smell the sweat of fear on her and see stains on her tan polyester pantsuit.

I did not walk straight into the house, as I had seen so many stupid-ass TV detectives do. I peeked through the gap at the door hinge and saw no one there. I felt the muzzle of a pistol's sound suppressor against the back of my neck. I should have recognized the strong scent of Brut aftershave before I felt the cold muzzle.

"Mr. Montecarlo, please raise your hands, leave your finger off the trigger and walk inside," Lenfant said. He removed the SIG Sauer from my right hand.

As I walked in smiling, his left hand found and removed the Kel-Tec P3AT pistol from my right back pocket. I gave a little jump, as if it tickled.

"Well, now, loaded for bear, were we?" he said as he placed my little gun in the inside pocket of his blue seersucker suit jacket. He did the same with the two switchblades clipped to my belt. Lenfant wore a royal blue shirt and yellow tie, like the wannabe Jimmy Swaggart he was. He removed my smartphone, turned it off, and placed it in his left outside jacket pocket. Ah well. *Gott lacht,* indeed.

Lenfant formed the third point of a dim triangle to my right and Mrs. Lenfant's left.

"*Semper paratus,*" I said, smiling. "Used to be a Boy Scout."

"I see," he said. "Mr. Bauer used to be a Boy Scout, too, but he went to Iraq and decided to put away Boy Scout things. The Army taught him some more interesting things, like electronic countermeasures. Your efforts to livestream this conversation were a waste of time."

"At the risk of sounding ungrateful, could you please tell me what's your point?"

From the shadowy hallway to my left, a woman's voice said, "The point, Mr. Montecarlo, is we want you to work with us."

#

56

The proposition

Thursday, Oct. 13, 2022, 8 p.m.

"Really, Delilah?" I asked, giving her a warm smile and the "'sup?" raised eyebrows of recognition. "You think it's a possibility? After what you've tried to do to Laurel?"

With a coquettish smile, Delilah stepped out of the shadows and raised the top of an electric camp lamp, which cast Halloween-like shadows around the room. Bringing with her a scent of Chanel Chance to wrestle with Louise's sweat, Delilah set the lamp on a built-in shelf. Wearing the NTOR uniform and Nike training shoes, the young woman motioned for Lenfant to light and place another nearby camp lamp on a counter separating the area where Louise sat from the kitchen of the empty little house.

"You ought to rethink your relationship with Ms. Traeger," Delilah said, her smile becoming more grimacey. "She's not good a good fit for you. You and I could own the world. Mimi thought so, and I'm sure she was right."

327

"And I thought Laurel was delusional."

Her face hardened, but the smile remained. "I could make you rethink her."

"If you had a firm grasp on reality, you'd realize how idiotic you sound right now," I said, giving her a shot of the Montecarlo Cackle.

She nodded at Lenfant, who hit me hard with the butt of my SIG Sauer on my ear, causing it to bleed.

"Ow," I said with as much sarcasm as I could muster, and chuckled. "My granddaughter hits harder."

Lenfant started to hit me again, but his twenty-something mistress held up her hand, threw back her head and laughed as if watching George Burns doing a talk show with Eddie Murphy as Gumby.

"You are a hoot, Pepe," she said as she recovered herself. "You don't mind me calling you Pepe, do you?"

"Only my friends call me Pepe," I said, still smiling as the blood dripped onto my right shoulder. "Friends don't try to kill the girlfriends of their friends."

"There are worse things we could do," Delilah said, grinning with fewer teeth.

"You have a point," I said. "State your proposition."

"Right now, we could frame Laurel Traeger for Juanda Falcon's murder, persuading a jury she was jealous," she said. "We've manufactured damning evidence. The recording you watched the other day is gone."

I turned my Pepsodent smile on Lenfant. "Just for shits and giggles, you killed her, right?"

Lenfant looked at Delilah, who nodded. "It was not I who killed her," Lenfant said.

"But I saw you chase her away with the sound-suppressed pistol you have in your hand now, and you carried her back," I said, unsmiling.

"I won't deny it."

I turned to Delilah. "Really, Delilah? What was the point in killing her?"

"I could not let her tell what happened before," said the woman who gave birth to Lenfant's child when she, herself, was a child. This evening, she spoke in a childlike voice. "Also, I had to prove to Philo, here, how important he is to me."

"And you hadn't killed anybody yet," I said, shaking my head with a sad smile. "And you knew how much your lover, role model and spiritual mother, Mimi Vega, enjoyed it."

"We heard you had a chance to view the Rex Vega video, but it won't do you any good," Delilah said. "We have destroyed that, as well."

At this point, I had a choice. Was I going to tell them how it was all well known? Not only was the video of Lenfant's torture of Juanda likely available to the police, but so was the Rex Vega video? If so, they might have changed plans and hit the road for parts unknown, giving up on any further violence in Pecan County, since it wouldn't do them any good.

But, given Delilah's budding taste for violence, I thought she might kill all the witnesses so she could start over elsewhere unencumbered by provable past crimes.

Also, dammit, I wanted to stop them, and I thought I could, although it might mean my life. Hey, it's been a good life. Can't say I haven't had more than my share of fun.

"I see," I said, nodding, my lips pursed. "So, you promise

to let Laurel go, leave her alone, if I join in with you, and we work some financial magic. What would be the first step?"

"Nut-Tree Orchard Resort belongs to me!" Lenfant said. "You will persuade Ms. Traeger to give up her claim on it. Marta Cena, who will soon die, will inherit it and leave the land to me."

"And do what with it?" I asked.

"It will become a Christian camp for wayward youth," he said.

"Ha-ha!" I said, chuckling with more of a Bart Simpson sarcastic tone. Do I watch too much old TV? "Those wayward yutes, of course, will be both male and female and just so cute!"

Lenfant didn't wait for orders. He hit me harder with the butt of my own pistol which knocked me down. I need to start carrying smaller, lighter guns with cushioned grips.

"That's my best pistol," I said, looking up from my hands and knees. It occurred to me I could access my thigh-strapped Kel-Tec P3AT from this position and shoot him. "You break it, you bought it." Lenfant moved closer to hit me – close enough for me to sweep his legs out from under him and elbow his windpipe before he could take another breath. But I needed more information.

"Stop," Delilah said, looking down at me with a benevolent smile. She may have realized I had forborne disarming her baby daddy.

I eased back onto my haunches, the way I had in Rex and Mimi's octagonal, mirrored abattoir, and looked up at Delilah.

"You have bigger plans, I guess," I said. "Such a camp will

be a way of cultivating a virtual army of 'mini-Mimis.' My humblest apologies to the entire cast of the Austin Powers movies."

"You are beginning to catch my vision," Delilah said with a broad smile. "Using sex and torture, pleasure and pain, to train a dozen people like Philo and Bauer and, yes, Adriana, to bring more and more minions under me could be … could be …"

"The Amway of psychopathy?" I said, rising to my feet. "A living 'multi-level marketing scheme,' as it were, drawing an ever-growing stream of resources – money, sex, pleasure, power – to you. I gotta hand it to you. It's a helluva vision."

#

57

Und Gott lacht (And God laughs)

Thursday, Oct. 13, 2022, 8:20 p.m.

"I hear a 'but' coming," Delilah said.

"In truth, it's a couple of buts." I gestured toward Lenfant and out beyond the house to whatever other minions awaited her orders. "I assume by 'more and more minions,' you mean the *Despicable Me* kind. So far, your team is not what I would call top level. In fact, these guys are quite a come-down from Rex, for example. They're like the gang who couldn't shoot straight."

Lenfant sneered and swung back to pistol-whip me again, but I just stared and grinned at Delilah, who held up a cautioning hand.

"For example, what was the point of sapping me the other

night outside the Hofbrau? And little old Laurel straightened them out? With a .32-caliber peashooter? Really, Delilah?"

Delilah looked down, chuckled, looked up again, shook her head.

"Bauer wanted to get you temporarily out of the way so they could eliminate your Nubian Queen, who turns out to be a formidable woman in her own right. Mimi considered bringing her onto the team, but thought Laurel wouldn't accept playing assistant queen bee, and I agree."

OK, couldn't hold back the Montecarlo Cackle.

"As Laurel would say, 'That's some mo' shiggedy right there,'" I said. "She may yet surprise you — and me, for that matter."

"Thanks for the warning. You said 'a couple of buts.'"

"One of the things giving me power – and you're right to think I'd be a big asset for your plan – is my little philosophy of the absurd," I said. "If the world is unknowable, if there is no cause and effect, if what we think of as laws and morals and good and evil are mere illusions, then there's no point in seeking."

She looked dumbfounded. "No point in seeking what?"

"Exactly."

She paused.

"Don't listen to this charlatan," Lenfant said. "He's like Bernie Madoff on crystal meth."

"Ha-ha!" I said, offering a bright smile as Lenfant raised the SIG for another blow. "Before you hit me, you better ask your baby mama whether she wants my gun shoved up your rectum. If she does, I'll sure do it. I'm pretty good at disarming cowards who shoot at defenseless naked women until they collapse into diabetic comas."

Lenfant looked at Delilah, who closed her eyes and shook her head.

"You don't have to show off your brilliance to me," Delilah said. "Explain it to me like I was a toddler."

"Seeking, in itself, is a pointless activity," I said, offering a sad grin and shaking my head in disappointment. "The moment you desire something – a person, an orgasm, some food -- anything you do not already have, that something has a ridiculous power over you. Imagine a Popsicle in the freezer over there. There is not one there. If you want a Popsicle, the imaginary Popsicle, an inanimate object, draws you to it, not the other way around. You see the absurdity? I'd appreciate a lime Popsicle right now, by the way, to hold against my ear."

Again with the laughter, this time like an infant watching a Laurel and Hardy routine.

"You are such a hoot, Pepe!" She giggled and wandered around the room behind Louise Lenfant, who resumed her whimpering. "So, from your perspective, I, who have been manipulating you like a chess piece since Mimi's death, am little more than a pinball bouncing between shiny objects."

"You are beginning to grasp the sad truth, Delilah," I said, giving her the big smile and the "'sup?" raised eyebrows. "You believe you were manipulating me, but your desire for me made you alter the course you had set for your life. Before that, your desire for Mimi made you alter your course to desire me, when she died. I'm sorry for your loss, by the way."

"You should save your sympathy for Laurel, who will not enjoy prison one bit. I'll make sure."

"You see?" I said, pointing at her, Louise and Lenfant in succession. "Your desire for me made you zing off to torture Mrs. Lenfant here, and continue hanging out with schmucks like Philo, here. Now it makes you zing off in another direction to think you can manage prison gangs. You're what – 25? Don't you have more fun things to do with your life than give me the power of making you do that?"

"All this is waaaay to deep for me," said a voice I had not heard for a few days. The last time, it was asking for my teeth. I won't lie: the hair on the back of my neck rose.

"Still looking for a good orthodontist, Mr. Bauer?" I asked, without turning. The odor of his sweat mixed with Chanel No. 5. I almost gagged on an initial pang of disappointment.

Feet shuffled behind me, and Bauer formed a fourth point of a rectangle, with Louise at the center. Louise looked at Bauer's left side, where Joanna stood with duct-tape across her mouth, her hands zip-tied behind her back. Bauer's left fist enclosed Joanna's right upper arm. She had a bruise over her left eye, half of a very angry green pair beneath her tousled hair. She wore blue jeans and a dark gray Teresienstadt YWCA camp t-shirt. As this meant she had not betrayed me, I was kind of tickled to see her, and I gave her a genuine smile.

Bauer wore a tan tactical vest with pockets over both breasts and at the waist. I spied with my little eye a two-gun shoulder holster underneath, getting stained by his shirtless torso. He wore cargo pants, a tactical belt and running shoes with olive drab calf-length athletic socks over the cuffs and pulled up almost to his knees, like old-timey puttees. Among defensive handgun aficionados, this was the "shoot me first" uniform. I shook my head and guffawed at the sight.

"I'll say one thing about Mr. Montecarlo, Delilah," Bauer said, waving a Glock 19 9-mm semiautomatic in his right hand toward me. "He's got balls the size of hay-bales. I see why you want him on our side."

Standing behind Louise but close to Lenfant, Delilah looked at Bauer, produced a small smile, gave Joanna the emotionless shark eyes, and looked at me with an air of disappointment.

"Pepe, what have you done?" she asked. "You brought a journalist to a meeting you knew full well was likely to be with the most dangerous person you have ever met. You must admit that, at least."

"Have you ever met Donald Trump?"

Bauer laughed and Joanna snorted derisively.

Delilah smirked, pulled my gun out of Lenfant's hand and put one bullet down through the top of Louise's head.

#

58

Psalm 23

Thursday, Oct. 13, 2022, 8:45 p.m.

"Sorry, Louise," I said, a sad grin on my face. "It really wasn't that funny."

Again with the laughter, but this was more like the giggling Mimi made late Saturday night shortly before her death. I cocked my head to look at Delilah, then back at the mess she had made on the chair, which did not include much blood spray. The bullet had gone down through her body, but the blood and bowel contents were spreading on the floor. Lenfant edged away from his late wife, perhaps to save his snappy two-tone gray and black expensive loafers.

I suppose I should have been thankful the bullet had not gone through Louise to hit me. Knowing Delilah, that was on purpose.

Joanna started crying, and her whimpering drew our attention.

"Shut the fuck up, newsgirl," Bauer said, shaking her upper arm with his large, hairy left paw.

Joanna's eyes were screwed shut in anguish. She stopped making noises, but moisture started spreading from the crotch of her jeans toward her Adidas training shoes.

"Ew," Delilah said, her giggle converting to grimace instantly. "Did I scare you, newsgirl? Sorry. You're not the one I want to fear me."

Lenfant edged forward, laid a hand on his late wife's shoulder, looked up and started muttering a prayer.

"Someone I know?" I asked Delilah, not grinning, trying to sound curious.

She looked at me as if at a disappointing pupil, and shook her head. "If you're not frightened, you're not as smart as I thought you were."

"If there's no point, there's no reason to fear," I said, gesticulating wildly with a grin on my face, trying to emulate Dennis Hopper's character in "Apocalypse Now." I should read more.

Delilah looked at Bauer, who shrugged and shook Joanna's arms to signify he was busy holding her.

"She's not going anywhere," Delilah said, pointing my gun at Joanna, who opened her green eyes in fear, saw what was happening and stood upright at attention.

Bauer let go of Joanna and moved between Louise's lifeless body and myself. Lenfant still looked upward and Delilah was to Bauer's right, maintaining a good view.

"I don't believe I've ever had such unwanted attention from a male suitor before," I said, smiling up at Bauer. "Did you acquire a new lust while you were in Iraq? Or did you have that before you went?"

"Don't flatter yourself," he said, and gave me a hard left jab in my nose, knocking me on my ass, breaking my nose and loosening an incisor. I tasted the ferrous blood in my mouth. Stars took a couple of seconds to clear as I assumed a kneeling position.

He turned toward Delilah and said, "You sure you want to work with such a smart-ass?"

"Given the massive talent for fucking up you two have displayed in the past week," I said in my best, monotonous business podcast voice, "I can't imagine why she wouldn't seek replacements."

Still with his back to me, I did not expect his powerful boot kick to my chest, which knocked me back on my ass.

I coughed some blood and chuckled as I shook my head. I stayed down on my back but raised up on my elbows, looking up at Bauer and Lenfant, then at Delilah.

"I suppose it's difficult for such a pretty young thing to find competent men to achieve an ambitious goal," I said. "Most men of any consequence don't respect youngsters your age. How did you persuade them you were the new Mimi?"

Bauer turned toward me and raised back his right foot to kick my left leg, which I shifted to lessen the blow.

"No," Delilah said. "Don't hit him yet. I want him to hear and understand."

I sat up a little more with my elbows on my knees, my hands clasped. I looked up at her as if I were a little boy hearing a story from Wendy in a scene from *Peter Pan.*

"Once upon a time, a beautiful queen taught a gorgeous

princess how to bring a man to the edge of climax," Delilah said. "Together, they brought that man -- and then several men, together -- to the edge again and again. On rare occasions, when these men had been really good, the queen and the princess let them achieve exquisite release."

"Okaaaay," I said. "But how did you convince these guys you were the new queen?"

"It seems there were some videos taken," Delilah said. "Some narrow-minded folks might object to what they did with underage girls and boys. Those recordings stay in my possession."

"Ah," I said. "So you literally fucked their minds and souls into submission. Impressive."

Bauer shifted his gun to his left hand and gave me a solid right cross to the left side of my head above the jaw. I sprawled to my right, and rolled onto my haunches.

I wobbled another loose tooth -- a molar, this time -- with my tongue as I grinned at Bauer. Behind and to Bauer's right, Delilah shook her head and smiled with disappointment at me. Lenfant looked down at me in disgust, playing Peter Lorre's Joel Cairo in *The Maltese Falcon.*

"I wonder if Joanna's station has a Dental Replacement Orthodontic Plan," I said, as I started to turn to my right and lifted my left knee, keeping my back-up, back-up gun on my thigh hidden from the audience's view.

Bauer looked up as if appealing to the gods for patience, then down, shaking his head.

"Do you, Joanna?" I asked, looking at her. She looked at me a bit confused.

Delilah looked at Joanna with similar confusion. Bauer

turned his head, not his body, to look at Joanna, then started turning toward me.

"Do you have a … DROP!"

Delilah's face took on a look of surprise and fear as the first shot from my Kel-Tec P3AT tore through Bauer's torso and the remains of Louise's head. Joanna dropped in time for a bullet from my SIG Sauer to pierce the space her torso would have occupied a moment before. My second shot got Bauer in the ribs as he tried to turn his Glock toward me, and he knocked over Louise, while Lenfant switched his own sound-suppressed semiautomatic (turned out to be .22 caliber) from his left to right hand and backed away.

I shot at Delilah, but she was around the corner. Joanna, her hands bound behind her, pushed herself toward the door as low and fast as possible on her back with her heels.

A siren started sounding in the distance.

"You might want to cut your losses, Reverend," I said, firing a shot through Bauer's left shoulder in hopes of hitting the scrawny nutsack behind the two dead bodies, but also to keep him from shooting at Joanna or me. "Surely goodness and mercy will follow you all the days of your life, because you are –" *BLAM!* "– the slimiest son of a bitch in the valley!" *BLAM!*

Joanna was out the door, and her tennis shoes made a quickly dissipating pitter-patter on the driveway and pavement, as sirens grew louder. The stench of Bauer's emptying bowels contributed to the scene's ambience.

Lenfant started laughing, stood from his position, his gun lazily pointed in my direction and peered out the window, unconcerned about the muzzle I had aiming at him.

"And you're not quite as bright as you think you are, are you?" he said. "Did you lose count? Only six bullets in a Kel-Tec P3AT."

"Always leave one in the chamber," I said. "Come on, give up. The cops are almost here. You're not getting away with it. Have fun with the prisoners. I'll make sure your daughter is taken care of."

The last sentence was my mistake. I thought he had a vestige of human affection for someone besides himself. I didn't realize he did not want to give up molesting his daughter.

His nostrils flared in anger and his pistol started turning toward me as I fired my last round into his chest. He was a wiry fellow. The hollow-point .380 bullet tore through his cold, cold heart, and his quieter shot went wide and broke a window.

I jumped up, bleeding from my nose, teeth and ear, grabbed Bauer's Glock and my extra Kel-Tec P3AT Lenfant had placed in his inside jacket pocket, and stuck it in my own cargo pocket. As I slid and stumbled through the house looking for Delilah, I tore off the extra Kel-Tec magazine taped to my thigh (Ouch! Not easy being hairy!) and reloaded the pistol I had just emptied into Lenfant.

The back door was open, the screen-door still oscillating back and forth on one of those shock-absorber closing devices designed to prevent closing with a bang. I took the hint. I followed a trail through the leaves and pine straw, beyond a chain-link fence gate into the fresh, loam-scented air and moonlit darkness of woods, which kept silent, save for the thump of my racing heart and the ringing in my ears from all the shooting.

\#

59

Lovely, dark and deep

Thursday, Oct. 13, 2022, 9 p.m.

I paused to listen. The wind rustled the trees above. The siren stopped in front of the meeting house. Car doors opened, releasing indistinct police radio chatter. I could only imagine what those cops thought when they entered and found the three dead bodies. I realized my guns had sent bullets into all the corpses. No doubt Wright could match the bullet that killed Louise with my SIG Sauer.

No birds called above. I had no idea if it was normal, but I took it as a bad sign I was not alone. Good. I wanted Delilah and me to find each other.

High above, a distant single-engine airplane's propeller chopped through the air en route God knows where. My father had been a general aviation pilot and instructor, and we had flown hundreds of miles to visit friends and relatives. Imagine such uncomplicated joy.

On the ground, like a World War I infantryman, I trudged through my own Argonne forest, trailing a mere kid to stop her from hurting more people and, if possible, to help heal her. It was my fondest hope.

Disturbed leaves and pine straw cast shadows deeper than the rest of the undergrowth. I found a five-foot-deep hollow, possibly left by an ancient tree, uprooted and hauled away before its disease could kill other trees.

Funny the crazy shit popping into your bruised noggin when you're focused on pursuing a quarry.

The pine straw appeared uniformly disturbed in the hollow. Wary of a trap, I circled like a curious cat behind trees on the edge of the hollow.

"Hello, again."

I heard the smile in her voice and felt the SIG Sauer's warm muzzle pressed to the back of my neck.

"Hello, darlin'," I replied, singing the Conway Twitty song and turning slowly. "Nice to see you. It's been a long time."

"Not so loud, please." She pressed the muzzle deeper into my neck, felt my pockets, found one Kel-Tec P3AT and stuck it in her pocket. "Please bend over and place the other two weapons on the ground."

The Glock was in my right hand, the still warm Kel-Tec P3AT in my left. It would have been an interesting gunfight.

"I want you to lead me to your car as quietly as possible, and I want you to drive me somewhere so we can talk," she said. "You see, I still have hope I can keep you alive. You see how much I care?"

"Yes, ma'am," I said, turning to view her. "I have the same hope about you."

She had camouflaged herself with a light tactical jacket, some green and brown makeup and a black wool toboggan. The change was quick — and interesting. She had anticipated the possibility of having to make an escape. She might be smart enough to see sense.

I started walking in the opposite direction from the Corvette.

"Really, Pepe?" she asked with quiet exasperation. "Really? I know that's the wrong direction. Head toward your car."

I wondered how she knew where I'd parked it.

"Bauer saw you pull up and go on your reconnaissance, and he texted me," she said.

"Gonna miss him?" I shuffled through leaves and pine straw, thinking it might draw attention from a neighbor's nervous dog or – just maybe – Tuffy, if she had somehow made it to the scene.

"Quit walking like an idiot," she said. "I can just shoot you and say we wrestled for the gun after you shot Louise."

I started walking more carefully.

"I'm unsure whether I'll miss him, yet," she murmured. "He wasn't as dumb as he looked, and he could get a hard-on if the wind blew. Kinda depends on you."

"Gee, I feel so honored to be in a league with such a paragon of manhood."

"Don't be so self-righteous," Delilah responded. "You've got the morals of a polecat, and we all know it."

"Do we?" I asked. "Who's chasing who?"

"Good question," Delilah said. "You could have stayed in

the house, waited for the cops and relied on Joanna's testimony to get you out of any trouble."

"Excellent point."

We had made it to the fence next to the road. She extracted wire-cutters from her jacket pocket and snipped six wires while keeping me in her gunsights. Were those her gunsights? Weren't those mine? Ours. Whatever. We walked through.

"I have to hand it to you," I said. "You thought of everything. You might have been a chess grand master."

"I'm an excellent chess player," she said, following me to the car. "But I'd rather play with people. Their possibilities are more intriguing. You drive."

"Are you like so many millennials, unable to drive a manual transmission?" I asked, removing keys from my pocket and opening the door.

"You may live to find out," she said, sliding into the passenger seat. "Drive forward carefully and quietly, leaving your lights off for now. I'll tell you where to turn."

We drove through the cool, dry air on Texas Highway 27, turned the lights on after the first turn, made several more turns and drove for about an hour. At last, we pulled across a cattle guard onto a dirt track, into a pasture sprinkled with trees and bushes at even distances. Could it be an orchard?

The engine stopped, and we listened to it tick as the hot engine began to cool.

"Sorry about what Bauer did to your car," she said, gesturing toward the dented hood with my pistol. "I didn't tell him to do it."

"Of course not," I said. "Bauer had a mind of his own. He

had a gift for belligerence. He knew how to push the buttons of an old fart who also happens to be a classic car nut. I can push buttons, too, as you may have noticed."

"True enough."

She inhaled the clean, Hill Country air, listened to wind rustling leaves and tree branches. A distant propeller plane buzzed overhead. Was it a new one? Or was the pilot of the old one lost in the dark? Welcome to my world.

"This is where you need to convince me I do want you on my team," Delilah said, raising her eyes to mine. "You have cost me two important players in this game. I need to know you're worth the trade."

"Funny, I thought you'd be trying to convince me to do whatever I can to please you, to save Laurel from your nefarious plans."

"Oh, she'll suffer, that's a given," Delilah said. "But how much? It's up to you."

"*Hoc posset esse peius.*"

"Excuse me?"

"Latin for, 'It could be worse,'" I said. "A Montecarlo family motto I made up."

Delilah nodded. "It could indeed be worse for Laurel."

"I was thinking it could be worse for all, you especially," I said. "But not much. Right now, you have at least one open-and-shut case of murder with kidnapping, which gets you the hotshot in Texas. If my attorney and I can convince a jury you had little control over your actions – not only did you not know right from wrong but did not even know such a thing as 'right' and 'wrong' exist –"

I did the air-quotes thing. Sorry.

"-- You might stay out of the death chamber and instead spend some time in the Texas Hospital for the Criminally Insane in Kerrville."

She started chuckling, trying to do such a broad impression of the Montecarlo Cackle I realized she was mocking me. I gave her a slight grin and shook my head at the thought of suing for copyright infringement. She shook her head in turn, looking down at my SIG Sauer, still pointed at me with her finger on the four-pound trigger. For your information, that's light.

"I begin to despair of our joining forces," she said, a wistful smile on face. "I don't suppose it would persuade you if I said you could have sex with me any time you wanted? Or my daughter?"

"As attractive as both you and your daughter are, the prospect pales in comparison with the delights of my Nubian Queen. And, by the way, EW!"

"But you won't have your Nubian Queen anyway. Wouldn't it be better to have us?"

"It's been a good life. I'll bear up under the strain."

Delilah frowned and advanced the gun's muzzle a little toward me from her position at the far side of the passenger seat.

"Set the brake and get out of the car very carefully. Keep your hands where I can see them."

She exited the Corvette with similar care, keeping her eyes and my pistol fixed on me the whole time.

"Strip," she said, as she moved around the car's rear fender and bumper to stand with me on the driver's side.

"Really, Delilah?" I asked, wondering for a moment

whether she wanted to show me some thrilling new oral sex technique.

"Strip, and I'll explain the next few minutes to you," she said.

I started undoing the buttons on my shirt.

#

60

Highway 27 revisited

Thursday, Oct. 13, 2022, 10:20 p.m.

"The story reported will sound something like this," Delilah said. She cleared her throat and tried to sound like a local TV news anchor. "Peter Paul Montecarlo, 63, award-winning journalist and millionaire whom some credit for causing the Great Recession, died on a back road near Teresienstadt sometime after 10 p.m. Thursday evening, apparently the victim of a hit-and-run accident.

"An avowed naturist, Montecarlo had been running nude along a curvy stretch of Texas Highway 27 when he had his fatal encounter."

"Leave your shoes on, by the way," Delilah said in her normal voice before returning to anchor-speak. "Why he was running at night is not known. Nor is it clear why he was out of the bounds of the Nut Tree Orchard Resort, a clothing-optional facility where he had rented a trailer and where he was often seen running naked."

"What is known: His guns were used earlier in the evening to shoot and kill Louise Lenfant, her husband the Right Reverend Theophilus Lenfant and Iraq War veteran John Bauer."

"Montecarlo and his paramour, retired high school clerk Laurel Traeger, who has ties to the Los Angeles gang world, were persons of interest in three earlier deaths: the alleged murder-suicide of Mimi and Rex Vega and the death by drowning of a Juanda Falcon, all at the Nut Tree Orchard Resort, over the past week.

"Sources close to the investigation speculate Montecarlo was despondent over the recent gangland-style drive-by shooting of Ms. Traeger, who is in the hospital under guard this evening."

I couldn't have stopped the Montecarlo Cackle if I tried, as I hopped with one foot on the ground, trying to extract the other still-shod foot from my cargo shorts. I finally fell over and just laughed.

"Life truly is absurd," I said. "Even in the tiniest of details, you sneak in an inaccuracy in the report. Of course, she's not in the hospital for the shooting, but for Adriana's poison attempt."

She moved forward a little to smile sympathetically down at me. "There's no real evidence tying Adriana to the poisoning. Joanna Metzger will find her credibility compromised. She may well face indictment for poisoning Laurel to get you."

I started to impersonate Etta James' singing style. "At last,

I found a woman more delusional than Laurel — about my attraction for women, I mean."

Delilah's eyebrows came down. "Don't sell yourself short," she said, wagging the pistol at me. "If you want, I can just kill you and bury you here, but the way I described earlier looks better for all concerned."

Conceding the point in my mind, I stood up wearing running shoes and a Smart Watch. At least I would know when my heart stopped.

"How, pray tell, are you going to get me out on the highway?" I asked. "I could just run behind those trees over there."

"Again, if you did, I'd just have to shoot you and bury you here," Delilah said. "No, you're going to sit on the door of the passenger seat as I keep the pistol aimed at you, and I'm going to drive us out to the highway a bit. Then you'll have a neat little surprise."

"This is like some elaborate James Bond movie killing," I said, still quite amused. "Do you have Bambi out there with all the other little woodland creatures with frickin' lasers attached to their heads? Are they ill-tempered woodland creatures?"

She laughed. "I will miss you truly, Pepe."

"Not dead yet."

"That's what I was hoping you'd think." She moved to the driver's seat, sat and closed the door while keeping the pistol trained on me with her left hand, and started the engine without looking down.

"Damn, I was hoping my anti-millennial car theft prevention device would have saved my ass again," I said. Among us old car nuts, that's what we call manual transmissions.

Chuckling, she said, "Go ahead and climb in and sit your bony white ass on the edge. Hold onto the windshield. This won't last long."

I have to hand it to her. She was adept at driving a stick shift one-handed. She backed up, turned and drove onto the highway, even avoided scraping the low-slung sports car's undercarriage on the pavement. She accelerated to about 30 mph toward a curve near the bottom of a hill in the road.

"*Adios*, Pepe," she said, and did an expert left-turn dough-nut, throwing me off into the middle of the road.

I was not surprised. I used my *aiki-jiu-jitsu* training to roll down the highway with some scrapes on my shoulders, elbows, knees and ass, but I kept my head off the pavement. Nothing broken, but this old sexagenarian was not moving too quick as I rose to my feet and saw her coming back down the hill to hit me. I ran straight for her but turned to dive to the side with a rock wall facing the road.

She missed me but also took a shot at me as she passed, ricocheting off the rock. Oddly enough, the little propeller plane still droned in the distance, although a little closer now.

Delilah did another doughnut – flat-spotting my tires in the process, dammit -- and started for me again. I started running toward her again. She fired two more times before I dove for the opposite side of the highway, which fell away a little into some woods, but I wasn't hit.

This time I continued in the same direction uphill on the road, thinking, *Is this how Sisyphus felt? Am I doomed to roll my aching, ancient ass up and down this hill forever?*

My wrinkled-yet-muscular legs were woefully outclassed

by the Corvette, no matter how old and dented. As I neared the top of the hill, my heartbeat competed with the glorious approaching sound of 300-plus American horsepower, the buzzing of the apparently lost propeller plane above and the occasional report of a poorly aimed shot from my pistol below. I decided it would be funny as hell to be die by my own machinery. I turned and stood on a narrow brushy shoulder that overlooked what would in daytime offer a lovely view of Hill Country autumn foliage. I couldn't help but laugh at the sight of Delilah, disappointed smile quickly growing closer, head shaking side to side, as she continued firing, left-handed.

#

61

Popsicle dominoes

Thursday, Oct. 13, 2022, 10:35 p.m.

As I lay dying ...

In a dream, I walked aching steps around the bodies of Bauer and the Lenfants in the otherwise empty death house to the refrigerator and opened the freezer door, hoping against hope for a lime Popsicle for my swelling ear and now, oddly, my throbbing right shoulder.

Inside, to my surprise, I saw dozens of lime Popsicles, unwrapped, standing on two sticks each along the door's interior shelf. Looking closer, I saw they were shaped like statues, each individually and intricately carved like Emperor Qinshihuang's terra cotta soldiers. At the end closest to the door handle stood a statue of myself, an eyebrow cocked and my mouth half-grinning. Adjacent was Delilah, her head popped backward in laughter. Behind Delilah stood a sneering Lenfant. Behind Lenfant stood his weeping wife. Behind Louise stood a glaring Bauer.

I stopped examining each one and looked at the hinge end of the freezer door. There, Mimi struck a sexy pose, hair covering one eye, a lascivious grin on her face. Her icy breasts' nipples touching the taller, thicker back of Rex, who wore the expression of resignation, sadness, disappointment and frustration which was the last I had seen of his face before its destruction by a .45 Colt bullet.

Shocked, I let go of the door handle and backed away. The door started to close, but before it did so, the Mimi-shaped Popsicle tilted forward against the Rex-shaped Popsicle, and then the next and the next followed suit like dominoes. Ultimately, the Popsicle carved to resemble myself magically dove off the door, followed by Delilah, Lenfant and all the others in succession, as if in an Esther Williams synchronized swimming musical. ...

In the dim light of the resort swimming pool, I hovered and watched the Popsicles cleverly swim upside down in a circle with their balsa-stick legs kicking in the air in time with the music of the Zydeco tune "Soulwood Train." I slowly descended, feet first, to stand in knee-deep water in the center of the circle. The circle of swimming Popsicles broke into two circles, then linked into each other forming a figure eight — or ellipsis, depending on how you looked at it — with the paths crossed between my knees.

How clever these Popsicles be, I thought.

But then I realized I stood at the deep end of the pool, draining fast with the Popsicles melting. Ultimately, I stared down at my feet straddling the drain with two Popsicle sticks lying parallel on the holey strainer itself, with one more stick crossing the two diagonally.

I wept.

\#

62

Lagrimas por una asesina (Tears for a killer)

Friday, Oct. 14, 2022, 3 p.m., *et sequitur*

I awakened to see Dr. Rodell looking down at me, shaking his head.

"What did I tell you about taking it easy?"

"What fresh hell is this?" I asked.

"He gonna be ah-ight," Eartha Kitt purred. "He crackin' jokes, he gonna be ah-ight."

I turned from Dr. Rodell to see Laurel's pink spikey hair over the cast on my right upper arm, elevated on a pillow above my heart to keep the swelling down.

"Eartha? Is that you? What did you do to land you in hell with me?"

With help from Joanna – Joanna? – Laurel stood up and showed me her lovely smiling face, a little grayish still from the poisoning but by no means dead. She bent way over my shoulder and gave me a kiss on my cheek. I didn't move and don't think I could have.

"What happened?"

"Well, Mr. Montecarlo, it's complicated," said Sgt. North, standing next to Dr. Rodell. "It appears you fainted, which might have saved your life. You got hit a glancing blow by a 1959 Corvette going about 50 mph that had bounced up off a the mostly buried tip of a small shoulder boulder hidden by brush. That car then sailed over a cliff and you, simultaneously."

"It gave you a compound fracture on your right arm, broke your clavicle and made your concussion a bit worse," Rodell said.

"*Hoc posset esse peius.*"

"Excuse me?"

"Nothing," I said, chuckling. "My humerus may be broken, my sense of humor is unbowed. Did Delilah make it?"

North cocked his head and looked at me. "I'm afraid not. Nor did your car. It fell about 100 feet, slammed into the rocky bottom of Goat Creek and burst into flames. Her remains are in the morgue now."

I couldn't help it. Tears blinded me.

Joanna looked at Laurel, who looked back and shook her head.

"Is he crying for the car?" Joanna asked.

"No," I croaked, and shook my head. "For Delilah. She was what the world had made her – her greedy, narcissistic parents, her perverted preacher baby-daddy, her psychotic grown woman lover, the brutal thug of a soldier-lover – all the sad, brain-dead influences in her life. She could have overcome all that, and I wanted to help her do it. For the part I played in her sad ending, I am truly sorry."

"Fuckin' amazing," Tuffy whispered from behind Joanna.

———————

The next couple of months might have been interesting for most people. The propeller plane I thought I heard? It was a drone operated by Joanna's cameraman, who shot much of the night's events from inside a van well away from the action. He was the one who called the cops. Joanna and my adventure in the house and afterward made the national news. He has gone to work for CNN covering various war zones -- Sudan, most recently, sad to say.

Far from having her credibility questioned, Joanna was also courted by national networks. She used some vacation time to mull options and cultivate her friendship with Laurel and me. When Laurel exited the hospital, Joanna took her to rent a new Camaro with an automatic transmission, dammit.

Quil came out of her coma and gave Tuffy and North the password to the digital recording of Juanda's death.

Sgt. Wright had managed to wipe clean Rex Vega's laptop by placing it next to an extremely powerful magnet in the evidence locker.

But, as mentioned earlier, Rex had given me a clue to the password for his relevant cloud files. My lawyer released the relevant files to the authorities after viewing them himself. He wanted to ensure his clients were not incriminated.

Oberst suspended Sgt. Wright, pending an internal

investigation. A relieved Tuffy expressed confidence "this particular fool" would be lucky to avoid prison time, much less ever work in law enforcement again.

FiddyShadesofBloo knew enough, when he was in a hole, to stop digging, so he never outed Tuffy's LtChocolock as a BDSM freak.

Wright's less fortunate brother – the W.O.W. to Sgt. Wright's B.O.W. – turned up headless in a cemetery in Piedras Negras, Mexico, across the border from where the Texas governor had stationed National Guard troops near Eagle Pass. W.O.W. had been absent without leave since the day after his arrival.

After my seven nights in the hospital, Dr. Rodell concluded my brain was out of danger. He also thought a 63-year-old fart with a fractured humerus and clavicle was unlikely to engage in another bar fight. I gained my release. Joanna drove Laurel and me back to the campground in Joanna's SUV, which was more comfortable for me with my arm still in traction than the Camaro would ever be.

DJ Ted and Sven were happy to see us and had made good progress in restoring the damaged reception area and offices. Laurel and I moved into one of the cottages from the RV, which would have been a bit cramped for me.

Jesse and Grace and returned to their home in Houston, but Doc and Tricia were still at NTOR, of course, along with Dean and Rose.

We hung out naked a lot. My white butt turned a nut brown. My cast got some interesting illustrations. Joanna often visited and gained a nice tan on her bikini areas, despite the cooling Hill Country autumn weather. Joanna and Laurel got to be pretty close, both in and out of bed. I left them to it. Little Pepe got an occasional ride from his Nubian Queen.

Ben showed up with his girlfriend Janis and Shawn-from-Manchester. They wanted to hear all about my adventure first-hand. They frolicked with Laurel and Joanna in the pool. The hot tub was open to guests, but Laurel wanted no part of it.

By mid-December, Quil had returned but was still taking it easy. She was happy with the work DJ Ted, Sven and a couple of new camp workers had done restoring her office and the lobby to its former antiseptic glory.

On Dec. 24, Dr. Rodell decided my arm and clavicle were healed enough for me to rejoin those of us who can scratch our elbows without the help of a friend and a wire coat-hanger. Bliss.

The vigor of aforementioned arm, my shoulder and much of the rest of me had diminished. I had been unable to run or workout or – ahem – perform any rigorous lovemaking for more than six weeks, so the truism remains true: what doesn't get used becomes useless.

But by the time NTOR's multi-night "New Year's Eve Ballz" rolled around, my physical therapy had begun to show a little progress. Over the holiday weekend, I finally got to run, although it was cold and wet much of the time.

#

63

The keystone to Delilah

Saturday, Dec. 31, 2022, 10 p.m.

It's counterintuitive, but big celebrations of any sort at nudist attractions catering to the swing lifestyle tend to feature fancy dress.

Jesse and Grace came to the party dressed as the cowboy from the Village People and Bo Derek from the movie "10." It sort of worked. Sven, wearing his black leather vest and chaps, kept giving Jesse the "come hither" stare.

Given Dean and Rose's BDSM lifestyle, they wore the usual – black leather with spikes for him, fishnet body suit and intricately tied ropes around breasts and bikini areas for her.

Doc came as a horny old doctor with a prosthetic penis poking out through his lab coat, and Tricia was his sexy candy-striper in nothing but an apron, white cap, white fish-net stockings and spike heels. Yummy.

Ben came as a sexy firefighter, showing an appalling lack of imagination. His lovely Janis came with a bikini made of red-rope candy and red-hots. Very hot.

Joanna came – which I convey in every sense of the word – in an exact copy of the costume worn by Diana Rigg in a notorious episode of *The Avengers* TV show, complete with whip, spiked collar, stockings and boots. Yowzah!

Laurel, of course, came as Cleopatra. "Tryin' to be cute," she said. She wore a *faux* gold snake necklace, a costume crown, a gilded brassiere, gold-colored satin bikini bottom, gold knee-high spike-heeled sandals. Pepe a lucky man.

I came as George of the Jungle, complete with Elvis-like black wig. I even shaved my mustache.

During a lull in the festivities, as Laurel led the crowd in a quasi-professional choreographed line dance to the tune of Michael Jackson's Thriller, I sat my bony ass down at a table, whereupon Joanna sat across from me, smiling coquettishly. I gave her my George of the Jungle square-jawed grin, to which she sighed and looked down at her gloved right hand, holding a plastic-tipped flogger.

She raised an eyebrow and looked askance at me as she slapped the flogger against the other hand. "Am I going to have to discipline you?" she asked.

"George swings!" I said, trying to impersonate Brendan Fraser in the live-action comedy. "George not dig pain!"

Joanna shook her head and set the flogger down between us.

"It's New Year's Eve," she said. "It's a time to let go of the past, set your sights on the future."

"George simple fellow," I said, cocking my head to one side. "Point not clear."

"You know what I want," she said.

I looked around. "Now? Here?"

Her head shook dismissively.

"You know," she said. "You used to be a journalist. You know how curiosity can eat at your insides. I must know what Popsicles and dominoes have to do with the night you saved my life."

Yeah, I recognized what she was going through and what she wanted. She told me the night they brought me back to the rented cottage at the campground.

———————

Friday, Oct. 21, 2022, 9 p.m.

"I rode with you on the way to the hospital that night, you know," Joanna said after Laurel had retired, exhausted. She sat on her ankles on an ugly olive-drab vinyl couch across from my comfy plaid recliner, her legs wrapped in a short blanket.

"Must be getting tiresome for you."

"I didn't want the man who saved my life to die without someone who loved him," she said.

I blushed.

"Uh, you know I'm committed to Laurel," I said. "We're getting hitched."

"I'm committed to Laurel, too," she said. "That's not what I'm talking about. I'm saying I heard you."

"Were the farts particularly noisome?"

She chuckled, shook a curl of hair before one of her dazzling emerald eyes.

"You kept mumbling about Popsicles and dominoes, and you were crying," Joanna said.

"Did I?" I said, starting to drift toward the Land of Nod. "Dead eye?"

Saturday, Jan. 31, 2022, 10 p.m.

"Jeeze, but journalists are annoying," I said. "Just think: people had to put up with me doing that for 35 years."

"I get the feeling you're hiding something, and it's important," Joanna said, looking serious at me with such a cute little mouth set firm.

"Oy!" I said. "Well, it was a hallucinatory epiphany of sorts, and it was very sad. You sure you want to hear it? You can't unhear it, as much as I'd like to."

She nodded.

"I realized the role I played in all those deaths and in all the suffering," I said. "It was just as if I had been sleepwalking through my life before. I kept trying to do the best I could, for my wife, for my kids, for the public at large. I worked hard to build my skills, to polish my 'self,' as it were."

Forgive me. I did the "air quotes" thing with my left hand.

"I had always been convinced I was not good enough for the people around me, especially family, but also for the world at large," I said. "I worked hard to make myself worthy. People noticed. Mimi noticed. Delilah noticed. I became a shiny object they had to have. They went to extraordinary lengths to possess me. It was a close-run thing. If Rex had not done what he did, Mimi might have got me."

"I was like that lime Popsicle in the freezer I talked about in the death house with Delilah, begging for me to use it to ease my pain. And I was like a domino. Once the other dominoes started falling, I did not stop. Could I have stopped it? Could I, like the keystone at the top of an arch, refuse to fill my hole, my role? I don't know. It appears to be my nature, like Sisyphus, to keep rolling this mortal fucking coil back up that hill every day, whether I like it or not. This Columbus Day week, I liked it not."

The dancing lasted until midnight, when the orgy started up in the Playhouse. Joanna and I used the swing while Jesse rode my Nubian Queen. I lost track of where, what and who else got done during the festivities. I do remember the glorious funk of lovemaking as Joanna, Laurel and I approached the Playhouse exit to return to our cabin. I also recall the fresh pine scent as Joanna, Laurel and I staggered, leaning against each other into the frosty night, with Laurel and Joanna shivering, sharing goosebumps and giggling together under Laurel's new ankle-length mink coat (a Christmas present — I'm spoiling her), which she had worn over her hastily discarded Cleopatra costume. Covered in every bit of my skimpy George of the Jungle costume, I held onto both of them with my good left arm as we crunched through the frozen leaves and pine straw.

The next morning, I awoke with my weaker right arm draped across Laurel. Joanna, spooning my (our?) Nubian Queen, had her left arm draped across my beloved from her other side. Laurel's left hand, sporting a new five-carat diamond engagement ring, gently stroked Little Pepe.

Pepe a lucky man.

#

64

Epilogue

Email

Date: Jan. 3, 2023

To: Pepemontecarlo@[REDACTED]

From: RaoulJones@[REDACTED]

Bud:

I didn't send all Rex's files to the Pecan County District Attorney's office. I sent only what I thought they would need to see you guys had no culpability in the mess at NTOR. My investigator went through all the files and found the attached recording you may want to listen to.

I gather Rex had a habit of recording his play sessions — at least some of them. Kinky.

To save you the shock of actually hearing the voices and action, I've attached a transcript of the relevant part, which the investigator generated. No one else — not my partner, not my paralegal — has audited the recording or read this material.

To be clear, in this transcript, the female voice is Laurel and the male voice is Rex.

BEGIN TRANSCRIPT:

Male (whispering): I have no doubt Mimi wants to take Pepe from you. She has big plans for him.

Female: She bett' not!

[Sounds of movement.]

Female: I'll take this knife and cut her from her skanky cunt to her lyin' lips, the bitch!

Male (whispering): Be quiet! You don't know what she's capable of! I'll stop her.

Female (whispering): Some mo' shiggedy. She got you so whipped, you'd never raise a hand to her. Oh! Sorry, didn't mean it that way.

Male (whispering): I know, I know, but I love you guys, and I can't let her hurt more people I love. I'll stop her somehow.

Female: You'd better. If you don't, I will, and it won't be pretty. You might as well know now. We won't be playing with you guys no more until this shit gets resolved.

[Sound of female giggling from a distance, getting louder.]

[Sounds of movement.]

Female: What you gonna do with that? Rex?

[Sounds of movement. Two gunshots and the sound of a falling body.]

END TRANSCRIPT

Bud, you're a grown man. You do what you think best. I destroyed the audio file and will soon destroy the transcript containing the above excerpt.

As your attorney, I'd advise you to do the same. If I were in your shoes, I have no idea what I would do.

As your friend, I ask you to forgive me for providing this information to you. Ignorance is bliss, but I have always understood you to be a man who wanted to know, rather than not know, the truth. As I've heard you say before: I could be wrong. I often am.

#

Acknowledgments and FYI

The author's heartfelt thanks are offered to friends at the Round Rock Writers Guild and the North Austin Fiction Writing Critique Group, and to the ten Beta readers who offered priceless assistance in bringing this work to life. To the extent that *Corpse on a Swing* entertains, informs and improves lives, the credit is theirs. To the extent that this work bores, misinforms or wastes people's time, the fault is entirely that of the author.

To learn more about the adventures of Pepe Montecarlo and Laurel Traeger, visit PepeMontecarlo.com, view the Pepe Montecarlo Facebook page or email pepemontecarlo1959@gmail.com